The Wonder,

Blood Red

A BASELINE PAPERBACK

© Copyright Nov 2016
James Devo

A CIP catalogue record for this title is
available from the British Library

ISBN–978-1-911124-26-9

Dedicated to

The Devo Girls

CONTENTS

Part 1
Keys to the Kingdom

Prologue	Chinsey, Capital of The Gramarye region	
	Grand Quillia	3
Chapter 1	The Glasslands The Gramarye Region	
	Grand Quillia	21
Chapter 2	The Gramarye Region Grand Quillia	41
Chapter 3	Near Talling/Maisy The Gramarye	71
Chapter 4	The Gramarye Region Grand Quillia	96
Chapter 5	The Gramarye Region Grand Quillia	107
Chapter 6	The Gramarye Region Grand Quillia	129

Part 2
Subterranean Homesick Blues

Prologue	The Gramarye Region Grand Quillia	151
Chapter 7	Beneath the Cathedral of Tales/	
	The Library of Senses	
	The Gramarye Region Grand Quillia	158
Chapter 8	The Glasslands/The City of Pearly	
	The Gramarye Region Grand Quillia	186
Chapter 9	The Cathedral of Tales/	
	The Library of the Senses	
	The Gramarye Region Grand Quillia	200
Chapter 10	The Cell The Cathedral of Tales/	
	The Library of the Senses	
	The Gramarye Region Grand Quillia	246
The Wonder Glossary – for those short of time		
and/or memory		268

THE DITCH

THE FAR MOUNTAINS 2.

1.

CHINS

3.

The Grama

5.

6

10.

MAISY

1. The Ditch

2. Attar Mountains

3. Chinsey

4. Slideways

5. Pyramids of Maisy

6. Ruins of Maisy

7. Glasslands

8. Gleave Lodge

9. Cathedral of Tales

10. Road to Moondock

PART 1

Keys to the Kingdom

Chinsey,
Capital of The Gramarye region
Grand Quillia

June 1856

Geraldine Bunce did not like lifts. She had no idea when it had been decided that walking up stairs was too arduous, but that was not the main reason for her feelings.

She definitely didn't trust them. The magic needed to build a bridge across a deep chasm, now you know somebody had paid proper attention to that, she thought. The slideways that enabled ice yachts to skate around the Empire, ditto. But a small room required to move up four or five floors of a building? Why apply yourself? Why expend any Wonder to alleviate the need to walk upstairs? Why help the lazy? Corporal Bunce had exercised before she'd joined the army – she'd had to. She'd been left to fend for herself at a young age in a rough part of the Empire. But it wasn't her disdain for the slovenly that caused her to hate lifts. Or

3

heights. In her main role in the squad, she was required to climb great heights, to find the higher ground, the highest tree and pick off all those she surveyed. Snipers did not need lifts.

No. The main reason Corporal Geraldine Bunce did not like lifts was because if there was a problem and it were to plummet from a great height, she did not want her crushed body to be ground into mince together with the other people in the lift with her.

Especially this lift.

Take Aaron Tork. He smelled of wet dog, he looked like a mean walrus with a moustache, and he could only speak in a growl or a whimper. Bunce had eaten mutton curry with more style, panache and intelligence.

Spicer, their commanding officer, a foot shorter than the bear-like Tork next to him, may have once had some charm, some modicum of manners, but all that had been burned away at around the same time his face was burnt off, leaving stubs for ears and nose. If the lift were to fall, if its magic were to fail, Spicer would be the crunchy burnt bits in the meatloaf they'd find at the bottom of the lift shaft.

And then the Squad's own hyperphysicist, an ex-army dabbler, Conway. God knows where he had studied magic – some grubby college in some failing military centre in the Empire's back alleys. This was probably the first lift Conway had ever been in.

Bunce felt another shiver of trepidation. Imagine if some reprobate hyperphys like Conway had designed the lift, his bony digits poking out of the fingerless gloves, melding the magic into whatever Wonder this lift needed to drag people up the inside of the building, his rodent eyes squinting into the workings as he pulled the required enchantments into being.

Magic spooked Bunce. She didn't understand it – she could see why people called it the Wonder. It was a wonder what some people had managed to do with it, even Conway occasionally. She also completely sympathised with those that called it *the dabble*. Mankind had found something buried deep in the earth. Some people said that it came from the bones of long dead dragons, others that it was from the roof of Hell itself. Whatever it was, it was useful. Useful for weapons, useful for energy, useful for speeding up everything, useful for shrinking the whole wide world. Useful for transporting people who don't like to take the stairs.

But mankind was dabbling. It didn't really know what this new-found power could do. It didn't know how long it would last. It didn't know what long-lasting effect it would have on those around it.

It was the great unknown.

Some people said that other civilisations had used the Wonder before and it had ruined them, changed them until they were no longer human, sucked them into the ground from whence the magic came. There were the remains of these people all over the world. Archaeologists were digging them up all the time, even in the capital of the Great Quillian Empire, but most had been found nearby, in the remote colony of The Gramarye. Superpowers clung to this lost knowledge as much as they battled to unearth important artefacts and their power source, the Wonder. The People of the Ditch apparently threatened Great Quillia at every turn, always hoping to steal some new piece of the Wonder that might make their lifts ascend that little bit faster than the Empire's.

The only things separating the Ditch from the Empire were the Attar Mountains, and if the Ditch ever dared cross the natural barrier the first place they would hit would be The Gramarye. Although there had been no incursions in living memory, nobody who had ever entered the Attar Mountains had ever returned, and rumours of Ditch spies insinuating themselves into the Empire were rife.

Bunce couldn't complain. All this paranoia meant there was a lot of work for freelancers – for privateers. Privateers such as herself and Tork and Spice and Conway.

They had been employed by the Trade, a commercial entity that ran much of the Great Quillian Empire's remote interests, to scour The Gramarye for a specific ancient magical device that could lead to a new source of Wonder. Another piece of dabble. None of them knew why the Trade wanted it so badly, and none of them, including Bunce, really cared. They'd acquired it and brought it back to Chinsey, the Trade's capital in The Gramarye.

And so here they were, in a lift in the Trade's regional headquarters, with a priceless chunk of ancient Wonder in a hessian sack slung over Tork's shoulder.

"I don't like lifts," said Bunce, to nobody in particular.

As soon as the lift ground to a halt, Sergeant Major Pendle hauled open the iron grate doors, his slender frame and pristine uniform hiding considerable brute force.

"You must be the Reclaimers," he said, taking in the four privateers.

He could feel the eyes of the clerks in the office behind him as the tip-tapping on their typewriters and clunking of their adding devices slowed. Pendle would have to reprimand them once this rabble had left.

Pendle looked the visitors up and down. They looked like the usual privateer scum found in this part of the Empire. Rough, ready, lacking in manners, etiquette, lacking in anything that would allow them to live respectable lives back in the heartland. If the regular populace of Great Quillia knew the sort of people their fortune was built on, they would shudder with shame. But then regular people probably hadn't heard of The Gramarye, except as a primitive, far off place that some of the Wonder came from, that same Wonder that made the slideways that transported them to work every morning, that powered the mills that spun the cotton they wore. The Wonder that forged the guns that built an Empire.

"I'm Lieutenant Spicer," said the man with the horrific face, pronouncing it the Imperial way – 'Lieutenant'.

Pendle regarded him with interest. His uniform was filthy, with some buttons missing and a torn epaulette; enough to put any of Pendle's clerks on punishment detail for two months. His weapons, however, were well oiled, some with sights and other attachments not of regular issue. Spicer's Twirler pistol crackled as the Wonder pulsed through its six barrels, its safety catch removed. Pendle found himself missing the old days of the battlefield, sabre in one hand, Twirler in the other, sending the natives packing. However, the mess of Spicer's face was enough to remind the Sergeant Major why Mrs Pendle had insisted he take a desk job.

Spicer wore his hair long – it touched the bottom of his collar; like many of the privateers who were keen to show they were a band apart from the regular army. But Pendle suspected this was a wig, albeit a good one, with real hair,

probably from the Imperial capital. The lieutenant obviously wore it to cover as much of his scarred head as possible,
for it resembled a walnut with a mouth and thick-lidded
eyes. Even for a veteran like Sergeant Major Pendle, it was
quite a battle to look Spicer in the eye, and he could hear
the sharp intakes of breath from the clerks as Spicer stepped
into the light.

He was followed by Conway, a grubby, wiry man who
seemed to exude grease, a man obviously more comfortable
surrounded by the devices of dabble and sources of Wonder.
As with most hyperphysicists, he was not in uniform, pre-
ferring a long leather coat, cut like the hyperphysicist's lab
coat, a leather hat that covered his ears, cracked goggles and
grotty fingerless gloves.

The woman, Bunce, was wrapped in ammo belts and
bandoliers, her uniform almost entirely obscured by ammu-
nition for the long slender rifle that hung from her back.
Her hair was short, her eyes dark, although she looked more
like a swarthy boy than a lady, despite the curves she tried
to hide. She did, however, smell marginally better than the
men, especially the last out of the lift.

Private Aaron Tork was enormous, his body built for bullying, his scarred hands always fists, his jaw always grinding.
He was the sort of pack animal Empire was built on, Pendle
caught himself thinking, not just the Great Quillian Empire,
but all of them. Tork's uniform was modified to terrify; the
sleeves removed to reveal arms like skinless hare carcasses,
and covered in primitive tattoos, some faded with age, some
throbbingly fresh. He wore bearskin over his shoulders, and
sheepskin chaps, anything to make him appear as a beast
from the woods. Tork smirked as he looked at Pendle's glis-

tening buttons, ironed tunic and shiny boots. Pendle was more interested in the hessian sack over Tork's shoulder.

"Do you have the device?" Pendle asked.

"Would we be here if we didn't?" Tork replied, watching Pendle as he checked out the sack.

Pendle was unfazed. He'd dealt with privateer insolence many times before.

"Major Franks has asked that I confirm the device is in your possession before I show you in."

"Anyone would think this Major Franks wasn't keen to see us," Tork sneered.

Spicer nodded acquiescence and Tork opened the sack in Pendle's direction. Pendle could make out the eerie blue glow of Wonder, and a dark ebony casing, resembling the underside of a fat cockroach. It certainly looked like the illustrations from the briefing, so he indicated for the squad to advance past the rows of clerk's desks to the door marked, "Mjr. R. Franks – Regional Enchantment Auditor".

Tork didn't like offices, he didn't like people who have offices, he didn't like being in offices and he didn't like meeting the people in them. He looked down on office workers because he was tall and they were stupid. If they weren't stupid, they were probably weak. Spicer wasn't weak and he wasn't stupid, unlike most of Tork's previous commanding officers. Spicer got him. He understood. Spicer didn't fit in either. People looked at Spicer the same way they looked at Tork. With horror. With disdain. Never with respect. Until they saw them fight.

Tork had never met someone like Spicer. He knew what everyone on his side should do in a fight, and he knew what everyone on the other side would do. It was like he had a sixth sense. Tork was not the same in this respect. Point Tork in one direction, just tell him where to get to, no need to tell him why, and Tork would get there. Never mind what was in the way, he would get through it and get to where he was told to get. He was no good with a Twirler pistol. He thought it resembled some effeminate pepper grinder, not a real man's weapon. So he was no quick draw, but he could fire a sawn-off blat gun and he could punch, hack and club all night long if need be.

Bunce could pop off the individuals, Conway could send up some dabbled fog or whatever, but leave it to Tork and Spicer to take care of the real thing, the fighting. The killing.

There was only one downside to being good at this stuff and that was meeting the pathetic squirts too scared to do it themselves.

Tork nodded thanks at the Sergeant Major as he held the door open into the Major's office, ducking his head to avoid the doorframe and squeezing himself into the tiny space with the others. The office had one shelf holding a few books. Your Majors and suchlike always have a few books hanging around to show grunts like Tork that they're busy while he's out doing all the work. Above the shelf was a small window showing the dusky sky as the sunset filtered through the red industrial smoke from Chinsey's few factories. Tork supposed some people would think it pretty. Others would be impressed that somewhere so provincial actually had a factory.

"Don't you people salute a senior officer?"

Tork blinked himself back into the room. He glanced over at the rest of the squad. None of them saluted. Tork turned to Spicer.

"Shall I show him the device now?" he asked.

"I don't want to see the damned device!" the Major snapped, pushing himself back from his tiny desk. The Major was a short man, shorter than most, which was unfortunate for him as it meant more people saw his bald spot, a palm-sized area on his head that he was desperately trying to conceal with a comb-over. It was a constant battle, exacerbated, he thought, by this pathetic back of beyond posting manned by a sorry bunch of ignorant provincials and visited by violent thugs, such as these disgusting Reclaimers. The only thing worse than them, their attitude and their stench was the ungodly device they had "reclaimed" and brought into his office.

The Gargoyle Key. An ancient artefact made of pure Blue Wonder by God knows who, God knows how.

Normally, as Regional Enchantment Auditor, Major Rupert Franks had to check the safety of industrial manufacturing centres that used Red Wonder, the source of energy for the Empire's lighting, the slideways, the weaponry: normal stuff. Very occasionally he had come into contact with Green Wonder, very rare in most parts of the Empire. It was rumoured that the Ditch had mastered Green Wonder, using it to lengthen their lives and raise entire armies from the dead. Only a few specialist hyperphysicists in the Empire were able to use it, including Doctor Axelrod, whose office was a few doors down the hall. Too few doors down the hall, in Franks' opinion.

Franks didn't like Green Wonder and he didn't like Doctor Axelrod.

But the Gargoyle Key. That was different. That was Blue Wonder, the real scary stuff. Banned around the world, hardly anyone knew how to use it, although there was evidence it was used in the past. Blue Wonder was the miraculous stuff, turning water into wine, letting people swim on the land, transforming music into monsters.

Everybody was scared of Blue Wonder. And there was a lot of the deep Blue to be found in The Gramarye.

"Go on, have a quick look," Tork smirked, opening the sack to let the pale blue glow leak into the room.

"No!" Franks squealed.

"It can't hurt you," reasoned Conway.

"How do you know? Nobody knows," Franks demanded of the hyperphysicist.

"He has a point," nodded Bunce.

"Look," grumbled Tork, losing interest and pulling the sack closed. "I haven't been in a city with a bawdy house for six whole weeks and my rifle needs oiling. Can you sign for this or whatever it is you have to do so we can get out of here?"

Franks was in full agreement with the large man with the big arms who seemed to be the custodian of the Gargoyle Key, but there was nothing he could do. He felt himself stutter as he replied.

"We have to wait for the Echo."

"What's that?"

"The E.C.O.," Spicer said, resting his hand on Franks' desk. "Enchantment and Chicanery Operative. The man who needs to check our prize and make sure it's the real thing."

"That's why I hate dealing with the blue dabble. Half the people are scared of it, and the other half don't even believe in it," Tork huffed, putting the sack on the table. Franks' face registered alarm, and he jumped at the rap at the door. Pendle's head poked in.

"Colonel Quine and his guests would like to see the Reclaimers, Major."

Franks bit his lip, attempting to withhold his unbridled joy at being able to relieve himself of these terrible people and their terrifying cargo.

"The Colonel has requested your presence too, Major."

Franks felt his face twitch.

Lieutenant Spicer followed the rest of his squad up the corridor towards the Colonel's office. He was tired. He knew that he'd let Tork get away with too much cheek. Normally he would slam the big man down, but there was something bothering Spicer. He felt like he'd forgotten to do something important. Or that something was on the tip of his tongue. Or that he'd just woken from a deep sleep but couldn't discern the reason. He got this feeling occasionally and it never led to anything positive. He tried to put it down to his tiredness. He also had a creeping suspicion it was the Blue Wonder getting to him. His parents had warned him about the Deep Blue. Don't get too close to it. It's dangerous. For everything good it seems to do for you, it will always make you pay twofold. Perhaps they were fairy tales they'd heard. Spicer had been brought up near a fairy colony and the little people certainly did like to talk and tell tales. Some people called it the dabble babble. At first, when he'd been very young, he'd been happy to listen, although nobody else seemed to take any heed except his parents. His few childhood friends had always scorned the fairies, and Spicer didn't want to be any more different than he already was. His burns were the result of an accident when he was a baby, and he couldn't remember a time without them. So Spicer turned his back on the fairies, just like everybody else.

As Pendle held the door open into Colonel Quine's office, Spicer's unease grew, with an oppressive sense of *déjà-vu*. One hand was already resting on his sword, and his other moved towards his Twirler pistol. As the Red Wonder of his gun tickled his fingertips, he entered the room.

"Major Franks, how good of you to join us. Which one of you is Lieutenant Spicer?"

Colonel Quine sat behind a desk the size of Franks' office in front of an expansive window, Doctor Axelrod at his side. Seated on a couch by the wall reclined an old man clinging to a walking stick, a gnarly individual Spicer recognised as Ambrose Willis, the Viceroy of The Gramarye.

"I'm Spicer."

He looked at the pot-bellied Quine crammed into his chair, his oiled hair glistening and his moustache sharpened to points, and at the ECO, Axelrod, a stick insect of a man, almost as tall as Tork but stooped, with a natural sneer beneath his hook nose. They looked like a natural double act, especially framed as they were by the broad window. The Viceroy was a different kettle of fish, lurking in the shadows, his eyes glinting with belligerence. He was no behind-the-scenes bureaucrat. This old man looked like he did nothing through the books. He regarded Bunce's feminine form and licked his thin lips through his yellowing teeth.

Beyond the glass, Chinsey, Grand Quillia's regional capital in The Gramarye, lay below them. On the outskirts were a few small factories and a mill, belching out red smoke as the Wonder kept things churning on into the evening. Many of the houses around the factories were tenements, with small shared yards backing onto dark alleyways. Slicing through the middle from beyond the city was a slideway, the ice glistening, leading all the way into Chinsey's central station, close to where they were, at the Regional Headquarters. Also discernible were the Trade barracks and the Viceroy's palace, imposing themselves over the rest of the provincial colonial town. In the palace's gardens, Spicer could make out a few ruins, from whatever town stood here before the Trade took over The Gramarye for the Empire forty years previously.

"May we see the Gargoyle Key, Lieutenant?" asked Axelrod, already drooling over the prospect of getting his hyperphysicist's hands on some real Blue Wonder.

"Of course."

Tork stepped forward, opening the sack.

"Perhaps Major Franks would pass it to us," Quine suggested.

Tork glanced at Spicer, unwilling to get involved in one senior officer bullying another, but Spicer's mind was elsewhere. Spicer felt like someone had just called to him from far away, and he had no idea who it was or what they had said. His hand tightened on his pistol.

"Here you go, Major," grinned Tork, removing the key from the sack and ramming it into Franks' quaking hand.

Franks walked towards the desk, holding the sack at arm's length, his face twitching, the auditor desperately attempting to retain some dignity in front of the Viceroy.

Spicer's gaze out of the window sharpened, and he found himself focusing on a wallet-sized patch attached to the outside of the glass. Then he realised what he had been feeling all day. Impending doom. And at that exact moment, Spicer felt his ears pop.

He pulled the Twirler pistol from its holster and spun the chamber to charge the Red Wonder's projectile force.

"Lieutenant?" Axelrod said.

Tork reached for the blat gun hanging from his shoulder.

"Explos…" Spicer began, before the window blew in, glass peppering them all. Spicer's ringing ears managed to pick out the whirring of other Twirler pistols as the glass showered onto the floor. Two figures in goggles and earmuffs, wearing lumberjack harnesses clipped to ropes swung in through the open window from the room above, red flashes thumping from their guns. One threw a long dark tube, like a documents holder, and as it span through the air, Spicer heard Conway shout two words.

"White out!"

As Spicer pulled his Twirler's trigger, everything flashed to pure matt white, as though a sudden snowstorm had buried them all at once, and then he couldn't make out a thing, like he had been struck by an avalanche. For a second he could feel the kick in his hand as the Twirler fired, then that feeling faded and there was no sound. He lowered the gun, worried he would hit the Colonel or the ECO who had been caught in the crossfire. His brain told his mouth to order Conway to bring up counter measures but he couldn't feel his jaw or tongue move. He'd been the victim of white out attacks before. It was Green Wonder, affecting the brain. There was no snow, and it was not deathly quiet, but he had lost all sensation. None of his senses were functioning. The tube grenade had unleashed Green Wonder treated to enter through the eyes and ears, hence the goggles and earmuffs on their attackers. He had known people who had suffered a fatal white out, unable to swallow food, imbibe water, or say goodbye to their loved ones. But this was already fading. Whoever had used the grenade didn't have the money for the good stuff so they obviously weren't military. These were freelancers, like Spicer's own Reclaimers.

The lieutenant slowly lowered himself to the floor, deciding to sit down and wait it out. With the combination of the white out and his uniform, he couldn't feel any of the glass he was undoubtedly sitting on.

When they'd first started looking for the Gargoyle Key, Spicer had heard there were others after it. He went down the list in his mind. Harcourt's group had been decimated by a Hump attack in the Glasslands. Goring's team had drowned when their chartered vessel went down off the coast of Livesey Island. The Albrecht gang had turned on each other in the dungeons of Kahleel, with no survivors. That left one crew with the audacity to embark on a raid in the Trade's own regional headquarters.

The wall of white clouding Spicer's vision retreated suddenly, as if someone had pulled a plug in the far wall and the pure white milky blanket had been sucked away. His hearing came back as though somebody had opened a heavy door to a loud party.

"…God's sake, Major. All you had to do was keep hold of it," Quine was snarling.

Spicer saw Tork shake his head clear, as though he was discouraging a bee from flying in his ear, while Bunce stared irritably at her boots as her sight returned. She rounded on Conway.

"What the Hell happened to you? I thought you knew how to deal with this sort of thing," she hissed, leaving Conway to shrug in reply.

Suddenly, the door was kicked open and Pendle stood at the door, his shoulders draped with ammo and a blat gun in each hand. Quine didn't even look at him as he waved him away.

"I'll get the caretaker, Sir," Pendle said as he closed the door behind him.

Tork helped Spicer to his feet, and the two of them moved to look out of the shattered window, the glass crunching under their boots. They looked at the hooks above where the ropes had been attached and down into the streets below.

Axelrod and Quine joined Spicer and Tork at the window, Axelrod with a pair of binoculars, which he used to scour the streets below.

"I take it this doesn't affect our fee, Colonel," Spicer said, not bothering to look him in the eye.

"Of course not, Lieutenant Spicer. You will receive your fee as promised," Quine licked his lips, savouring the moment, "once the Gargoyle Key is safely in my possession."

Spicer rolled his eyes in Tork's direction.

"Anything, Axelrod?"

Axelrod shook his head.

"The perpetrators would need to know exactly where the key would be taken - on this occasion to you, Colonel. They would need to know how to gain access to a Trade building. And they would also need to be able to get their hands on weapon-grade Green Wonder and know what to do with it once they had it," Axelrod surmised.

"It can only be Rickenbacker," Quine spat, "Rickenbacker, and that gaggle of fools led by Sir Evan Mandell. But why would they want the Gargoyle Key? They would never work for the People of The Ditch. Why would they steal it from us?"

"To stop us having it," said the Viceroy, picking glass from his lap as he remained in his spot on the couch, "You know how difficult Rickenbacker likes to be."

"We should have killed him all those years ago," said Quine, "when he was still working with us."

"Colonel," said the Viceroy, tapping his stick on the floor. "Send the lieutenant and his Reclaimers with an Immolator Squad to get the key back. They found it once and they will find it again."

He raised his stick and pointed it directly at Spicer. "Rickenbacker cannot be allowed to use that key."

"Rick who?" Tork asked, surprised he was interested.

Axelrod answered, "Professor Hilary Rickenbacker, once one of our own but his hyperphysical studies sent him crazy. Too much Wonder, Green or Blue, who knows? Now he can only be described as..."

"...a terrorist," Quine interrupted. "A terrorist, Mr... whoever you are," he added, looking Tork up and down.

"Where is he heading with the key? What does the key open?" Spicer asked.

Axelrod moved to a large, newly torn map of The Gramarye across the wall, "The Cathedral of Tales," he said, his thin finger tapping at the location, "in the middle of the Glasslands."

"An extra twenty per cent if you bring the terrorist back with the key," the Viceroy offered.

"Dead?" Tork asked.

"I don't care in the slightest."

Spicer had something on Rickenbacker and Mandell's crew. Something that would prove to be very useful.

"Fine. Let's go," Spicer shrugged and headed for the door.

"One last thing before your bring Rickenbacker to us on his knees, Lieutenant," Quine said, looking up at Tork.

"Sir?"

"Make the big one salute me before you leave," said Quine with a coy smile.

CHAPTER 1

The Glasslands
The Gramarye Region
Grand Quillia

June 1856

As Professor Hilary Rickenbacker steered his pony through the Glasslands in the sunlight, the Gargoyle Key in a pouch on his belt, he felt like he was riding in starlight, through constellations in daytime. Each tree had been turned to quartz, each leaf to glass, every blade of grass to amber. The sound of the leaves recalled xylophones playing a gentle ode to delicacy. It was indeed magical.

He looked up at the spire of the Cathedral of Tales rising high above the treetops of the Glasslands and wondered what the Gargoyle Key would reveal to them on their arrival, should they survive the journey. One road cut through the glacial forest, Aspic Lane, now deserted since the Trade had built a slideway bypassing the entire godforsaken area.

The transformation of the forest had occurred hundreds of years before, and to this day academics argued as to how it had happened. Most concurred it was caused by deep Blue Wonder, but nobody agreed why. One school of thought explained it away as an act of war, in which, having obliterated the city that had originally housed the Cathedral of the Tales, an evil force had deprived the survivors of fuel for their fires, meat and security. Some said it was punishment by God on a city of sin. The more fanciful speculators blamed dragons, hunted to extinction, laying waste to the beautiful woodlands as a final dying act of spite.

Both hyperphysicists and the opponents of dabbling had agreed it could be an accident, the result of mutation through the overspill of deep Blue, too powerful for the fools who thought they could control it.

Professor Hilary Rickenbacker considered himself a romantic and a gentleman, and so he preferred to believe the Glasslands had been created as a memorial to a greater time, to a people who had embraced the Blue Wonder as a force for good. As an academic and historian, he could find nothing to disprove his theory.

It was a pinnacle of what the Wonder could be, and he felt a flutter of excitement as he thought about the potential answers offered by the Gargoyle Key finally in their possession, snatched from the hands of mercenaries under the noses of the Trade.

He was sure they would be pursued by the Trade, but their enemies would have to face the same danger as his own group. Although no predatory wildlife could survive on a land made up entirely of minerals, there were the blood-thirsty Humps to look out for. Like camels, the large humps on the Humps' backs were both a burden, full as they were with cumbersome moisture to keep them alive, and something that gave them real freedom. They could go anywhere, live for months without water touching their lips. And they were happy eating raw flesh, so didn't need a fire. Their Neanderthal brains believed they absorbed the power of those they consumed, so their favourite diet consisted of humanity. Eat a bird and you gain the soul of a sparrow. Banquet on man, you get the power of the most vicious two legged beast of them all. The exact source of the Humps was another academic argument that continued to rage in the gentlemen's clubs of the Grand Quillia. Some said they were mankind's ancestors, left behind by progress when we started to create our homes nearer rivers and wetlands. Others said they had lost some great war and had been ostracised by society, so they had then adapted with the growth of their humps and the loss of civilised behaviour.

Whatever they were, everybody agreed they were best avoided.

They were not native to the Glasslands, but they had thrived, just as they did anywhere that was inhospitable to man. Deserts, salt flats, volcanic areas – places where man clung to life by their fingernails, the Humps were there to make it harder, to snatch hope away.

Rickenbacker felt a chill and kicked the flanks of his pony to get closer to his comrades. He looked over his shoulder to check Teddy was right behind him. He had familiar pang of guilt about dragging the boy into this. Unlike the others, Teddy wouldn't be able to defend himself against Humps, against anyone. Teddy would have trouble against a feral kitten, Rickenbacker admitted to himself. Teddy was the nephew of Rickenbacker's landlady in Fairport, when he was lecturing, and had come to work for the Professor as his manservant. When Rickenbacker discovered the existence of the Gargoyle Key and decided to pursue it, Teddy had stayed by his side. He had warned the boy that his decision to pursue something that may bring them up against The Trade could lead them into choppy waters, but the boy, never demonstrative at the best of times, had shrugged his shoulders and packed his things into the same leather case that hung incongruously from his saddle amongst the pack bags.

Teddy's eyes swept the forest, and Rickenbacker could see his slender knuckles were white as he gripped hard to the reigns. The Professor really didn't need anybody to make his tea or lay out his clothes any more. He carried no teapot and had just one change of clothes. Once they got back to civilisation, Rickenbacker would make the boy redundant - with as generous a payoff as he could manage, of course.

As Rickenbacker made his decision, he noticed that the man named Pinkerton had slowed down to ride alongside the boy.

"All alright there, Teddy, my boy?" Pinkerton asked in his lilting accent from the Western Isles.

"Yes, sir, thank you, Sir, Mr Pinkerton, Sir," Teddy replied, his lips trembling.

Teddy seemed just as scared of the enormous boxer as he was of the forest and Humps. He avoided looking into Pinkerton's battered face, framed by the man's cauliflower eyes, heavy bridge of a brow and awesomely plush sideburns meandering down his face to skirt the edge of his mouth. His eyes got as far as Pinkerton's battle-scarred hands and went no further. He had seen the handbills and posters the man carried around like business cards. Everybody had. Whenever the beer started to flow or wine glasses were filled, which they would be all the time if Pinkerton had his way, the man would unfurl the posters and tell his stories.

The posters called him Ten Fingers Pinkerton the Gentleman Pugilist, and his most famous fight had been a bout that lasted eight hours and twenty-four minutes, bare-knuckled on Langtry Common. His opponent, Bill Edlington the East Country Masher, had broken Pinkerton's arm in two places, but still Pinkerton battled on, finally knocking Edlington spark out with an uppercut to the jaw after a quick one-two, as the sun turned blood orange red over the Great Quillian capital.

Occasionally they would meet people who had heard of Pinkerton, and once they met a drunk who claimed to have been at the Langtry Common fight, but that same drunk had also claimed to have once dined on his own ear, an assertion disputed by both ears being healthily in place either side of his head.

Pinkerton had already been riding with Sir Evan Mandell when Rickenbacker had first met them. Rickenbacker and Teddy had been fleeing The Trade's militia through the back streets of Allenbridge and had stumbled into a dead end behind a pub. Mandell later recalled he had seen the militia, weapons drawn, advancing on the Professor and his manservant, and had been in the process of flipping a coin to ascertain whether he should finish his meal - a rabbit and bean stew with potatoes and leeks, and a fine specimen of it at that - or head straight out and intervene. His decision had been made for him when Rickenbacker had used a burst of Red Wonder to deter his attackers, accidentally smashing every window on that side of the pub and showering all the occupants, as well as Mandell's stew, with slivers of glass.

It was when the pub's regulars joined the militia in demanding their pound of flesh from the Professor that Pinkerton had reminded Mandell of their decision to become gentleman adventurers, and the two men had joined the fray, naturally taking the side of the underdog.

Sir Evan and Pinkerton had been riding with the Professor for the three months since, and had seen many sights to provide stories their grandchildren would become rich reciting. They had seen the Professor wield magic like a weapon straight from pure unmediated Wonder, both Red and Green, and had broken into a Trade Headquarters, (albeit a regional one, but not all parts of the story need be stressed) to steal a prize from the renowned Reclaimers commanded by the unscrupulous Lieutenant Spicer, a privateer ruffian and all round bad egg.

The final member of the group advancing through the Glasslands was the fair Lady Elena Melody. The rest of them knew little about her, except for Sir Evan, who had managed to see her naked twice, and had seen her breasts a total of five times. Unfortunately the last time he had been spotted ogling said chest, which had been a fearsome embarrassment that could only be salved with copious amounts of alcohol, this time a fulsome brandy from a roadside inn on the other side of Chinsey.

Lady Melody explained she was a widow, although this made her no more susceptible to Mandell's attempt at seductive charm. Her husband Lord Runciman Drew Hynes Melody was from the respected Drew Hynes Melodys who, four generations ago, had sponsored the Drew Hynes Melody Wing at the University of Fairport, where Rickenbacker had lectured in a History of The Wonder. Although he had never met Lady Melody, Rickenbacker had met Runciman fleetingly when the ruddy-faced Lord had twice visited the University for a Founders Day or some other black tie boozy bash. Despite the few rushed introductions, the Professor had apparently made quite an impression. Elena told the story that on his death bed, Runciman told his darling wife to seek the Professor out and study with him, help him in any way she could and that is what Elena had dedicated herself to for the last month. She had discovered Rickenbacker at a provincial records office, when he had started planning the raid on The Trade's Chinsey headquarters, and hadn't let the Professor out of her sight since.

She proved to be quite the tomboy, able to ride with the best of the men and fire dual Twirlers from the hip, something she put down to her background as the only daughter in a family with thirteen brothers.

Elena was the first in the group to hear the Humps' approach. She pulled her pony up and tilted her head to listen. Mandell had seen enough of Elena's skills to trust her instincts better than his own, and drew his pistol. It was an antiquated pre-Twirler one-shot Spinner pistol, the heirloom of a military family. He spun the chamber on his thigh to charge the single shot, looking over at Pinkerton, who was pulling his blat gun from its saddle holster.

"What's happening?" Teddy asked.

"Humps," Elena hissed, before pointing to the side of the road, "coming from that direction."

"Professor," Mandell called, squinting into the woods, "Any tricks up your sleeve?"

The ponies started to spook, as did Teddy. It was then the rest of the group heard the approach. Like the sound of grit being shaken in thousands of glass bottles simultaneously echoing in a tunnel full of wind chimes, the Humps crashed through the Glasslands, unable to surprise the party on pony back. They knew their prey's ponies would get skittish, and that would only help them.

"Throw me the bag," Rickenbacker demanded from Teddy, whose pony twisted as he reached round the saddlebags desperately searching for what Mandell called the Professor's 'bag of tricks'. Elena's Twirlers hit their optimum spin, a noise akin to a swarm of mosquitoes, and she was the first to fire, pulling the triggers on her guns three times each. The bright red shots of Wonder carrying the projectiles lit up the crystal trees around them as they hurtled through the woods. Teddy's young eyes could make out the dark shapes of the Humps thundering towards them, seeing two in the front fall to the ground leaving arcs of blood as the shots hit their targets.

"Teddy!" Rickenbacker shouted over the gunfire, desperate for his tools.

Teddy tore his gaze from the Humps and returned to finding the bag, the sound of the ponies' screams, glass shattering and Twirlers blasting deafening him. Over the cacophony, Teddy could make out the booming blat, like a huge dollop of mud dropped from on high hitting the ground, accompanied by Pinkerton's imaginative torrent of abuse and occasional roars of laughter at either his own invective or the results of his violence. Teddy thought they were all crazy. Why would anyone choose to live like this? If his mother were not twice as terrifying as your average Hump, Teddy would have been home months ago. The fact his mother had probably moved house and hadn't replied to any of his correspondence implied he had nowhere to return to anyway, but still.

Finally, his hands clamped around the felt bag and he pulled it from the saddlebag to hand to Rickenbacker, who grasped for it eagerly. He looked up and found the woods themselves suddenly thick with Humps; some naked, some clothed, all of them dark with blood, their own, that of their comrades and probably that of their victims. Teddy whimpered and his pony spun. Rickenbacker's fingers slipped from the bag as Teddy let go, and it dropped to the floor between them. Teddy tried to look at the Professor, hoping to see some forgiveness or something that said, "Don't worry," or "None of this is happening." This was not forthcoming, however.

"Hurry, Teddy!" Rickenbacker yelled, wishing his legs were thirty years younger so that he could swing down to get it himself.

Mandell glanced over and spurred his pony to stand between Teddy and the advancing horde. He continued to spin the pistol against his thigh between each shot, and each shot seemed to count. He pulled his cutlass and nodded encouragement to Teddy as the boy dismounted. His pony twitched its head, yanking the reins from Teddy's grip, and Teddy found himself deposited painfully onto the muddy road, the felt bag tangling around the pony's hooves. Teddy reached for the bag but the pony continued to trample, and, as Mandell rained fire at the oncoming Humps, the pony kicked higher. Suddenly the Humps broke the tree line, two throwing themselves at Rickenbacker as he looked on with helplessness at Teddy scrambling around on the ground. Elena dispatched both with her twin guns before more Humps broke towards her. Mandell holstered his pistol and turned his pony towards Elena, waving his cutlass as he approached, casually hacking down more Humps on the road.

Finally, Teddy's pony stumbled clear of the bag and Teddy pounced on it, clasping it tightly to his chest.

"Professor, I've got it" he exclaimed, as he felt a Hump's hand grasp at his coat.

"Look out!" Rickenbacker called, kicking Humps away from his own steed.

Teddy was spun around so the Hump could look him in the eyes before taking his first bite. Teddy shook his head, hoping to convince the Hump out of his nature, as the smell of rot became as suffocating as the Hump's grasp. He saw the back of the Hump's head explode in red, like a peacock's tail unfurling, before he heard the blat of Pinkerton's weapon.

"Throw the bag, pipsqueak!" Pinkerton bellowed into his face, before taking out two more Humps with one shot.

"Take that, you misshapen heathens!" he chuckled, as he watched the bag fly through the air into Rickenbacker's hands. Teddy hadn't seen Pinkerton dismount but he was standing alongside his pony, grinning, covered in blood. With the big man alongside him giving him some strength, Teddy took stock. Elena and Mandell's ponies were next to each other in a yin-yang formation, Elena using her Twirlers, Mandell his cutlass. Pinkerton blatted two Humps as they approached Rickenbacker, who was rummaging in the bag.

"Take this and sit on that," Pinkerton ordered, ramming the blat gun into Teddy's arms and throwing him onto his pony. Then he turned to face the stream of Humps, teeth bared and fists ready, shouting, "Come on then, you fat-backed jessies!"

Teddy straightened himself on Pinkerton's pony, and looked back into the woods, and at more Humps. The smile had finally left Mandell's face as he hacked without the aplomb or class which he had merrily displayed before. Elena was trying to spur her pony further down the road but the animal was stumbling on the corpses and wounded Humps around its hooves.

"You cheeky buggers!" Pinkerton howled, as three Humps grabbed his arms, one biting deep, sinking its rotten teeth into the muscle. Now two Humps had found Teddy and he clubbed at them with the blat gun, unsure whether it was blood, sweat or tears running down his face.

"Pinkerton! The trees!"

Pinkerton walloped one Hump in the face and shook off two others to frown in the Professor's direction.

"Climb, Pinkerton!"

Pinkerton noticed the Professor pulling a round wooden box no bigger than a cricket ball out of the felt bag, and immediately understood. He growled with exertion, shook off his attackers like a bear swatting away dogs in a circus pit, and threw himself at the nearest overhanging glass branch. He roared in pain as he caught it, the sharp edges slicing his fingers, and the Professor threw the ball straight down at the floor.

Teddy felt his ears pop, and then he couldn't hear gunshots or glass smashing or the howls of the subhuman. He heard a deep hearty hum and he saw the muddy lane turn a shadowy blackberry-violet colour. He saw blood running down Pinkerton's forearms and then he saw the gold tooth in the boxer's mouth as the man gave him a broad grin. His eyes moved to the Professor to see his employer close the felt bag and wipe his brow with relief. It was then he noticed Humps retreating into the woods at speed. He looked at the two who had been attacking him, but they were bent over double, pulling at their feet, tearing at their ankles. As his hearing returned, Teddy was aware of the childlike howls of terror coming from his ride. He heard the gunshots as Elena finished off the Humps near her ride, which was also screaming. She dismounted, raised her pistol, and put a round through her pony's head. Pinkerton let himself drop from the branch and walked around the Humps who had been attacking him. He grabbed the heads of the two nearest Teddy and cracked their skulls together. They lolled backwards but stayed upright, despite being out cold. Rickenbacker calmed his pony before climbing down to undo the saddlebags.

"What happened?" Teddy asked as Pinkerton started to unpack the saddlebags either side of the boy.

"The old boy happened," Pinkerton smirked, casually throwing belongings he no longer needed over his shoulder.

"We have to walk from here," Rickenbacker said sombrely.

"What was that, Professor? What did you do?"

"That was the Wonder, my boy," he said. "Very old Wonder," he mumbled. "I wasn't entirely sure it would work,"

"That was the green, wasn't it, Professor?" Elena asked, wiping blood from her riding gloves onto her pony's corpse.

"I'm afraid it was, Lady Melody."

"You did good, old man," chortled Mandell, slapping the Professor on the back. "I thought for a minute we were reaching a less than rousing finish."

"I'm not so sure it was good, Sir Evan."

"We're alive, aren't we?" Mandell asked, prodding a dead Hump with his foot.

"For the minute. We have no ponies and the Humps have tasted blood."

"Only Pinkerton's. That'll give them heartburn at the very least."

"But what was it, Professor? What green magic?"

"Originally mentioned in Ember's Study of Green Wonder from the Sixth Epoch," he looked at the results, "You may remember the paralysing floor from its use at the Meander Canyon Massacre."

"Paralysing floor?"

"I've heard of that," Elena nodded, "it sticks anyone to the floor like quick-drying mud. Even those inches above can be affected."

"Like flies in aspic," Mandell suggested, picking brains from his double-breasted tunic.

"How long does it last?" Teddy asked, glancing at the struggling Humps nearby.

"Thirty seconds," Pinkerton joked, teasing a Hump as it grasped at him.

"Forever, Teddy. None of these creatures will ever leave here."

Rickenbacker turned back to emptying his saddlebags.

"Come on now, Teddy. We need to move on."

Teddy stared at the Humps, the ponies, the corpses and Pinkerton's bloody handprints on the crystalline tree and shuddered.

"Does the thing we got from the Trade do this sort of thing?" he asked.

Elena paused to listen to the Professor's response.

"It's Blue Wonder, not the Green, Teddy, and from what I've read, the Gargoyle Key protects us from all..." he waved his hand around, "...this."

Elena put a reassuring hand on Teddy's shoulder. Rickenbacker regarded the worry on the boy's face. This time he would definitely leave the boy at the next town.

"I hate this pony," Tork remarked, as the animal started wheezing under its load. "Is there any type of dabble that could make it stronger?"

"Or anything that could make Tork lighter?" Conway snorted.

"He could eat less," Bunce suggested.

"I will happily kill you both in these woods and leave you here for some Humps pudding."

"I doubt they'll need pudding if you're the main course," Conway shot back, winking at Bunce.

"I reckon that old bird Rickenbacker was already the main course. They're probably picking their teeth with his bones right now."

"I didn't know dental hygiene was important to Humps," remarked Conway.

"Do we really need to be having this conversation?" Spicer interjected, without looking back.

Conway and Tork exchanged glances. The boss had definitely changed since they'd found the Gargoyle Key. He was morose, as if a realisation of some great darkness had shrouded his mind.

Tork had never wanted to embark on the Gargoyle Key job anyway. He preferred the proper reclamation jobs, the work that had earned them their name, reclaiming land that rightfully belonged to the Trade, as opposed to this ancient unknowable artefact dabble mumbo jumbo.

"Where are the Humps anyway?" Bunce mumbled, looking into the Glasslands as she stroked the butt of her rifle.

Spicer had not noticed her bloodthirstiness before. It bothered him now, but he couldn't discern why.

"I reckon they're scared," Tork grunted.

"Of you?" Conway again.

"Of them," Tork said, flipping his thumb at the Trade Immolation Squad marching behind them.

The Immolation Troops were the elite corps of the Trade's private army. They were inscrutable, silent and deadly soldiers in full battle armour; not the greatest fighters but they never questioned, and so, despite their name, were worth much more than simple Wonder fodder. They wore leather armour with full-face helmets and goggles augmented with Red Wonder, which crackled around them like Saint Elmo's fire. Nobody outside the corps saw beneath the masks, ensuring rumours were rife about their true identity. Their commanders communicated with them remotely, using ancient Wonder skills that nobody else truly understood. This meant nobody could take out their leader, as he was concealed far behind his own lines. They could not be taken prisoner. If a trooper was wounded, he immediately self-immolated, an inferno terrifying to the enemy.

Wherever the Trade were in The Gramarye, the Immolators were there, like a beacon of terror. The Great Quillian parliament turned a blind eye on the commercial organisation's use of Blue Wonder, as long as none of the regular suburban citizenry caught sight of the Immolators, of course. They were happy for them to exist as the shadowy bogeymen of the Empire, but they didn't want the people on the home front questioning exactly how the Trade went about the business of wringing out the rest of the Empire's resources in its farthest corners.

The Immolation Squad marched in formation behind the Reclaimers, always keeping up with the privateers, despite them being on pony back. Spicer knew that no matter how strong Tork's pony was, or how fast it would gallop, the Immolators would be right behind them. It gave him another chill. He still hadn't shaken his sense of foreboding since the Gargoyle Key had been snatched, and, as they turned a corner of Aspic Lane to be confronted by the results of Rickenbacker's paralysing floor, he knew the feeling was not about to leave him any time soon.

Axelrod's apprentice gasped, eyes wide.

"What is it?" Quine asked, looking over the boy's shoulder into the crystal ball on the plinth in front of them.

"Rickenbacker," Axelrod groaned as he nodded at his apprentice to halt the Immolation Squad in his command.

The Colonel and his Enchantment and Chicanery Operative were deep beneath The Trade's regional headquarters in Chinsey, in an area below the basement. The architecture was completely different from the Trade building above, ornate in a way different to the Imperial edifices of Great Quillia. This was delicate curved stonework that celebrated art and having the time to spend on creating beauty, rather than being designed to be oppressively impressive. The beauty surpassed anything the Trade had built in these remote parts of the Empire, which was exactly why the Trade had demolished the rest of the structure to build on top of it. The ruins in the garden were there to remind the natives of their power. Nobody outside the upper echelons of the Trade knew about the existence of this subterranean vault, however.

A few of the vaults had been found around The Gramarye, most of which had already been pillaged for their crystal balls. It had taken over a decade of study before they discovered a beneficial use for the stunning chambers built around the surviving crystal balls, and this particular chamber was the only one they had managed to operate effectively. The activation of the ballroom corresponded with the proliferation of the Immolators around The Gramarye. The ECOs had conceived of a name bitter in its innocuousness, considering the chamber's ability to control brain dead homicidal troops. They named these control centres the Ballrooms.

Secure in the Chinsey Ballroom, Quine, Axelrod and his assistant peered at the perfectly round blackberry stain blighting Aspic Lane, seen through the eyes of their lead Immolator.

"Where did Rickenbacker get something that could create a paralysing floor?" Axelrod hissed, almost to himself.

Quine started to pace. He didn't like this one bit.

"Do we go round it?" asked Tork, sounding less than interested.

Bunce dismounted and walked slowly towards the blackberry stain.

"Is it still active?" Bunce asked, poking at it gently with the butt of her rifle.

"It is for those poor devils," Spicer replied, tying his pony out of reach of the stain.

There was a loud discharge of a blat gun as two surviving Humps were blown apart, remaining upright in death. Tork started laughing, swivelling his blat gun at his hip to point it at another stuck Hump.

"For God's sake, Tork," Spicer snapped. "Conway, do we need to go round it?"

Conway shrugged. Bunce shook her head with disbelief.

"Erm, sorry."

One of the Immolators broke ranks and marched steadily towards the stain, knocking Bunce's shoulder on the way. Without a pause it stepped into the blackberry stain and marched on the spot, a ludicrous sight that almost seemed to taunt the corpses left by Rickenbacker's group earlier.

"Looks like smiley here has answered our question," Conway said, folding his arms.

"Okay. We ride through one at a time. Let's go."

Spicer swung back into his saddle and kicked it gently forward. He waited for his ears to pop, for the searing pain, for the world to fall in, for anything to validate his dark feelings, almost willing it. But unlike the majority of those in the blackberry stain, Spicer and his pony remained in complete control of all their limbs and faculties. He turned back to reassure the rest of his group as the Immolators marched past him as if he wasn't there.

After two hours of walking, Rickenbacker and his companion rounded a bend on Aspic Lane. Looking up, they saw a unique sight towering above the glistening treetops.

"Please tell me that is where we are going," Mandell huffed, while Teddy thought the exact opposite.

"The Cathedral of Tales," Elena marvelled, dropping her bags to the ground and planting her hands on her hips.

"That's right, Lady Melody," Rickenbacker nodded, "although we don't know if that is what it was named by its builders."

"Professor, sometimes you sound remarkably like a Professor," Pinkerton grinned.

The Cathedral of Tales looked black against the whiteness of the crystal vegetation, its stonework darkened by time. The main walls jutted above the trees, vase shaped window frames reaching towards the absent roof. But the most impressive aspect of the Cathedral was the tower, soaring into the heavens before arching back over, so that the chamber at the end hung halfway down.

"It looks like a snowdrop," Pinkerton murmured.

"How did they build it?" Elena gasped, "I mean, I know it was the Wonder, but how is it still up there?"

"This entire area is still incredibly rich in the Wonder, my dear."

"Then why isn't there a trade strip mine exactly where we're standing? It's not like the Humps have scared them away. Send in an Immolation Brigade and the Humps would..."

"There is more to be worried about in this part of The Gramarye than Humps, Sir Evan."

"Like what, Professor?" Teddy asked, shuddering.

"Deep Blue Wonder," Lady Melody said, her eyes still on the slender neck of the curving tower.

"Exactly, milady," Rickenbacker nodded slowly. "Whatever built the Cathedral, whoever had the power to change these woods around us, who's to say they have left us? Nobody has ever returned from the Cathedral. Nobody knows who or what is in there."

"I hear it's gold and silver carved with Wonder, to melt the hearts of the fairest maidens," Sir Evan suggested, glancing towards Elena.

"Perhaps it's a pretty dress and some high-heeled shoes with oh such delicate buckles," Pinkerton chuckled, clasping his paws beneath his chin like an eight-year-old in love.

"What's that?" Teddy asked, pointing to the north-west, where a thin column of dark smoke rose into the clear sky close by the Cathedral, nearby to where Aspic Lane led.

"I've heard there is a way station for the weary traveller, the last left on Aspic Lane," Rickenbacker said.

"Is it run by Humps?" asked Sir Evan.

"We will ready ourselves there before we use the Gargoyle Key to enter the Cathedral," the Professor stated, before setting off down the lane.

"I do hope readying involves fair maidens and much inebriation," Sir Evan winked, following the Professor.

Elena continued to stare in awe at the enormous building.

"Milady?" Pinkerton prompted.

"It's incredible, isn't it, Mr Pinkerton?"

"That it probably is, Miss. Perhaps we should catch up with the others."

"What do you hope to see before we enter that place, Mr Pinkerton? In case..."

Teddy paused to hear the boxer's answer.

"A dog, milady. I'd like to tickle the hairy chin of a large mutt and feel his wagging tail slap against me before I enter another hellhole from which I may never return. I like dogs, Miss."

"As do I, Mr Pinkerton, as do I."

She indicated to him to lead on, and, with one last glance at the wilting architecture of the Cathedral of Tales, the three of them made their way down Aspic Lane.

CHAPTER 2

The Gleave Family Lodge
The Gramarye Region
Grand Quillia

June 1856

The path leading from Aspic Lane was well tended, gravelled with enough room for a large carriage to enter. The trees hung over the path, making a glass tunnel, and as the sky bruised and the sun dipped, the Glasslands turned a warm ruby red.

"This really is..." Elena caught herself saying.

"...Magical," Teddy finished, pausing to take in the whole environment.

"I can imagine retiring here," confided Pinkerton, "if the service weren't so abysmal, I mean."

"Why haven't the Humps come back, Professor?" Teddy asked, feeling a little more secure with the familiar feeling of swept gravel beneath his feet.

"The good thing about Humps is they're not as stupid as they look. They are just as petrified by the Wonder as…" Sir Evan cleared his throat, "…other people can be."

"Some would say the intelligence of the Humps is the biggest problem," said Pinkerton, rubbing the bite mark on his arm.

The crystal tunnel came to an end, so they could make out a building, two stories, with large bay windows and an accompanying empty stable. The brickwork at the front was host to ivy, turned to crystal long ago, and a light shone in the porch. Thick curtains were pulled across the windows, and to one side, bright green against the antiseptic crystal-lisation, pots of vegetable and herbs grew on large veranda that looked out over a large pond. The smoke that left the chimney was dark, with a touch of red to it. The new arrivals stopped and took in the incongruous scene. A dog, large by the sound of it, started to bark from inside.

"Looks like you got your wish," Elena said to Pinkerton.

"Wish?" asked Rickenbacker.

"He likes dogs," Mandell, crossing his arms across his chest. "Now there's a hell of thing."

"Why is there a hotel here? Do people come on holiday here?" Teddy asked, not believing his eyes.

"It's a lodge," Mandell said. "A hunting lodge."

"But what is there to hunt?" Elena frowned.

"Humps?" Pinkerton suggested.

Rickenbacker harrumphed.

"I sincerely hope that is not the case."

He straightened his jacket and hat, picked up his saddle-bags, and marched towards the front door. Teddy scampered after him, slicking down his forelock with a licked palm.

Mandell and Pinkerton glanced at each other, shrugged, and followed them. Elena regarded the house curiously and looked over her shoulder back down the gravel path, unable to see Aspic Lane beyond. She glanced back into the woods, pulled her Twirler, and checked its six barrels nervously before returning the pepper pot-shaped weapon to its holster and walking across the gravel to the lodge.

The porch was large, with a curved entrance and foot scrapers for the weary traveller to clean his boots. The front door was one enormous gnarly piece of oak, a sibling of what were now diamond ghosts of the surrounding trees. Above the door was a crest and words carved in a dead language. Rickenbacker squinted up at it.

"What does it say?" Elena asked.

Rickenbacker recited the foreign words. They sounded guttural and angry.

"Freedom through the Hand of Might," the Professor translated.

"Whose hand?" Elena asked.

"The Gleave family, judging by the coat of arms. Once they were a powerful force to be reckoned in the Gramarye." Rickenbacker said, reaching for the doorknocker.

"Once?" Pinkerton asked.

"Then the Trade arrived."

"It's the snowdrop," Elena said.

The knocker had the same curve as the Cathedral tower, its surface worn smooth by many visitors seeking entrance. Rickenbacker pulled back the knocker and let it drop back onto the fist-shaped metal plate embedded in the door. He knocked twice and the deep thud seemed to bounce around the woods.

"I hope they have wine," said Mandell, licking his lips.

"I hope they have hot water," added Elena.

"I hope they're friendly," murmured Teddy.

They heard two heavy bolts slide back and watched as the large door handle turned slowly. Teddy shrank behind the Professor and Mandell's hand tightened around his cutlass. As the door opened a couple of inches, a large black blob of a nose rammed itself through the gap and an enormous dog pushed itself into the open.

"Don't let the dog out!" came a voice, and Pinkerton's thick finger slipped beneath the hound's collar and held fast. The dog kicked the door wide open, and Pinkerton was spun round, knocking Elena and Mandell into the wall, and dragged into the gravel by the Western Isle Wolfhound, a magnificent example of a fine beast.

"Alexander, you come back here," said the man behind the door, as the wolfhound threw its paws onto Pinkerton's shoulders and commenced licking his face. Rickenbacker placed a gentle hand on Mandell's, and Sir Evan slid his pistol back into his holster.

"You're a good dog, yes you are," Pinkerton informed the dog, struggling to his feet while keeping a firm grip on the collar. He removed his neckerchief and wiped his sodden moustache.

"Sorry about that."

As is generally the case, the owner of the Wolfhound resembled his dog in all but size. He had large, kind brown eyes, shaggy hair that curled around his full eyebrows and a badly trimmed beard. He stood with an uneven gait, as though he had recently carried a very heavy shoulder bag, and his feet were turned outwards. He had the battered hands of a labourer and the dark leathery skin of a life spent outside. Around his neck and secured at his waist hung a blue and white striped apron, which made the fearsome carving knife in his hand a little less threatening.

"I'm Brennan," said the man, reaching out a hand to be shaken, "I expect you'd like a drink."

Mandell clasped the man's hand and shook it vigorously.

"Mr Brennan, I cannot possibly share with you accurately just how very pleased I am to make your acquaintance. I can already tell that we are set to become extremely firm friends."

"That's good, then. If you'd like to leave your luggage here in the hall, I'll send the boy to take it to your rooms. That is if you do plan to spend the night. I do not recommend travelling the Glasslands once the sun has set."

"Do you have room?" Rickenbacker heard himself ask.

"We always have room, sir. Alexander, get IN!"

And with that, they all followed the Wolfhound and its wagging tail into the lodge.

"Is it on the map?" Spicer asked, looking at the column of smoke through a looking glass Conway had provided.

Bunce traced Aspic Lane with her finger until she found the Cathedral. She could make out the small block next to the Cathedral and squinting, read the tiny smudged words. The Immolators stood silently alongside them.

"It says it's the Gleave family lodge."

They all looked at each blankly.

"Show it to our friends. Let's see what they suggest."

Bunce approached the lead Immolator with some trepidation, folding the map so only the relevant part showed and holding it up to the enormous armour clad warrior's face.

"Very interesting," Quine stated several hundred miles away, still pacing while he consulted his own map in the Ballroom.

"Why would there be a lodge there?" Axelrod's apprentice asked, rubbing his eyes as he gazed into the ball, "There's nothing to hunt, Sir."

"Oh, the Gleaves were always able to find something to hunt. A truly disreputable bunch of butchers with blood on their hands that ran all the way to their shoulders."

Doctor Axelrod raised an eyebrow as he saw the admiration in the Colonel's face. He turned to young Cobb, his apprentice.

"Centuries ago, before Grand Quillia even knew of its existence, the Gleave Clan fought for freedom in the Gramarye, leading a rebellion that annihilated their original ruling parties. Those they couldn't murder were banished, never to return. Some say it was these original rulers who built these Ballrooms," he said, motioning around them, "who created the hyperphysics that enabled our control over the Immolators."

Cobb couldn't recollect the Gleave name in his classes, and hid his ignorance by continuing to contemplate the ball in the centre of the room.

"The Gleaves banned magic from all of the Gramarye. It is said they created the Glasslands by discharging all the Wonder the rulers had accrued, twisting the woods into what you see before you, keeping people from the Cathedral of Tales. The Cathedral has defences of its own, however."

"Hence the Gargoyle Key," Quine nodded.

"The last of the Gramarye rulers wanted to use the Cathedral as a rallying point. The Gleaves built a lodge on the only road to the Cathedral."

"So this family lodge…" Quine said, turning away from his map.

"…Was one big honey trap. Rest here for the night, stay the rest of your life."

Cobb nodded, impressed at the treachery.

"Are the Gleaves still there?"

"It looks like our friend Rickenbacker is about to find out…"

In the Glasslands, the lead Immolator pointed at the smoke rising above the treeline.

"So that's that, then," Tork shrugged as he kicked his pony onwards.

As Brennan locked the door with two bolts behind Rickenbacker and his companions, the warm smell of a rich beefy stock reached their noses from an adjoining door. Teddy's stomach rumbled in excitement as he looked around at his surroundings. He generally entered buildings of this calibre through the tradesmen's entrance, so he paused to wipe his feet on the large mat. The rugs on the floor, although too worn to be described as sumptuous, looked like they cost more than his mother's old tenement. Coloured glass in the leaded lights cast shadows on the oak-lined walls as candles flickered on a large dresser. All the soft furnishings looked well used but still overstuffed, and none of the wooden pieces had sharp corners, smoothed away by years of touch. Teddy looked up at the high ceiling and noticed a gallery encircled the whole room. The wood-panelled walls were made up of light and dark patches, with old nail holes in the lighter areas, as though shield-shaped hangings had been removed.

"If you leave your luggage here, the boy will take them up to your rooms," Brennan informed them. Initially, Teddy though Brennan was instructing him to take the bags, but a young man of Teddy's age entered, checking out the visitors with what appeared to be friendly curiosity. He had hair lightened by the sun, strong arms and a thick chest. He picked up a couple of the saddlebags with ease, nodded and departed to climb the stairs to the gallery above. From the same door stepped a woman, thick auburn hair bundled atop her head, a full womanly figure with a small waist and a pinny around her lap.

"So these are our latest guests," she said, placing her hand on Brennan's shoulder and smiling a broad, warm, welcoming smile that took up her whole face.

"Laurel?" Mandell stuttered.

"It's not like you to remember a girl's name, Sir Evan," the woman chuckled.

"Let me look at you," Sir Evan said, placing his hands on her shoulders and looking her up and down.

"You are still without doubt the most beautiful woman to have ever graced my bedside."

He hugged her and she hugged him back.

"I was his nurse after he was wounded at the Battle of Sceptre Hill."

"Wounded? I nearly died."

"You had the energy to pursue every single nurse in that field hospital within a week."

"But I was only ever interested in you, Laurel."

"Were you just practising on the others? Now quit your habitual flirtations and introduce your friends."

"How can I notice anyone else in the roo..."

"Hello, I'm Lady Elena Melody," Elena butted in, pushing Mandell aside to shake Laurel's hand.

"You'll have to excuse our dog," apologised Laurel, as she noted Alexander at their side.

"Dogs have less drool and more manners than Mandell," said Pinkerton, leaning in. "I'm Pinkerton, gentleman pugilist and keen adventurer, winner of the Four Bells Trophy three years running."

"Milady, Mr Pinkerton, it is a pleasure to have such esteemed visitors and it is a relief to meet some people who are willing to put a muzzle on Sir Evan."

"I do not really see why I have to be a figure of fun here," grumbled Mandell.

"I am Professor Rickenbacker and this is my boy Teddy."

Rickenbacker clicked his heels together in greeting while Teddy blushed a deep crimson. Women with looks like Laurel's bothered him in an awkward way.

"A lady, a gentleman, a Professor, a lecher and a teddy, well you are all welcome. Please make yourselves at home in the lodge. I take it you're here to raid the treasure of the Cathedral?"

Her conversational tone surprised them all, and she noted their surprise before continuing.

"Nobody else comes here, except the occasional fugitive. Why else brave the Glasslands?"

The boy came out of one of the doors above and walked around the gallery back down the stairs to take the remaining bags. There was a silence in the room.

"And you, Madam," Rickenbacker managed, "What is this place, so far from civilisation in such unforgiving lands?"

"Civilisation isn't all it's cracked up to be, Professor. Now step into the sitting room and warm yourselves at the fire. Brennan, open the good wine to accompany dinner. We don't want to raise Mandell's ire. Perhaps I shall bore you with a potted history of the lodge over some meat stew. If you'll excuse me..."

She nodded at Brennan and returned to the kitchen, Alexander the wolfhound alongside.

"The sitting room is this way," motioned Brennan, delivering a toothless smile as he considered how much Pinkerton's jacket would have to be altered before it would be comfortable on his own shoulders.

Rickenbacker noticed Brennan's eyes flickering across the boxer's torso, could feel the capriciousness of the grinning man, but despite the incongruity of the sumptuous lodge in the Glasslands, and the fact that he could no longer see the carving knife Brennan had held at the entrance, he did not feel threatened. He speculated whether he was the victim of some form of Wonder, that he had been enchanted into complacency, but he hadn't felt the pressure change, the telltale popping of the ears, and he couldn't smell any of the ingredients required for this sort of thing. Perhaps the gorgeous smell of the stew was to conceal it. Mandell's recognition of the girl also helped him relax, although he wished that he knew the woman's surname, as she was obviously well connected to the lodge, and from what he remembered of the Gleaves, they were not to be trusted.

As they entered the lodge's sitting room, and Rickenbacker saw the well-tended fire in the broad fireplace, smelt the familiar rich scent of tobacco and saw the worn leather sofas, most of his doubts blew away like smoke in wind.

"You may hang your coats over there, and the drinks cabinet is by the window. We run an honesty bar here, so leave whatever money you think you have drunk in the platter there. The rooms are twenty Great Quillian pounds or three thousand Gramarye shillings each, and breakfast is included. The view, however," Brennan explained, waving his arm in the direction of the enormous panoramic window, "is completely free, while the booze will definitely take its toll."

The words tripped off the older man's tongue as though he had said them a million times, and his eyes continued to trip over the visitors' belongings with longing.

"What…oh!" Mandell exclaimed, throwing off his great coat in Teddy's direction and marching to the drinks, Pinkerton close behind.

"Thank you, Mister Brennan. Your hospitality knows no bounds," Lady Melody said, taking her gloves off finger by finger.

"Well that all depends on who you are," came a weasel-toned voice from one of the three high-backed chairs by the fire.

"Mr Kendrick," Brennan replied, without turning to face him, "you are welcome to leave at any time."

"You couldn't afford me to leave," said the man, pulling himself out of his chair and ending up shorter standing than he was while seated. His thinning hair was scraped across his broad flat head, his eyes shone from cat-like sockets while his thin lips were locked in a grin. His sloping shoulders and tiny frame were draped in a well-made suit with more buttons than it needed at its cuffs and ankles, and his torso was longer than his legs, which ended in tiny feet in well shone shoes. A small cheroot hung from his bottom lip.

"Hello, fellow travellers. My name is Kendrick. Aldo Kendrick."

He marched like a precocious child up to Elena and Rickenbacker, his clammy little hand outstretched. Elena offered the tips of her fingers to be shaken, regretting that she had removed her gloves.

"Mr Kendrick can introduce you to our other residents, so if you don't mind, I will be taking my leave."

"Thank you, Mr Brennan," Rickenbacker replied, as his hand was taken by Kendrick's little fist.

Mandell and Pinkerton raised full glasses as Brennan left.

"My card."

As Kendrick reached into an inside pocket, Teddy caught the man's odour, old sweat ground into old clothes, and the boy was pleased to be ignored by the man. Kendrick handed cards to Rickenbacker and Melody before moving to Mandell. He looked Pinkerton up and down, the card remaining in his hand.

"Can you read?" he asked the boxer.

"Do you bleed?" Pinkerton replied.

"Oh, that's very good," Kendrick chuckled, "I could use a man like you."

Mandell looked down at the card.

"Aldo Kendrick, Esquire. Fixer. Entrepreneur. Friend."

Mandell raised his eyebrows. Nice card. He really had to get some new ones. He just had the family card, with the crest, but this Kendrick fellow's was inspiring. *"Sir Evan Mandell. Hero. Lover."* As soon as they returned victorious from the Cathedral, he would find a printer and then find some previously unknown young ladies to introduce himself to.

"So which one of you strangers discharged a paralysing floor on Aspic Lane?"

Melody and Rickenbacker glanced at each other uneasily, while Kendrick raised his eyebrows theatrically.

"Leave them alone, my boy," wheezed another voice from the chairs by the fireplace.

An older gent struggled to his feet and turned to face the visitors as Kendrick slithered back into the shadows.

"Don't mind him. He's not a fan of the old dabble."

The speaker was clothed in the scarlet dress uniform of the legendary Gramarye Torchlight Cavalry, his boots, buckles and buttons shining through the dark sitting room as brightly as the old man's eyes. The pips on his collar showed him to be a Brigadier, while the large half empty brandy glass in his shaking hand suggested he was an inebriate. While his immaculate uniform was impressive, the man's hair looked like it had been cut with shears, his chin managing to display both stubble and shaving cuts. Although in his late sixties and glassy-eyed, something about the Brigadier demanded respect.

"Name's Beasley. Don't believe in business cards. Ruddy good to meet you all. Welcome to the lodge and jolly congratulations on getting this far. Damned good show."

He shook the hand of Mandell with sincere enthusiasm, accompanied by a quick mumbled "and who are you?"

"Well met, my man. Sir Evan Mandell, son of Prince Edmundsen of the Bullen Protectorate and brother of Lord Ethering of the Great Quillia Parliament," but Beasley had already moved to Pinkerton, so Mandell continued, "and this is Corporal Pinkerton, er..."

Pinkerton couldn't help but salute, possibly for the fourth time in his life. The Brigadier saluted back tightly, with his chin in the air before moving on to Elena, looking to Mandell to continue with the roll call.

"This is Lady Elena Melody, granddaughter of the Bishop of Waring and widow of Lord Hynes Melody."

"May your husband rest in peace," Beasley said, bending to kiss the woman's knuckles.

"I'm not actually related to the Bishop of Waring, I should point out."

"And why's that?"

"I said it to Sir Evan to dampen his ardour."

"Well done, you," Beasley said, his face unchanged from pleasant curiosity as he moved to Teddy, "and who is this strapping youngster?"

"Teddy, Sir. I work for the Professor."

"Well that must be inspiring, Teddy," Beasley said, reaching out a hand to the Professor.

"I'm Rickenbacker."

As Beasley took his hand, Rickenbacker saw the final chair at the fire push back and its former occupant turn to face them, silhouetted by the flames with a fearsome sword in his hand.

"Professor Hilary Rickenbacker, scourge of the Trade and infamous evil Professor who misuses the Wonder for his own nefarious ends," said the man.

Mandell saw the man's blade glint and pulled his cutlass, Pinkerton right behind him.

"I advise you, Sir…" Sir Evan said, before his cutlass was tipped up by the man's blade and embedded deep in the ceiling beam above. Mandell reached for his pistol but felt a jolt as his gun, belt and holster tumbled to the floor, cut through where the leather meets the buckle. He heard Pinkerton growl and looked up from his pistol on the floor to find the barrels of the man's Twirler in his face and the man's sword at Pinkerton's throat. Melody drew her pistols but the old Brigadier already had a small Schrödinger pistol against her chest.

"It would be a pity to ruin such a pretty breast, my dear," said the old man.

"Professor?" Mandell whimpered, his arrogance shaken, fear flickering in his eyes.

"Please could we all just drop our weapons?" Rickenbacker said, holding a Red Wonder grenade in front of him, the string to the trigger looped around his thumb.

"I wish I could, Professor," said the man, returning his Twirler to his holster and letting the blade drop from Pinkerton.

Melody looked down to see the Brigadier's pistol had disappeared back to where it had materialised from, while Mandell blushed a deep crimson, indecisive whether to heave his cutlass from where it was buried or to pick up his weapons belt. Pinkerton folded his arms, impressed, as Rickenbacker slipped the grenade back inside his jacket.

"You should look before you leap, boy," the man said to Mandell, keeping his eyes on Rickenbacker.

The door to the sitting room opened and Laurel stepped in. She glanced around and raised her eyebrows in exasperation.

"Brigadier, I told you to keep an eye on Kendrick," she groaned.

"It wasn't me this time, Miss," Kendrick smirked.

"Well, for whatever happened, I can only apologise," said Laurel, her eyes washing over the man as he sat back down, out of sight. "As you can imagine, visitors to the Glasslands are sparse and generally lack table manners. Sir Evan, what on Earth has happened to your belt? If you'll follow me, I'm sure I can find you a replacement. If there's one thing I've learnt about you, it's that we really need to keep your trousers on."

She took Mandell by the arm and led him out of the room, leaving his cutlass hanging from the beam and his belt on the floor. Pinkerton watched them go, scratching his moustaches.

"Can somebody tell a poor simple Western Isle boy what just happened?" he asked.

"You just met Hilt," Kendrick explained, picking up Mandell's glass and sniffing its contents before draining it.

Laurel led Evan through the galleried hall, lit a lantern and opened a small door off the main hall to reveal a steep winding staircase.

"Age before beauty," she laughed, letting Mandell go first.

He suddenly felt naked without his cutlass and pistol. The air of the cellar was fetid and, if he wasn't such a gentleman, he would have definitely let Laurel go first. He ran through what he knew about this woman. He had almost lost a lung at Sceptre Hill, to a piece of shrapnel from an explosion that decimated most of his men. His family sent out a surgeon to the field hospital, where there had been many nurses, but Laurel had been different and he had tipped the doctor to get her as his personal nurse. She had been confident around the men, unlike the other nurses, who had spent their youth in charitable organisations run by various virginal old matrons. As Laurel had nursed him back to health in a house rented near the field hospital by the Mandells, he discovered that she had not spent her teenage years surrounded by old spinsters, but in the gold rush towns of the Empire, where she had performed a dance hall act having run away from foster parents.

Mandell paused in the darkness of the stairs. Did he really trust this girl and her colourful history, which had never been corroborated? She may have nursed him back to health on the battlefield, but now they were in the middle of nowhere. This was every man for himself.

"What's up? Afraid of the dark?" she quipped, flipping an auburn curl out of her dark eyes.

He could feel the cold dampness of the cellar below, the lightness of his step without his weapons, and he realised he was alone without Pinkerton or the other companions. For the first time he could remember, with a woman who had saved his life once before, Sir Evan Mandell suddenly became extremely aware of his own mortality.

Colonel Quine considered himself a leader of men. That said, he was not happy to be leading a Trade Platoon into the Glasslands to check up on the Reclaimers and Immolation Squad. Axelrod had been right; If Rickenbacker was able to create something as powerful as a Paralysing Floor, then he may have some defence against an Immolator. And the added complication of the Gleave family being involved, despite being just a footnote of Gramarye history, had also caught his attention.

Hence the platoon of human troops, the majority of the Trade soldiers in Chinsey. It was just a pity Quine couldn't trust anybody else to lead them.

His only recompense was the fact that, besides having Axelrod at his side, he was also being joined by that desk jockey Major Franks. Looking back, he saw the pathetic worm of a man with terror in his eyes as he clung to the reins of his pony. If anything, Quine hoped Rickenbacker or the Gleaves had the power to rid the world of Franks before they killed the Professor and took back the Gargoyle Key.

"Perhaps you would like a drink," Beasley suggested, lining up three glasses, "The brandy I can recommend with extreme sincerity."

"Thank you," said Elena, her eyes on the back of Hilt's chair.

"Take a seat," Beasley suggested, indicating two large sofas by the panoramic window.

"Will you be joining us, Mr Hilt?" Elena called to the back of the chair.

"No."

"He's even grumpier in the mornings. If you wake him up…" Kendrick ran a finger across his throat.

Pinkerton sat down on the sofa, realised Teddy and the Professor were waiting on Elena to take a seat, and stood up again. It was easier being a pugilist that a gentleman, he ruminated. Beasley passed a brandy glass in Teddy's direction.

"Teddy, see if you can help in the kitchen," Rickenbacker suggested.

Teddy looked from the glass to Rickenbacker, back to the glass and left the room, wondering where he'd find the kitchen.

Elena caught sight of herself in the mirror. She looked grubby and tired. She unclipped her hair and shook it out, letting it fall to her shoulders.

"Lady Melody?" Beasley said, proffering a glass.

"Is there somewhere I could change? Freshen up?"

"Upstairs my dear. I'm sure Alfie will bring up some hot water for you."

"Thank you, Brigadier. If you'll excuse me."

Elena left the room, leaving Beasley to offer the glass to Rickenbacker.

"I don't drink," the Professor informed him.

Mandell heard Elena's footsteps as Laurel led him further into the cellars. From the lantern in Laurel's hand, he could make out small doors with small barred windows lining a damp central corridor.

"What is this place?" he asked the woman.

"Not all of us are left castles and mansions by relatives. Some of us get badly located hunting lodges with scary dungeons in the cellar."

"Relatives? I thought you were an orphan."

"I was. Then one day this representative from some big Great Quillian legal firm found me in the hospital and told me I wasn't an orphan after all."

"I don't follow."

"My mother put it in her will that on her death her daughter would be contacted and informed of her heritage. And I am that daughter."

"So who are you?"

"Sir Evan Mandell, may I introduce Miss Laurel Elizabeth Gleave. Charmed, charmed, charmed..." she curtsied to Mandell. "Welcome to my family dungeon," Mandell replied, finding himself nodding back automatically.

She opened a door into a small cell and held up the lantern to cast more light into the gloom. Mandell jumped nervously, as he thought he saw a head glaring back at him, and was relieved to make out the shape of a full-face helmet.

"You should be able to find a replacement for your belt in here. Take anything you want," Laurel suggested.

Mandell saw, piled up to the ceiling, a plethora of equipment, luggage, clothing and weaponry, some recently designed, others dated; rucksacks, backpacks, cloaks, boots, holsters, scabbards, some still containing their weaponry; crossbows, more helmets, and a variety of belts.

"Are these the Gleave family heirlooms?"

He tugged out a sword and the pile collapsed somewhat, revealing more of the same.

"Do you think you are the first chancers to attempt to enter the Cathedral of the Tales? Adventurers and other ne'er-do-wells have been coming here on their way to their imagined unimaginable riches for years. They all think they'll be back," she shrugged. "None of them have been."

"And this is what they left behind."

"Exactly. I lock it down here to keep Kendrick's grubby little mitts off it."

Mandell grabbed a belt and pulled it free.

"You don't mind my taking it?"

"Needs must," Laurel said.

Mandell started to thread the belt through the loops in his trouser as Laurel put the lantern on the floor.

"Perhaps you shouldn't be in such a hurry to put your belt on," Laurel suggested.

"Hurry?"

Mandell was confused.

Laurel stepped close, yanked the belt out from the loops and started to unbutton Evan's trouser. She kissed him passionately on the mouth and Mandell was no longer confused, although he was a little intimidated.

"So what exactly are you a Professor of, Professor?" Beasley asked, seated on the sofa next to Rickenbacker.

Pinkerton was moving around the room, pretending to examine the paintings, their canvasses blackened from decades of tobacco smoke and grime, while attempting to get a clear look at Hilt.

"I lectured in a history of the Wonder at Fairport University, Brigadier."

Kendrick glanced towards the fireplace at Hilt.

"That sounds interesting," Beasley said, staring into his brandy glass.

"And then you decided to move into fighting against the Trade," Hilt said.

"I am not necessarily fighting against the Trade. I prefer to think of myself as fighting for freedom," Rickenbacker replied.

Hilt stood up, his sword still in his hand. He was tall, with broad shoulders, lean, with hair in his dark haunted eyes. He resembled an Alsatian, with proud bearing, defined cheekbones and an attentive air. He also looked very tired and very angry.

"Whose freedom are you fighting for?" he asked, leaning against the high back of his chair.

"While in the employ of the Trade, I discovered something, something that could shame all humanity."

"Something to do with the Wonder?"

"I take it by your tone, Mr Hilt, that you are not in favour of the Wonder. Are you against progress, Sir?"

"I'm sure we've both seen what progress can do on the battlefield."

"I believe it can be used to shorten conflicts."

"By killing people quicker?"

"My studies have shown that the Wonder has also opened the world up, connected people, made things easier for those in jeopardy."

"And made things easier for those in power."

"Hilt. Let the Professor rest," Beasley sighed, "He has had an arduous journey to reach this far, and I cannot see why you have a quarrel with him. You are not the biggest fan of the Trade by any means."

"Thank you, Brigadier," said Rickenbacker. "Mr Hilt, I can only apologise if my companions or I have in any way offended you. Perhaps we could all relax a little more if you were to lay down your sword..."

"I am afraid my friend..."

"I can speak for myself, Brigadier."

"May I see?" Rickenbacker asked, reaching towards Hilt's sword hand.

He regarded the Professor with suspicion before moving closer, like an abused dog. He held out the blade.

"This is the sword of a noble man," Rickenbacker noted.

"Noble men don't need swords, Professor."

The Professor turned Hilt's hand over and shook his head with sadness. Pinkerton, looking over the Professor's shoulder, whistled through his teeth. The man's hand was melded with the sword so that flesh, steel and leather pooled together, like rock pools at the foot of a cliff.

"I haven't..." Rickenbacker started.

"So you'll excuse me if I'm less hopeful about the dabble than you are, Professor," Hilt stated, withdrawing his hand and sword.

"Mr Hilt," Rickenbacker said sagely, "from what I have seen, sometimes I think hope is all we have left."

The sun had set and the moonlight glinted cold blue through the trees. Spicer's Reclaimers moved down the gravel path with their weapons drawn, using the crystal trees of the Glasslands at the edge of the path as cover. The Immolators remained stationary at the end of the path furthest from the lodge.

"Why aren't we waiting for Quine's reinforcements?" Conways whispered over Spicer's shoulder.

"If that bastard or any of his men get their hands on that Gargoyle key before we do, do you think he'll find it in his heart to pay us?"

"We could get Tork to salute him again," Conway grinned. "He seemed to like that."

Spicer hissed and continued to creep down the path towards the light of the lodge.

"Give me the lantern," he instructed Conway, "and stay back."

"No problem there, boss."

Spicer continued on alone. He reached the end of the path, covered the lamp with his great coat, and lit the wick.

Elena dried her hair with the towel she'd been provided with, and stared out of the window. She felt more refreshed than she had in weeks. She couldn't remember the last time hot water had touched her body.

Then she saw the flash of light. She frowned and looked in earnest where the path to Aspic Lane ended. It flashed again, paused, flashed again twice, paused, flashed once again, and then repeated. Elena moved to the lantern in the bathroom and covered it with the towel, then copied the rhythm of the flashing light outside. She was tired of Mandell's desperate testosterone bluster. It would be nice to see Spicer again, she thought to herself.

As Laurel straightened up her clothes and dusted herself down, Mandell lifted the lantern high and checked out his surroundings.

"How much further does this cellar go on for?" he asked, casting a lascivious eye over Laurel.

"Is this your attempt at post-coitus, Sir Evan?" she replied, watching him blush. "This is about all of it. There's a water fountain or something at the end."

"A water fountain? In a dungeon?"

"Hey, anybody can get thirsty."

"Does it still work?"

"Never has."

"So how do you know it's a water fountain?"

"I don't. Want to come see it?"

Mandell had had his fair share of women. Some would say he'd had more than his fair share, and that it may have occasionally encroached on other, less fortunate men's shares, but then all was fair in love and war. Well, fair game, anyway. But Laurel was different. She always seemed to turn away from him first. And not in a game-playing way. He never felt like she was doing it to keep his interest up. He had a worrying feeling that she really didn't care what he thought about her. Which never happened to Sir Evan Mandell.

And the more he got to know of her, the more she became an enigma to him. Was she joking about the water fountain? Was he supposed to care or not?

Sometimes Sir Evan had a creeping suspicion that Laurel just wanted him for his body.

"I'd like to," he said.

"What?"

"The water fountain?"

"What water fountain?"

"Erm... the... water fountain that isn't...?"

"I'm joking with you, Mandell, you big kid."

Mandell chuckled awkwardly and squinted into the darkness. Laurel stepped forward and took his arm.

"Come on, let's have our first date," she laughed, taking the lantern off him.

They took about ten steps and reached the end of the corridor, which did indeed look like a water fountain. A distorted beast's head stretched from a large black plaque on the wall, like an evil dog emerging from pitch. In the flickering light from the lantern it looked like it was moving, swaying, with drool curling down its dark teeth.

"Oh my God," Mandell uttered.

"It really is quite horrible, isn't it? When I redecorate, that is the first thing that goes."

Mandell walked slowly up to the plaque and tentatively brushed his fingers against it.

"It's freezing."

He thought he could see a cloud of condensation come from his mouth. He reached up to touch the beast's face.

"WOOF!" Laurel suddenly shouted, and Mandell felt the blood leave his soul.

"Stop it! For God's sake, Laurel."

"So you are scared of the dark."

"It's not the dark I'm scared of. It's what's in it."

He shuddered again, straightened his shoulders and adjusted his hair. He reached a fist up and knocked hard at the plaque, bravado overriding everything else. A slithering fluttering noise echoed from beyond the plaque as the knock bounced around in the gloom, sending chills up Mandell's back. Something slid around his waist and he screamed. Laurel yelped in terror.

"What?" she demanded.

"I felt something. Around my waist."

"It was me."

"Why did you do that? It scared me."

"I was scared. I was putting my arm around you."

"I think we should go back upstairs," he suggested, taking her hand as his breathing returned to normal.

"You're right. This is a shit date."

This time, he knew Laurel was joking. But he also had no idea why.

Elena came back into the sitting room having changed and washed. Her hair was down and she'd even managed to find a little make up in her pack. Her Twirler was at her hip and two stiletto knives hung from her belt. Pinkerton was lecturing Beasley and Kendrick, while Rickenbacker was flicking through a book from one of the shelves. Hilt leant against the window frame, looking out intently.

"So I gave him an uppercut, crack, and his feet actually brushed my shins as he took to the air," Pinkerton was saying, reciting another old boxing tale, handbills from previous fights laid out in front of him.

"Jolly good show," Beasley mumbled, his eyelids heavy.

Elena closed the door as loudly as she could without slamming it and cleared her throat. Rickenbacker nodded to her, as Beasley led Kendrick and Pinkerton in standing up to greet her.

"My Lady Melody," Beasley said sleepily.

"Don't let me disturb you, gentlemen," she said, moving towards the drinks.

She could see Hilt's eyes reflected darkly in the window as they followed her across the room. She reached the drinks and filled two glasses before approaching him. The other men resumed their own preoccupations.

"I poured you a drink," she said, handing him the glass.

His eyes weighed her up suspiciously, but he decided to take the drink anyway.

"Thank you, Milady."

"Please. Call me Elena."

"Elena."

"Do you mind if I ask your name? I mean, Hilt can't be..."

"Hilt is fine, Elena. My old name doesn't matter. My old life no longer exists."

"Do you miss it?" she asked.

She could feel his curiosity grow. He lifted his sword and tapped it gently against the base of the window.

"It's generally best not to look back, I've found."

She looked him in the eye and moistened her lips, pleased to see he was no longer looking out of the window.

"Shall we take a seat?" she asked, keeping her eyes on his.

He couldn't say no, so he pulled back the other chair in front of the fireplace and they both sat down. Elena could smell Beasley's cologne. It smelled of old man, tobacco and booze.

"Why the interest?" Hilt asked, moving his eyes from hers to stare into his drink.

"Not really a ladies' man, are you, Hilt?"

"I've never had the need."

He looked at her evenly. Perhaps he could have a little tournament with one of the strangers after all.

"Is there any way I can interest you in a conversation or is this all one way?" she asked.

"You seem like just another dabble-dunker to me, Milady."

"Dabble-dunker?"

"Do you like to woo the Wonder, Lady Melody. Just another little girl who gets off on the smell of it? Did your late husband lack a little spark? Did the magic go out of your relationship?"

"You think I'm interested in you because of your... wound?"

"I think you're only following Rickenbacker because he knows his way around a magic wand. As for your interest in me? Brennan's too old, Beasley's too drunk, Kendrick is slightly too sticky and Alfie the kitchen boy is otherwise engaged slopping out."

"Alfie the kitchen boy? I'll make a note but until I do get my evil claws into the child, why don't you tell me how that happened," she replied drily, one finger pointing towards his hand.

"No slap around the face? No storming off?"

"Not even indignation, Hilt, or whatever your name is, was, whatever. I'm bored and you've got a sword stuck to your hand." She paused to sip her drink. "I find it incredibly sad that you still need to prove you're the alpha male when you're surrounded by, as you say, drunks, old men, kitchen boys, and whatever you called that foul Kendrick fellow."

"I don't need your pity," Hilt growled.

"You need something though, don't you? You're a needy man who doesn't know what he's missing, who doesn't know what he needs."

"You know what I don't need, Milady?"

"Someone like me?" she said, her voice sounding tired, hoping to cut off his insult at the tongue.

Hilt stared into the fire.

"Oh, you'll do, Elena. What I don't need is psychotherapy and a full set of cutlery."

He looked up at her so she saw the exhausted honesty in his face, as a tiny smile tickled his lips. She raised her drink.

"Cheers," she said.

Their glasses touched gently.

"Why are you here, Elena?" Hilt asked.

"One could say I have a taste for adventure."

"I bet you do."

"What about you?"

"Adventure leaves a bitter taste in my mouth."

"I'm not sure that was always true. Your friend the Brigadier's uniform, his medals, what remains of the uniform you're wearing..." She indicated his cavalry boots and riding britches with a distinctive broad stripe down the seams. "You were there, weren't you? Both of you. You're survivors of the Meander Canyon massacre."

"You have a surprising sense of history."

"Anybody would recognise that uniform. You are a member of the Torchlight Cavalry."

"You tell me."

"The Trade sent a thousand privateers against two hundred members of the Torchlights, the last remaining native defenders of The Gramarye."

She stood up and started to pace to chase her memories. Pinkerton moved closer to listen, while Rickenbacker placed the book he was examining back on the shelf. Beasley had closed his eyes while Hilt leant back to regard Elena.

"The Torchlights were trying to keep the road to the Moon Docks open when they were ambushed by far greater numbers in the Meander Canyon," Elena continued. "But somehow they fought back. They started to win."

"There were no winners in the Meander Canyon."

"What did happen?" asked Pinkerton, always interested in an old war story.

"Perhaps the Brigadier and our friend would prefer not to relive the story this evening, Lady Melody," Rickenbacker suggested.

"I relive it every night, Professor. I'm sure the Brigadier would too, if he were ever sober enough."

CHAPTER 3

The Meander Canyon
Near Talling/Maisy
The Gramarye

October 1840

The Meander Canyon is located in the deep south of the Gramarye, in a torrid, sun-scarred region called Maisy, renamed from Talling by the Trade. When Great Quillia first arrived in the Gramarye and explored the area, Talling had offered little; no crops, little livestock, few people, and a small uninspiring fishing port called the Moon Docks, named after the shape of the bay in which it was located. The food was also uncomfortably spicy, which the first explorers found curious considering the lack of water.

But one day an explorer desperate for some form of recognition, be it through the discovery of new forms of flora or fauna, anthropology or anything, came across the Pyramids of Talling, great shiny black edifices almost impossible to look at as they reflected the sun, invisible in the darkness of night, centuries old and obviously brimming with the

Wonder. Once he reported his findings to the Great Quillian Council of Alien Architecture, the Trade contacted him. The explorer showed them where the pyramids could be found, and the Trade, in return, allowed him to name the area Maisy, after his mother, of whom he had been very fond. The explorer returned to Great Quillia a happy man, and wrote countless books about the same thing for the rest of his life. He died knowing that something previously unknown was now known, and, even better, it was known by his dear mother's name.

The Trade approached the Pyramids of Maisy with aggressive avarice, desperate to chip away at the reflective marble-like exterior of the buildings, ship some back to the capital's museums to prove their love of overseas culture, and then tap whatever Wonder was therein.

Unfortunately the Trade could not get inside the Pyramids of Maisy. They drilled, hammered, scraped and dug, but nothing could break the dark surface. After a decade or two, one particularly lateral minded individual brought in an Enchantment and Chicanery Operative to try to find a way inside using the new techniques of hyperphysics. The ECO let off a rudimentary grenade and the pyramids came alive. Shards of red light burst into the sky and shot across from one pyramid to another. A latticework of luminescence glowed from deep underground, leading to enormous lakes of light, a light that shone with great Wondrous power.

The Trade got to work, excavating the subterranean Wonder beyond the pyramids, and, as it did so, the great lights from the pyramids started to fade, the darkness of their surfaces turning to grey. The largest underground pool was located directly below the town formerly known as Talling, but renamed Maisy, and so the Trade recruited private Reclamation Squads from all over the Empire to empty the town of its inhabitants.

The benefits of using freelancers allowed the Trade to blame any truly reprehensible behaviour on these privateers, and these individuals knew this. So they took to the job with a terrifying zeal.

The people of Maisy fought back desperately and rallied a militia, made up of some five hundred dragoons, to fight off the rapists, murderers and thieves doing the unholy work of the Trade. The dragoons were called the Torchlight Cavalry, as they were seen as the defenders of the pyramids' light and their surrounding lakes, and also as representatives of truth and justice.

But the Torchlights could not keep out the influx of Reclaimers.

Many civilians of the Gramarye heard about the troubles and ships were despatched to evacuate the people of Maisy. The infamy was such that the atrocity became known as the Disenchantment of Maisy, and it became the basis of many shanties and nursery rhymes. Even former civilians of Great Quillia settled in the Gramarye were ashamed. Some went so far as to name themselves Grama-Quillians, to distance themselves from the brutal new arrivals reclaiming a peaceful town in the name of Empire.

The distance between Maisy and the Moon Docks was just five miles, but the Reclaimers had surrounded the town, cutting off the road to the port and back inland. The only hope of the people was the remains of the Torchlight Cavalry, now numbering just two hundred.

By now, many of the Reclaimers had suffered at the hands of the Torchlights, and they wanted recompense, so the Torchlights decided to offer them the opportunity.

John Widdershins had joined the Torchlights as soon as he had received the call. He had returned to Maisy to find his widowed mother had been thrown off the family farm because it sat atop a seam of Wonder leading from the pyramids. He had already fought for the Trade so that he could support his mother once his father had passed, and there had been some scepticism when he had arrived at the recruiters. But all the doubts were assuaged by his best friend Crispin "Kip" Edlington. Kip's family had always lived in Maisy - indeed, his grandmother still knew it as Talling - and they were well loved and equally respected. Kip had met young Widdershins at school, and they immediately became thick as thieves. Kip came out to learn to ride on the Widdershins' farm, where the urbanite helped his hick friend with his reading and writing. Just as Kip excelled at writing and became the first editor of the Maisy Chronicle, so Widdershins became the greatest rider in all the region. Once spotted by a captain of the Trade, it was only a matter of time before he was lured away to chase down glory. Widdershins made his name escorting Trade caravans through the Hump tribes of the Tattershall Scrublands, and throughout his adventures he had kept in contact with Kip through letters. He always enclosed the majority of his pay for his mother, which Kip duly passed on.

When the Reclaimers arrived, it had been Kip who had printed the first call to arms for the people of Maisy, and his newspaper offices and printing press had been turned to ash the following week. As soon as Widdershins received word, he resigned his commission and returned to Maisy. It was a measure of the respect he had earned that the Trade forces allowed him to keep his horse, a beautiful mare named Estella. If they had known where Widdershins and Estella were headed, they may not have been so keen to give his steed away.

Once Kip explained that Widdershins would do anything for Maisy, they accepted the battle-hardened cavalry officer with the twin pistols, and he started to train the rest, including Kip, whose family were terrified for his safety, but whose twin sons were thrilled that daddy was becoming a hero instead of writing about them. Widdershins proved to be invaluable in his first few skirmishes with the Reclaimers. He was soon introduced to the leader of the Torchlights, Brigadier Mycroft Beasley.

Beasley, a hardened veteran in his early fifties, recognised Widdershins as one of his own, and the two of them worked closely together planning guerrilla tactics to discourage the Reclaimers. They had enabled the Maisy civilians to build a rudimentary defensive wall around their town, with one gate leading inland and one gate leading to the road to the Moon Docks.

But now they were surrounded by a vast force of Reclaimers, and fires had started to break out at the walls. It was time to evacuate to the ships, and the only way to do that was through the enemy.

The townsfolk had gathered in the square, while the Torchlights were lined up facing the north gate that led to the road inland.

Kip's family had supplied a carriage with its cyan roof and the Widdershins two white horses to pull the survivors of the two families to safety. Kip lifted his two boys inside and kissed them both on the forehead.

"You keep your heads down until your mother says otherwise. She knows best now and will know best for the rest of your lives, do you understand me?"

"Yes, Father," they replied in unison.

Then he turned to his wife, who stood ashen faced holding his horse. She looked him up and down, her beautiful husband, the clever man of letters, with pistols at his waist and a sword hanging from his belt. He read her thoughts and took her face in his hands.

"Remember my love for you. Nothing else matters," he told her.

"Come back to me."

"Always," he replied, lifting her into the carriage to join her children and John's mother, Mrs Widdershins.

He looked at the four of them as his wife took the boys under her arms, and felt everything inside him squirm with dread. He managed a smile, saluted the boys and closed the door. His grief pounded further into his heart with each step he took away from the carriage, as he approached Brigadier Beasley, Widdershins and the newest recruit, young Talisker, a recent graduate of Fairport University, where he had been studying the Wonder. Talisker had been the only child of Maisy who had ever studied the Wonder, as the people of the Gramarye had mistrusted the power beneath their feet for generations.

"I've just been telling Talisker. Some news made it through the line. The bastards have a dabbler. No offence," Beasley said, nodding in apology to the boy.

"It doesn't make any difference to the plan, Brigadier," Widdershins said. "We should be on our way. Are you ready, Kip?"

Kip looked around at his hometown, hardly recognisable from his youth, windows blown out like the eye sockets of skulls, dark burns smudged across shops, houses missing walls so their contents spilled out like guts.

"I'm scared, John," Kip said, almost smirking at his inability to hide his honest feelings.

"Good. It'll make you ride faster. Let's mount up and save some lives."

Kip and Widdershins turned and saluted the Brigadier.

"Good luck, my friends," the warrior said, shaking their hands, "and look after this one, Kip. He may be our secret weapon."

The Brigadier mounted his horse and nodded to the bugler, who sounded the order.

"See you on the other side," said Kip to his oldest friend. They hugged briefly, "Let's go, kid," he prompted Talisker, and the three of them mounted up.

The two hundred dragoons formed up and faced the north entrance, Beasley at the rear with Widdershins while Kip and Talisker stayed in Maisy town square with the townsfolk and a small detachment of Torchlights. Beasley looked down and winked at a young lad, who scampered southwards.

"Prepare to open the gates," called Beasley, straightening his back like the proud Brigadier his troopers had always been honoured to serve.

From the roof of the town hall, a lookout called, "They're coming around to meet us!"

On the other side of the north gates, the privateers started to mass, keen to get a first crack at the do-gooder scum who had been so arrogantly bothersome.

"Then let's give them what they want!" Beasley called, unsheathing his sabre and piercing the sky with it.

The bugler called the charge.

Kip felt his ears pop and felt a surge of wind, a sudden humungous gale burst at his back. The southern gates had been obliterated in an explosion. The smell of Red Wonder filled the air. As his hearing throbbed back, he heard the Brigadier's call.

"Charge!"

The Torchlight Cavalry turned as one, each horse on its hind legs, and barrelled south towards the hole left by the explosion, weapons drawn. A part of the town square had been left clear and the empty main street allowed them to get up to speed, the air was full of the roar of the warriors, the thunder of hooves and the rattle of sabres. The privateers who had survived the explosion turned in panic, desperate to flee the cavalry charge.

The Torchlights raced outside the walls of Maisy, Beasley leading a break to the left, Widdershins to the right. As the convoy of townsfolk galloped out of the town square heading south, kip felt his heart beating with a mixture of terror, excitement and hope. He saw Widdershins fire off his pistols, raise his horse to crush nearby Reclaimers as he swapped one pistol for his sword and then hack down at other attackers. Widdershins wiped his spinner against his thigh and fired again, his face glowing with a righteous anger. The convoy rumbled as quickly as it could manage out of the south gates. For the first time, Kip saw the devastation, limbs and blood and life scattered in the mud. He saw his horror reflected in Talisker's face.

"Kip!" his wife called from the carriage.

"Don't look back!" he started to cry, but suddenly the wood of the carriage splintered as buckshot thudded into it, tearing back some of the cyan fabric. Kip looked over his shoulder and saw a squad of six privateers on horseback pounding towards them, one holding the blat gun that had been used to pepper the carriage.

"Stay with the convoy," he ordered Talisker, before peeling away on his horse, pulling his spinners and rotating them hard. He felt the rhythm of the horse below him, and, as he pitched upwards, he aimed low and fired at the privateer with the blat gun. One bullet blew out the man's chest and he swung back in his saddle. Kip holstered the pistols and went for his sabre. The blade was halfway out of his scabbard when the privateers were on him. He felt a slash across his shoulder blade, like a punch followed by a sudden freezing cold. As he slumped forward under the blow, he saw another Reclaimer's spinner angle towards his chest. He heard two shots, and nothing else seemed to hit him, so he pulled hard on his reins and struggled to sit up. He looked over his shoulder and saw two Reclaimers already on the ground and another with Widdershins' sabre deep in his stomach. The Torchlight hero snatched the spinner from his enemy's hand and fired at another member of the squad on horseback, hitting him in the middle of the face. Kip spun one of his pistols and despatched the last of the squad before taking his horse alongside his friend.

"Thanks," he shouted over the sound of the carnage.

"Protect the fucking dabbler!" Widdershins roared, before spurring his horse back into the battle. Kip scanned the area. The last of the townsfolk had left Maisy and were racing unhindered down the road to the docks. He saw Talisker, still alongside his wife's carriage, and urged his horse towards them, knocking aside any Reclaimers en-route. The bulk of the privateers were starting to emerge from the north side of Maisy's walls, and he heard the Torchlight bugler as Beasley led a detachment to head them off. Kip reached the young hyperphysicist quickly.

"Are you okay?"

"Yes. Yes."

Kip ducked down to check inside the carriage, expecting the worst, but saw three pairs of eyes stare back at him with love and relief, while Mrs Widdershins gazed out of the opposite window, hugging herself tightly. Kip straightened up and for the first time felt the pain in his shoulder.

"You're hurt," Talisker told him.

"Don't worry about that," Kip called back. "Just look after yourself."

He looked back over his bloodied shoulder and saw black smoke belching from Maisy. He could hear the faint echo of the bugle but it was harder to make out the Torchlights themselves against the swarming Reclaimers.

"What's happening?" Talisker asked, as if Kip would actually have an answer. "We're losing, aren't we?"

"We have to get the people to the Meander Canyon. They'll be safe there. Come on," ordered Kip, kicking his horse further on towards the head of the convoy, Talisker behind him.

The horizon changed as the canyon came into view. Cliffs rose up and the road disappeared into the slash that cut through them. There was no way the Reclaimers could have scaled the cliffs and so once they were in the canyon, Beasley and Widdershins believed the Torchlights would have a bottleneck they could defend while the others made it to the port. They knew that just claiming Maisy would not be enough for the privateers after such a bloodthirsty siege.

As a boy, Kip had never liked the Meander Canyon. It twisted and turned in shadows, the sun never able to warm its corners. He never would have dreamt he would ever be relieved to see it. As they approached the head of the convoy, he was surprised to see a solo Torchlight, a young man named Dunst, leading the way.

"Dunst, where are the others?" he called, slowing his horse to match the boy's.

"Dead, Sir," said Dunst through gritted teeth without turning to look at Kip.

Kip noticed he was holding the reins with one hand, with the other was clamped against his stomach. Dark blood stained the boy's tunic. Finally the boy turned to look at him, and they immediately understood each other, in a way Kip had never felt with anybody else. This wounded young man, holding his guts in place, looked back at Kip taking in his wounded shoulder, and they both knew what had to be done.

"Kip!" Talisker called.

Kip turned and saw Talisker motion ahead. At the mouth of the canyon, he could see the red flashes of spinner fire. He looked back at Dunst but the boy was gone.

"Stay back," Kip warned the dabbler.

He took one last glance over his shoulder, hoping to see his family's carriage with its distinctive cyan roof, but all he could see was the dust of the convoy and the smoke from the town rising above it. He clenched his teeth and dug his spurs deep into the horse's flanks, bending down low as he picked up speed. Kip drew his sabre and screamed into the wind as he felt bullets buzz past him.

"Charge!" he shouted as he threw himself towards the mouth of the Meander Canyon.

The Reclaimers from the north side of Maisy had slammed into the thin scarlet line of the remaining Torchlights spread across the road, but the cavalry held. Fired up by the sight of their home's destruction, they stood their ground. Those that had lost their horses used the defences the privateers had built during the siege of the town. Their comrades pulled back to absorb the charge of the enemy before swooping back around to chop them down. Widdershins roared with a wicked bloodlust as he repeatedly plunged back into the fray, a sword in each hand now, his spinners proving to have been too slow to take down the press of attackers around him. Estella, his horse, was ankle deep in blood, with raw wounds gushing crimson into the froth of her sweat. Beasley saw the bugler hit once and the boy jolted back in his saddle but stayed upright. The Brigadier hacked his way to the boy's side and grasped his tunic with one hand to keep him on his horse while he swept his sabre at the Reclaimers around him.

He surveyed the battle and knew they had done the best they could, that they had given everything to ensure the townsfolk would have the best chance to reach the canyon.

"Sound the retreat, my lad!" he hollered at the bugler, but, from the dead weight he could feel through the man's uniform, he knew the life had left him.

"Retreat!" he bellowed, raising his horse up and heading back down the road.

As the horse rose, so that horse and rider looked like some great memorial statue in the centre of Great Quillia, Beasley felt his stead stumble to the left.

"Steady, my girl," he muttered, and then his horse toppled.

He felt an enormous thump against his back and he was thrown towards the bugler's horse. Then he heard Widdershins' voice.

"Stay alive, you bastard!"

As the bugler's corpse fell, it dragged Beasley so he could reach the edge of the dead man's saddle as he kicked his feet free of his own stirrups. Widdershins slapped the horse's arse with the flat of his sabre, and the beast bolted. As it pulled itself free of the throng, Beasley yanked himself into the saddle and took the reins.

"Ride, my love," he hissed into the horse's ear as he galloped down the road without looking back for Widdershins.

Only a small group of Reclaimers guarded the mouth of the Meander Canyon, made up of cowards who had not wanted to be within range of the walls of Maisy during the siege. But this did not improve Kip's overall situation. He fired out of the cover provided by his horse's corpse without aiming as he wiped blood from his eyes.

As the front of the convoy got closer, the riders and their steeds were spooked by the armed men at the mouth of the canyon. They scattered off the road, earlier corpses acting as psychological roadblocks.

Kip lent back against his horse and spun both pistols, unable to hear the mosquito buzz of the spinner chamber above the sound of the approaching convoy. Then he saw Talisker tearing towards him, the boy's horse's tongue lolling with exhaustion from the side of his mouth. Kip growled, ignoring the fresh bullet hole in his thigh and rolled over. He fired his pistols at the upturned wagon the Reclaimers were using for cover, span them against the horse's hide and fired again. He continued until he heard the hooves of the dabbler's horse. He glanced over his shoulder and saw the grenade in the boy's hand. Bullets rammed into Kip's horse and he realised the Reclaimers thought Talisker was on a mission to rescue his fallen Torchlight comrade. They hadn't seen the grenade.

"Go on, you beauty," Kip called, firing both spinners as Talisker's horse vaulted over Kip's position and kept going.

The boy launched the grenade at the wagon and it sailed over them, struck the cliff behind and exploded on impact. Kip's ears popped but he knew the sound would echo all the way down the canyon. Dust and rock filled the air, and Kip heaved himself up and dragged himself towards the entrance to the canyon, his pistols gripped tightly. He could vaguely make out the sound of the convoy through the ringing in his ears, and saw the ghostly shadows of the former townsfolk of Maisy flash past him.

The air cleared, and Kip saw that a massive section of the cliff had fallen outwards, collapsing on the carriage and flattening the Reclaimers. Midway between him and the rubble, the crumpled body of Talisker the dabbler lay next to the road. The convoy rode through the dust cloud into the darkness of the Meander Canyon, scared faces staring at the stone grave of the Reclaimers.

When Beasley saw the explosion ahead, his heart burst with relief. Talisker had sealed the entrance to the canyon behind the convoy and the townsfolk were saved, as they had planned all along.

He slowed the bugler's horse, took one last look at the red cloud as it rose into the air like a victory flag, turned the horse off the road and galloped into the desert, a broad smile plastered across his face.

Widdershins also saw the red cloud, but he knew it was not the outcome they had planned. If the grenade had sealed the mouth of the canyon, the cloud would be darker with the stone dust of the canyon itself. Whatever this explosion had destroyed, it had happened in open ground. He kicked and slashed his way out of the frontline towards the road and saw Beasley heading west at full tilt, head down.

And so it fell to him, John Widdershins, the man the Torchlights hadn't wanted, who wasn't welcome, to save the day and keep the Reclaimers from the townsfolk.

"Rally to me," he commanded. "Rally to me!"

As he saw the Torchlights turn towards him, he spun and kicked Estella southwards, knowing his comrades were right behind him. And on their heels were five times as many Reclaimers. He felt a wave of relief that his best friend Kip was up ahead, looking after their families. He knew he could trust Kip.

"For Maisy!" Widdershins called, and he heard the cry go up behind him.

"For Maisy!"

Kip turned Talisker onto his back and wiped the muck from his eyes and mouth.

"Don't die on me now," he told the dabbler.

Talisker coughed and opened his eyes.

"Are you okay?"

"No," Talisker replied, letting Kip help him sit up. "Are you?"

"No," answered Kip, "Shall we go?"

"What happened?"

"Your grenade happened."

"A grenade couldn't do all this," Talisker said, looking at the destruction.

The two men helped each other to their feet as the Maisy refugees passed them. Kip, pale from the loss of blood, his arm going cold and his thigh trembling, prayed he'd see the cyan-topped carriage, hoped it would stop and his family would take him in, his sons would cheer and his wife would hold him tight. He heaved a sniper's rifle from the rubble that had once been the Reclaimer's defensive position and shifted it under his arm as a rudimentary crutch. He re-alised with bitterness that the crutch could have been the weapon that fired the shot that had caused the wound to his thigh. He decided not to share this speculation with Talisker.

"Was that your only grenade?" Kip asked instead, stand-ing by the side of the road.

"I've got one last trick," Talisker replied, "Have you ever heard of a paralysing floor?"

When Widdershins was a mile from Maisy, he looked back for the first time to see who was with him. He saw twelve bloodstained and exhausted Torchlights on the road with him. Beyond them he could see about two hundred and fifty Reclaimers starting towards them, having dispensed with the last of the Torchlights who had dug in near Mai-sy. Surveying the land ahead he could make out the peaks of the cliffs and knew they were nearly at the canyon. He spurred his horse on, a plan for a last ditch defence forming in his mind.

Kip felt relief at seeing the scarlet uniforms approaching, but also felt a sense of real helplessness when he saw the lack of numbers. He was not surprised to see Widdershins leading them, but cursed when he saw the Brigadier was not there too. He stopped himself from thinking of all the others that were lost; the bugler, Dunst, Philips, Bellenden...

And then he saw the huge cloud of dust being churned up by the Reclaimers behind them, and felt a shiver of darkness.

"Is that everybody? All that's left?" Talisker gasped.

The last of the refugee column had already entered the canyon. Kip calculated that they were five minutes ahead of the Torchlights, and that the front of the convoy should break out of the canyon and reach the Moon Docks in ten minutes. If the Torchlights could hold the Reclaimers for just five minutes, then there was still some hope.

Estella reared up as Widdershins halted next to the dabbler and his friend.

"Where are they?" Widdershins demanded, ignoring the fact that the mouth to the canyon was still very much open.

"Five minutes ahead," Kip replied as he felt his friend size him up.

"Does that sniper rifle work?"

Kip looked down at his crutch and felt his shoulder ache as he shrugged.

"Don't know."

The rest of the Torchlights reached them and stopped.

"They're right behind us," one Torchlight stated through his exhaustion.

"What's the plan, Widdershins?" asked a boy with broken nose and a gaping gash above his eye.

"It's time for the caracole manoeuvre, gentlemen. You know what to do," Widdershins replied, turning to face his remaining cavalry. They glanced at each other with trepidation and resignation before nodding consent.

"Get ready, Torchlights," Widdershins commanded, and the men saluted before getting into two rows of six. Two rows of six against two hundred, Kip thought to himself.

"What can we do?" Kip asked his friend, indicating the dabbler next to him.

"Has the dabbler got anything left?"

"A paralysing floor, Sir," Talisker replied.

"Okay, we'll slow them down at the front, which will mean the bastards in the middle will bunch up. Once they're in the crush, make your move, Mr Talisker. Kip, you need to go to ground and protect him."

Kip nodded, looking for cover, seeing Widdershins doing the same for him.

"Can you climb?" Widdershins asked, looking at the chunk of cliff that had fallen into the Reclaimers' position.

"I can try."

Widdershins held out his hand for the rifle, checked it over quickly and handed it over again.

"This'll work. Talisker, help him up that rubble. If anyone sees you, kill them. Do you understand?"

Kip saluted his childhood friend.

"Yes, Sir."

Widdershins saluted back and turned to the Torchlights.

"Listen up, men. We get as far as we can through this canyon and then we form up. Are you with me?"

"Yes, Sir."

"Good luck, Kip," said Widdershins.

He nodded once at the dabbler and spurred Estella forward.

"Let's go," he called, pulling his sabre.

"See you on the other side," Kip called to the Torchlights' backs as they galloped past.

And then they were gone, while the dust cloud around the approaching Reclaimers grew bigger and closer.

When Maisy was still known as Talling, and Talling was a tiny hamlet, the townsfolk had spoken a very different language, the same language found on the inscription above the Gleave family lodge's front door. And in that language, the word "caracole" meant "snail". The caracole manoeuvre had been used by native cavalry to defend the Gramarye when the Trade had first started using force, but it had never been the most successful defence. However, as soon as Widdershins ordered it, the other Torchlights knew immediately that in the confines of the Meander Canyon it was an inspired tactical move, not just a final patriotic gesture against a much stronger force.

As the Torchlights weaved through the canyon, Widdershins felt a rush of adrenalin. He loved being astride Estella at speed and the high walls either side of the thin trail made the ride thrilling despite the circumstances. He realised he had sped way ahead of the others, and slowed. He could see a trail of mules tethered to the rear of a cart and knew he had reached the stragglers from the Maisy column. He took in his surroundings. He was in the middle of an S-shaped bend, the corner going into it was thin and the central straight had some length. This was the place.

"Form up," he ordered, as the last of the Torchlights arrived in the middle of the Meander Canyon.

Kip and Talisker lay on their bellies in the rubble looking down at the mouth of the canyon as the Reclaimers piled inside, the weapons drawn.

"How do they hope to stop them?" Talisker asked.

"They just need to slow them down enough for you to use the paralysing floor."

"But there are so many."

"You think I'm going to kill them all with this?" Kip asked, patting the rifle by his side. "Get ready, dabbler. This looks like the last of them."

The stream of Reclaimers slowed to a trickle. As the final privateer entered the canyon, Talisker helped Kip back down to the ground from the pile of rubble.

As the Reclaimers turned the corner, they came across the Torchlights in two rows of six, one in front of the other. The privateers roared with delight and pure aggression upon finding the last of their enemy. Then the rear row of the Torchlights fired their twin pistols, bringing down the frontline of the enemy. As the other Reclaimers piled over the corpses of their comrades, the rear row of Torchlights trotted calmly past the front row, which turned and fired a salvo from their pistols. More Reclaimer bodies thudded to the ground in the bottleneck. The Reclaimers slowed as their horses stumbled over the dead, and the Torchlights repeated the manoeuvre so that the onslaught never ceased, the pistols never stopped pouring fire into the advancing army. The Torchlights continued rotating, the hoof prints their horses left behind resembling snail shells, and the continual movement meant that they never presented a static target to their enemies. Twenty Reclaimers went down. Thirty. The Meander Canyon began to be dammed by the dead.

Kip saw the first of the Reclaimers retreating towards them and sighted down the rifle. He fired once and the man was flung from his steed.

"Grab the horse!" Kip ordered as he re-sighted on the next privateer racing to escape the might of the twin guns of the remaining Torchlights.

"Is it working?" Talisker asked as Kip brought down the second Reclaimer, using the wall of the canyon to steady himself.

"Never underestimate John Widdershins," Kip grinned, spinning the chamber of the sniper's rifle and preparing for his next coward.

Kip and Talisker were the last to hear the explosion. First, the gale force ricocheted down the canyon, and then the noise followed, like a crack of thunder during a stampede.

"What was that?" Kip asked as the wind threw sand and dust into his face.

"They have a dabbler," Talisker stated, holding the reins of the horse he had managed to capture.

"Why didn't they use him at Maisy?"

"Because he was waiting for us at the other end of the Meander Canyon," Kip replied. "They've boxed us in. It all depends on the Torchlights and your piece of wonder now."

Widdershins felt the explosion before Kip and immediately knew what it meant.

"Hold the caracole," he ordered the remaining eight Torchlights when they looked at him with terror in their eyes.

Then he kicked his horse forward until he reached the end of the immigrants' column again. All he could hear were screams of mules, horses and people. The sun couldn't break through the dust so everything was in shadow. He had no idea how many of the townsfolk had got through or if they were encased in the rocks that now completely blocked the canyon. All was devastation, coated in a thin film of red dust. An unholy glow seemed to emanate from under the ground, as if hell itself was rising up to greet them.

Widdershins dismounted and bent low to investigate the ground beneath his feet. The power of the pyramids had brought the Trade to Talling, and that same power would kill them all. The Wonder beneath the earth was amplifying everything the dabblers had done. That was why Talisker's paltry grenade had brought down a whole cliff onto the Reclaimers' position. And that was why Widdershins had to stop the boy. If the Trade's dabbler had caused the whole canyon to collapse by being this close to the subterranean red Wonder, what would the paralysing floor do, amplified like this? And if the boy unleashed it, it would be Widdershins' fault. Beasley had resisted using the dabble but Widdershins had made it a major part of the escape plan. As the surviving townsfolk on this side of the rockslide staggered about in shock, he knew what had to be done. He tore off his shirt and dropped his gun belt to the floor. He kicked off his boots and undergarments, and, naked, climbed back into Estella's saddle with one spinner and his sabre. He headed back down the canyon towards the Torchlights at speed.

He turned the corner to find the final three Torchlight dragoons with sabres drawn, clashing with the Reclaimers who had managed to stumble over their dead to get at them. Nobody had a chance to see that their commanding officer was naked, and Widdershins didn't stop. He powered through the Reclaimers and drove Estella over the tens of dozens of dead warriors, hacking and kicking and swearing at anything that tried to stop him, and then he was through the final corner of the S-bend and onwards he galloped. Joining the Reclaimers who had chosen retreat over attack, Estella carried him onwards, faster and faster, feeling her rider's desperation. The privateers who noticed the naked warrior moved aside, not sure what side he was on. All they saw was a berserker galloping from the explosions they had heard behind the enemy's lines.

As more Reclaimers raced towards him, Kip removed his distinctive scarlet tunic and leaned back against the wall of the canyon to let them pass. As the privateers started to cram the canyon floor in their retreat, Kip grasped Talisker's arm.

"This is it," he told the young man, checking his face to ensure he'd be able to perform.

Talisker looked back, nodded once and reached into his pack for the paralysing floor receptacle, an ugly, roughly made wooden tube made up of three different compartments each holding a different measurement of Wonder and other ingredients. Talisker had made this himself taking instruction from ancient books of Wonder he had managed to smuggle from Fairport University library and Kip found himself worrying, as he had seen sleeker, more obviously fatal grenades in museums when he had visited Great Quillia, round balls with obvious triggers, like the explosive grenade the boy had used earlier. Talisker started twisting and turning the different compartments.

The canyon wall above them exploded, and they both ducked. Kip span the sniper rifle and raised it to his shoulder. Charging towards him through the dust churned up by the privateers, he could make out the shadowy figure of a rider. He fired once and saw the rider's shoulder flick back with the force of the bullet. As he spun the rifle's chamber and attempted to supply cover for the dabbler, another two rounds burst above his head.

"Throw it! Throw it!" he screamed at Talisker as the rider got closer.

He fired once and saw the horse skip as the bullet scratched his side. Then the horse was over and the rider tumbled into the dirt floor.

"Talisker!" he yelled, preparing for another shot as he saw the rider pull himself up.

Kip sighted and fired but hit another fleeing Reclaimer. The rider had lost his pistol but flashed his blade at a Reclaimer, grabbed the man's pistol and fired. One bullet hit Kip in the shoulder, spinning him round to allow a second bullet to tear into his throat. He slumped back against the wall, moving his mouth and feebly indicating with his hand to Talisker.

"No!" Talisker cried.

He wanted to grab the rifle, kill the man himself before he threw the tube of Wonder, but he knew this was his last chance. He scraped his way up some rocks to get higher before turning the final part of his Wonder conundrum and throwing it. The rider fired one last shot, hitting the wooden tube as it flew through the air. He dropped his pistol, and was about to throw down the sword when another Reclaimer swung at him. He blocked the swipe, and countered with a slash to the chest.

Widdershins leapt into the air as soon as he felt his ears pop. The Wonder burst from the tube as it hit the floor, unleashing the dark power of the paralysing floor. As the blackberry stain hit the floor, there was a blinding red flash from beneath the earth and the howling of every horse, every man, woman and child in the valley, as the paralysing floor followed the red seem, crackling with ferocious energy from one end of the valley to the other.

The red wonder reacted with the paralysing floor, multiplying the power so that everything fused, not just whatever was touching the floor. Skin welded to clothing, rider merged with horse, and man folded into rock. Widdershins hit the floor and kept running towards Kip and the young dabbler.

"Kip" he called. *"Kip!"*

He reached his childhood's friend's side and saw the shock, fear and complete bewilderment in his eyes before the life left them.

"I'm so sorry, my friend," Widdershins said, before turning to the dabbler.

Talisker was crying, tearing at the clothes now embedded in his skin.

"How? How? *How?*" he said, over and over again.

Widdershins looked down at the sword in his hand to see that his hand was now that sword. And then he walked out of the Meander Canyon. He stopped at the entrance to take the clothes from a Torchlight corpse and then kept walking, his only bullet wound received from his own side, his best friend whom he had killed. He never looked back at Talisker, he never listened to the screams, and he never investigated what had happened to the carriage with the cyan roof.

CHAPTER 4

The Gleave Family Lodge
The Gramarye Region
Grand Quillia

June 1856

The room fell silent as Hilt finished his story. He never disclosed his name throughout the tale, and at one point, when Beasley had looked like he may rouse himself from his dozing, Hilt's voice grew quieter. The fire was now just embers, and even Mandell, who had entered after the story had started, had held his tongue.

"Have you ever been back?" Elena asked.

"Why would I go back? There's nothing to see but corpses and dust."

"I've heard there are still some pockets where the paralysing floor is still active, and catches people as if it had just been cast that day," said Pinkerton, shaking his head.

"That is a truly sad tale," Rickenbacker commented, "and my heart goes out to you."

Hilt looked at Rickenbacker as if he was checking that the man of books was being serious, and he nodded slowly.

"Maisy was raised to the ground, a few survivors got to the fishing port but a Trade frigate was waiting there, with their dabbler. They were all cut down where they stood, made an example of. Children, parents, even the horses."

The door opened and Laurel entered. She immediately felt the funereal chill in the air and cleared her throat before speaking.

"Dinner is served."

The visitors looked at each other and filed out of the room. Elena paused and glanced at Hilt, who remained in his chair.

"Are you coming?" she asked. "I would be honoured if you would escort me to dinner."

"I need to wake the old man," Hilt said, looking back over his shoulder but not catching her eye.

Brennan, mashing potatoes at the central island workspace, noticed Laurel's demeanour as soon as she re-entered the kitchen.

"Kendrick?" he asked.

"Worse. Hilt again," she groaned in reply.

"Meander Canyon?"

"The same. I mean, fine, he's a big hero, the sole survivor, the heart-broken martyr and avenging angel, but does he have to be all that just before dinner?"

"It's because that Professor used a paralysing floor," Brennan reasoned.

"Professor Rickenbacker had to use the Wonder. We was being attacked," Teddy heard himself say.

"Of course you were, my boy," replied Brennan, "Now take some pickles from the pantry and take them to the table."

Spicer had been joined by the rest of his Reclaimers at the end of the path, having deployed the Immolators to surround the lodge so there was no hope of escape without being spotted.

"What do you think they're eating?" Tork asked, glumly licking his lips.

"Shut up, Tork. Honestly."

"Did you see Elena? I mean, did she look okay?" asked Bunce.

Bunce missed her friend. She would never tell Elena she'd missed her; after all, she'd never divulged that she considered her a friend, but she liked having another strong woman around. It meant people didn't look at her like she was a freak. One woman in a band of rough and ready men seemed to bother people, especially people who considered themselves civilised. But when another woman was around, nobody seemed to care. And Elena was different. Tork liked a fight. Spicer had nothing else he could do with his facial scarring, as people didn't want to be reminded that people got hurt. Conway seemed to hang around just to be petulant and practise his Wonder skills. Bunce, if she was honest, was doing it because she had never felt right in a dress. It made her feel uncomfortably invisible. Powerless. After some of the things she'd been through, she always felt she should look and feel strong, and working with the Reclaimers was perfect in justifying that. But Elena seemed to be there, working with them, out of choice. She enjoyed it, craved the thrill, was entertained by the sort of people they were, and the adventures they endured. She was adventurous and thrilling.

Then it struck her that she wasn't even sure if Elena knew her first name was Geraldine, and it made her feel sad. Bunce really liked Elena.

Mandell had found the soup under-seasoned, so was happy for Pinkerton to finish his portion for him, but the stew, served with mashed potatoes and fresh herbs from the veranda, was rich and homely, complementing the wine perfectly. The pickles were also very acceptable. The young knight was rather keen for a quick doze, which would be the perfect end to a dinner. Having killed a few Humps and humped an attractive woman, Mandell felt he deserved a nap.

"Can I see it?" Kendrick was asking.

As Rickenbacker took the Gargoyle Key from his bag, Brennan and Kendrick both leaned over the table to get a closer look, Kendrick managing to dip his shirt cuff in the remaining sauce on his dinner plate.

"And you stole it from the Chinsey Trade headquarters?"

Pinkerton nodded, surprised Mandell wasn't leaping forward to recount the story, as he tended to with every other adventure in which he could paint himself the victor.

"How does it work?" Brennan asked as Laurel started to clear the plates.

"I'm afraid that just as the interior of the Cathedral of Tales is a mystery, so is the means of entry," Rickenbacker replied.

"He doesn't know," Elena clarified, smiling.

"Can I touch it?" Kendrick asked, reaching for it.

Rickenbacker did not stop him but the greasy man dropped it back onto the table immediately.

"It's freezing," he exclaimed.

Brennan rolled it gently over with his butter knife.

"What are these?" he asked nobody in particular, prodding six grooves in the dark sides, "They look like teeth marks."

"Perhaps somewhere in the distant past the dabble was used by mystical orthodontists," Hilt suggested.

"Perhaps Gargoyles have bad teeth," Elena smiled, feeling Hilt's eyes pass over her.

"So you don't know how it works or what's inside the Cathedral," Beasley asked from the head of the table. "What's your plan?"

"Actually, I'd quite like to hear that too, Professor," Pinkerton admitted.

"Sometimes plans get in the way."

"Interesting," Kendrick smirked.

"I'm not even sure where the key should be used, Mr Kendrick, but then nobody alive does. But at least by possessing the key we are a couple of steps ahead of the opposition."

Hilt shook his head, but for the first time Rickenbacker didn't feel any antagonism from the man.

"You have a lot of nerve, Professor Rickenbacker, I'll give you that. Here's to you," said Beasley, raising his drink.

Rickenbacker was surprised when Hilt also raised his glass. Elena also caught a toast from the Torchlight dragoon, and then she caught his eye.

"Smoke?" she asked, pulling out a box of cheroots nobody else in her party had ever seen.

"Why not?" Hilt said, standing up to help Elena out of her chair so that they could adjourn.

"Where are we going?" she asked.

"I like a smoke on the veranda after lunch," Hilt admitted.

"Outside?"

"That's generally where verandas are. The smell of the herbs by night reminds me of being... elsewhere."

"What about the Humps?" she asked, suddenly aware she would rather Hilt be anywhere but outside.

"I'll take a weapon," Hilt stated, before opening the door for them to leave.

Laurel and Brennan exchanged surprised glances. Hilt was not generally a ladies' man.

Bunce raised her telescopic sight and watched as Elena was escorted onto the veranda.

"Who's the guy with the sword?" she asked Spicer, passing him the rifle.

The lieutenant took a quick look and shrugged.

"Perhaps she's trying to tell us to look out for him," Bunce suggested.

"I'd say he needs to look out for Elena," Spicer replied.

Elena followed Hilt onto the veranda, watched as he lit a lantern and covered the match as he lit her cheroot. He leant against the wooden railing and looked out into the woods beyond. She rested her back against the barrier and let her hair fall down over her shoulders. Elena had used any weapon she could to protect herself in the past, and didn't see how using the fact people found her attractive to be any different. She slid her weight onto one hip and blew her smoke into Hilt's face.

"I bought these the last time I was in the capital," she told Hilt, who seemed to be studiously examining the woods beyond, exactly where she did not want him studiously examining, "from a tiny shop run by a delicious little man off the Regency Boulevard. Hand rolled."

Hilt turned to look at her, leaning against the railing with the sword dangling towards the floor.

"Did he roll them himself?" Hilt asked, his face in shadow.

"Sorry?"

"Your delicious little man off the Regency Boulevard?"

"I do believe you're laughing at me, Mr Hilt."

"You make me smile, Lady Melody."

Elena had mixed feelings about making this lost man smile. When he had called her a dabble-dunker, he had to a large extent been correct. She had always been attracted to powerful people until they had tried to exert power over her. Her late husband had built his fortune in slave mines, sourcing volatile Wonder for the slideways of the Empire. He had beaten his slaves, mistreated his staff, conned his business partners and hounded his first three wives to early graves. Elena, a young lady of extremely easy virtue, had learnt all this months before marrying the bastard. Any people related to, working for, or even simply in the vicinity of, Lord Runciman Drew Hynes Melody would have congratulated her had they known she had murdered him.

In her youth, her mentor, an underground kingpin known only as the Pick, had educated her in both how to please a man and kill one, and she had put both skills to the test. The Pick had become famous subsequently, in penny dreadful and weekly instalments in the newspapers, primarily for his gang of pre-teen cutpurses, but the Pick had always been careful to keep only the vaguest shadow of a mention of a character like Elena in these stories. He had never touched Elena himself, and she always suspected he preferred his gang of little boys, something she had teased

Tork about many times, as the two of them had originally met through the criminal overlord.

And now here she was, flirting with a legend, the last of the Torchlights, making sure he didn't realise that the lodge was surrounded. Sure, Spicer and his crew were here for Rickenbacker and the key, but it didn't seem that Hilt would welcome Reclaimers into his current home. It was a pity really. She was starting to grow strangely fond of him, despite his being the opposite of useful to her.

"How long have you been here at the lodge?" she asked him.

"A while."

"Why?"

"After the Meander Canyon, I found myself in a pretty dark place. This is about as civilised as I can manage nowadays."

"Dark?"

"The last time you were in the capital you were buying tobacco from a delicious little man. The last time I was in the capital I killed fourteen people. Have you ever heard of the Creeper?"

"That was you? You're..."

"Dark."

"But you're a hero."

"Depends what side you're on."

"Were all the Creeper's victims..?"

"They all had some connection to the disenchantment of Maisy. The press labelling me a serial killer seemed a good cover. It meant the others weren't expecting me."

"So you killed them all?"

"All the ones I could find."

"And then you came here."

Elena had to admit that this murderous side of the great Torchlight legend served to make him a little more attractive to her, which she felt should probably bother her but she knew the numbers, she knew how many thousands died in Maisy. And besides that, she knew other people who had killed more than fourteen people with a lot less reason.

"I was brought here. Beasley found me. The lodge needed someone for security and I was all out of revenge."

"I suppose a retired serial killer could be good for home defence."

"So here I am."

"Here we are."

There was a pause. Hilt looked down at the butt of his cheroot before flicking it into the crystal trees beyond.

"If you excuse me, Lady Melody," he said, stepping off the veranda.

"You have a prior engagement?"

"I need to do my rounds, check for humps, a touch of serial killing before I retire to bed."

Elena put her hand on his wound.

"Perhaps there is something else you could do before bed."

"Lady Melody. Elena."

"Mr Hilt, this could be my last night on earth. Anything could happen in that cathedral tomorrow. Please stay with me."

He turned to look at her and she stepped closer. She could smell tobacco, brandy, the fire, and something else. She was surprised to realise that he smelt of aftershave as they kissed.

Bunce lowered her rifle and looked at Spicer.

"Told you he was in trouble," he said.

"Kiss of the Spiderwoman," Tork said, taking some salt beef from his rucksack and ramming it into his mouth.

Kendrick watched as Hilt led Lady Melody up the stairs to his room. He stepped onto the veranda, saw Elena's cheroot butt, sniffed it for quality, and slipped it into his jacket pocket. His eyes glanced over his shoulder as he heard something, but the woods beyond seemed the same as ever. Any Humps around would have to get through Hilt, and if he was too loved up, there was Brennan's son Alf, Brennan himself, all these well-armed strangers, before they got to him. He would sleep well tonight. Better than Mandell anyway, who was being jostled to one of the guestrooms by Laurel, always relieved to be visited by fresh nubile flesh. As he crept through the house, he took stock. Beasley was asleep in front of the fire, as always. Rickenbacker was reading a book from the shelves seated on one of the sofas, his boy curled up asleep on the sofa opposite. Brennan and his son were locking up, sliding the bolts across the front door and securing the window shutters. As he climbed the stairs, Kendrick heard a scratching, and, when he reached the landing, he saw Pinkerton open his bedroom door to allow Alexander the Western Isles wolfhound inside.

He opened the door to his room and entered. He looked forward to his bed every night almost as much as he looked forward to breaking into the cellar and rifling through these new visitors' belongings. Except the dead had no belongings, these were just items once their previous owners had disappeared into the bowels of the cathedral. Kendrick was astounded at the endless stream of self-proclaimed heroes and treasure seekers passing through the lodge. Would they never learn? He sincerely hoped not, as he had calculated that one more bunch of idiots would probably supply him with enough booty so that next time he got a lift into Chinsey he'd be able to afford to stay there, get a place of his own. Perhaps not a big place, but a place nonetheless.

Then he noticed the gravy stain on his cuff. He removed his suit and hung his shirt outside his door, for Alf to pick up on his nightly rounds. He considered how much he'd miss the lodge. Laurel cooked and cleaned for him, Hilt defended them all, and the procession of fools meant he could loot enough money to pay for the others' services, he could stay here forever. Also, nobody except the regulars was ever there long enough to form a real dislike of him. Kendrick knew he was pretty unlovable, as it had been pointed out many times, but it didn't really bother him. It saved him spending money on bouquets of flowers or romantic evenings out. But he had grown bothered that nobody seemed to like him, or was even remotely fond of him.

As he climbed into bed, he found himself relieved he was tolerable. If he wasn't vaguely tolerable, then they might ask him to leave the lodge, and then who would press his shirts? No. Perhaps Kendrick would stay here a little longer. He felt safe here in this lodge in the middle of a cursed wood surrounded by malformed cannibals.

Two hours later, when she thought everybody would be asleep, Elena set the plans in motion to allow the Reclaimers into the Gleave family lodge so they could steal the Gargoyle Key.

CHAPTER 5

The Gleave Family Lodge
The Gramarye Region
Grand Quillia

June 1856

Alf enjoyed the late nights and early mornings alone in the lodge. He scrubbed at Kendrick's shirt cuff by the light of the moon shining through the kitchen window. As everybody else slept, he could imagine that he actually had some semblance of a life, a life that didn't revolve around the lodge or its occupants, be they regulars or guests. That this was his finely tailored shirt.

His mother had died in childbirth. No midwives or doctors were willing to brave the Chiming Wood to visit the lodge, and they had no means to reach a hospital. Any animals left in the stables ended up as bait and then a feast for the Humps, so the difficulty of getting in and out meant most medical conditions went untreated until Laurel had inherited the lodge and brought her nursing skills with her. Laurel had also brought her feminine wiles, as her father

called them, something so many visitors seemed to find ir-
resistible, although Alf generally saw her as an extremely
bossy big sister. A big sister who was also a bit of a slut, truth
be told. His father doted on her, which nagged at Alf, but
then she could sell the lodge any time and they'd be home-
less. Admittedly, he didn't know much about real estate, and
the Chiming Wood wasn't exactly prime location, but they
still owed her.

He had met the occasional old friend of his father's,
and had managed to ascertain that until his wife's death,
Brennan had been more boozy than broody. On his few visits
to Chinsey with his father, Alf had seen the old townsfolk's
sneering and tittering as the old man passed by, and worse,
had seen pity in their eyes when they realised he had a son.
His father had taught him not to judge people, but he had
learnt to understand others by the way they judged his
father.

With the trickle of visitors through the lodge, he had
learnt to work out the liars and the cowards from the brave
and true, the ignorant from the hopeful, the sympathetic
from the patronising. He had learnt what was good. Which
was why when his father took him to a whorehouse in
Chinsey, he had been unable to enter. He knew why his father wanted to help, and he knew why it was wrong to take
advantage of the offer. He had discovered his virginity was
indeed a virtue.

He had succeeded at everything else. At Hilt's instruction he had learned to fight and win, to outwit an opponent,
be they Humps or some of the more nefarious visitors to
the lodge. He could hunt, snare, skin and cook most beasts,
not that there was any food running about in the Chiming

Wood. He could grow herbs and vegetables from seedlings. Basically, Alf could live in the middle of nowhere with great success. He could also wash and iron clothes, which were skills not so regularly required in remote areas. Laurel had always told him he'd make someone a good husband one day, while Kendrick had told him he'd make someone a good wife. Following this comment, Kendrick had unwittingly eaten all his meals seasoned with Alexander the wolfhound's drool, which had greatly improved Alf's mood.

When Rickenbacker's manservant had arrived, Alf had realised perhaps he should not be so hard on his own life. This poor young chap couldn't fight, had nothing to say for himself and was terrified of everything, including some food. Alf suspected the boy would never change, whereas Alf knew his life was just beginning, that he was on the verge of a great adventure, once he left the lodge. And one day he would meet a girl, they would fall in love and he would lose his virginity. And they would live happily ever after.

Then he heard somebody slide back the bolts on the front door.

Elena had spent some of the night in Hilt's arms, which she would have enjoyed had he not had a cavalry officer's enormous sabre attached to his hand, the blade of which was inches from her face now he was asleep. He had been a generous but very quiet lover, which neither surprised nor disappointed, and, as he had dropped off, she had listened to Mandell's cries of ecstasy emanating from Laurel's room. She had heard soft footfalls creep up and down the hall within the last hour, but now everything was quiet. Elena breathed out and held her breath, listening to Hilt's heavy exhalation. Sure that he was asleep, she moved his left hand from around her waist, pushed back the blade extending from his other hand and swung her feet onto the floor, leaving her weight on the bed. She reached over to her bag and dragged it towards her, pulling out a pair of handcuffs. She considered which hand to secure to the brass bedstead and chose the riskiest, the hand with the sword. Having clicked both sides of the handcuffs in place, she pushed herself from the bed and grabbed her clothes from a chair. She slid the pistol from Hilt's holster, opened the door to the hall, took the key from the lock on the inside, and locked the door behind her, slipping the key into her pocket. The hall was dark and silent. She looked over the gallery into the hall below and then dressed quickly before tiptoeing down the stairs towards the front door.

She reached downstairs and crossed the hall quickly. She hadn't heard Rickenbacker leave the sitting room, and risked opening the door to peer inside. Her eyes had grown accustomed to the darkness, and she could see the Professor out cold on the sofa, sitting up with his chin against his chest, the boy Teddy across from him. She considered attempting to steal the key for herself, but if anyone awoke and the front door was still bolted she'd be trapped with just lies and excuses to fight her way out. She let the door close slowly and crept further towards the front door. There was no light coming from the kitchen, but she could hear a scratching and a scrubbing, which she put down to rats or that enormous dog. She reached the front door and, as quietly as possible, slid back the first bolt. The sound of metal grinding on metal was so loud to her ears that she was certain the rest of the lodge would spring awake immediately.

Her fingers reached for the second bolt and pulled. Then the kitchen door opened and the young lad stood there, a wet shirt in his hands.

"Can I help you, miss?" he asked.

"I thought I'd go for a walk, Alf," she offered, turning the door handle.

"I wouldn't do that around these parts," he suggested. "Perhaps try the veranda if you need some fresh air?"

Then, as the moonlight crept through the crack in the door, Alf heard feet on the gravel outside and saw Hilt's pistol in her hand.

"Are you expecting someone?" Alf frowned.

Elena spun the Twirler as Alf threw himself backwards through the open kitchen doorway. The mosquito sound filled the air and then she fired, the gunshot echoing into the hallway beyond. The bullet flew past Alf's chest as he tumbled to the floor and slammed the door closed with his feet.

"Elena! Silencer!" she heard Spicer call, and as she opened the front door wider, one of Conway's brutalist handmade containers flew past her head. As it hit the wall, it smashed into a cloud of multi-coloured wonder and the world went deathly silent.

Elena immediately recognised the silencer, a simpler version of the white out weapon Rickenbacker had used in Chinsey, a piece of wonder that will kill any sound in a specific area. It meant nobody in the lodge would be able to warn anybody else of this breach, but it also meant the Reclaimers couldn't communicate either. She hoped Spicer had a plan.

The first one to wake in the lodge was Alexander the Western Isle wolfhound, closely followed by Pinkerton, who was wrenched from his sleep by Alexander's large paw stamping into his nether regions as the dog leapt off the bed towards the door. Alexander had heard the bolt and decided that, although it wasn't his normal exercise time, Brennan must be treating him to an early walk.

They both heard the gunshot that followed, and then their ears popped. Pinkerton watched in shock as the dog howled in silence, before he grabbed his blat gun with one hand and pulled on his trousers with the other. He glanced out of the window and was shocked to discover the dark figure of an Immolator, weapons drawn, standing at the treeline. Pinkerton swore, but no sound came out.

Laurel and Mandell woke up with a start as the shot rang out, without knowing what had dragged them from their sleep. They hardly noticed their ears pop in their drowsiness. Laurel leant across and kissed the man on his lips. He moaned with pleasure but nothing could be heard. They disengaged from their embrace and looked at each other in shock. They both started to talk but neither could interrupt the other as neither said anything. Then they were out of bed pulling on their clothes with as much desperate eagerness as they had originally felt when removing them.

Teddy's eyes burst open as soon as the sound of the gunshot reached the sitting room. He lay there petrified, waiting for one of the old veterans snoozing nearby to do something, anything, preferably tell him which way to run. But both slumbered on.

The his ears popped and he saw Rickenbacker's eyes flicker, then slide open into a squint as his eyebrows came down. He focused on Teddy and saw the lad's terror.

"What's wrong, boy?" he mouthed, and then he could smell the Wonder and knew somebody had used a silencer.

He pointed at Beasley, indicating Teddy should wake him, while picked up his bag of tricks.

Brennan slept on.

Hilt was wide-awake, as if the gunfire that had woken him was from a starting pistol. He sat up immediately, eyes wide open, swung his feet onto the floor and then turned to look at his sword hand cuffed to the brass bedstead. He looked over at the chair and saw his holster was empty, and that the key to his door was missing.

"Bitch," he said, and then his ears popped.

Kendrick woke up, moved his slumber to under his bed, taking his sheets and pillows with him. He had done it before and it had been just as comfortable then. As he went back to sleep he considered whether to move his sleeping arrangements to under the bed as the norm.

Spicer pointed towards the kitchen door and Tork nodded. He raised his blat gun and kicked the door open as the others advanced into the main hall.

Elena put both palms together, raised them to her cheek and then pointed at all the doors around the gallery. Spicer nodded once to Bunce who knelt down and covered the doors above, her rifle resting on a chair arm. Elena then twisted her wrist, indicating the key, and pointed to the door leading to the sitting room. Conway and Elena followed Spicer as, for a second time, he approached his final objective, the Gargoyle Key.

Tork rolled into the kitchen, taking cover behind the central island. He glanced over the counter and saw steam rising from the sink, spreading condensation across the moonlit window. He stood up slowly and slid the primer on his blat gun. There were two other doors, the side door and the door to the dining room. He trained the blat on the dining room door and walked towards the side door, the steaming sink to his left, the central island to his right. He was pleased the silencer meant he needn't tiptoe. He felt a man should never tiptoe.

Alf clenched the cleaver to his chest as he watched Tork's shadow cross the opposite side of the central island. He was holding his breath despite the complete lack of sound as he started to move in the opposite direction, so that the two of them circled the table, Alf in darkness, Tork's enormous bulk silhouetted against the window and casting a shadow across half the kitchen.

Tork reached the side door. Taking all the weight of the stocky fat-barrelled gun in his right hand, he reached out and turned the handle of the side door with his left. It was locked. He moved the hand back to the blat, rolled his head to loosen his neck, flexed his fingers and moved towards the door to the dining room.

Alf allowed himself one glance over the top of the central island, and saw the big stranger with the blat gun approach the dining room door. He edged backwards towards the pantry, and with his hand behind his back found the handle. As Tork kicked in the door to the dining room, Alf opened up the pantry and ducked in amongst the pickles, dried herbs, cured meats, tins and preserves, pulling the door closed towards him.

Tork squinted into the darkness of the dining room, the dark slab of the dining table in front of him. He fired the blat three times, splintering the vast oak antique. Then he looked at the heavy curtains across the large window and fired the blat into the fabric, tearing it apart, shattering the windows and blowing holes in the shutters, so that the eerie moonlight reflected by the Glasslands lit up the room. He walked towards the scraps of curtain, prodded them with the blat and noted an Immolator posted outside. Then he shrugged, and, remembering he had only eaten rations for weeks, decided it was definitely time to raid the kitchen. Grinning, he strolled back into the kitchen, looked around, and noticed the door to the pantry was ajar. As he approached, the pantry door burst open and a boy swung a cleaver at his head. Tork took a step back and felt the breeze as the cleaver missed him by an inch. He grabbed the boy and pushed him to the floor, aided by the boy's own momentum. He put his foot on the boy's back as he slid the primer on his blat gun, and shot Alf point blank in the back of the head. He then turned to see what he fancied eating from the pantry. He decided to start on the preserves first, and chose a raspberry jam.

Pinkerton followed the dog out of the bedroom door, and then saw the mutt's feet sliding on the floor as it desperately tried to turn around. There was already one large bullet hole in the wall next to his door, and two more appeared, getting closer to his own head. Without the sound of the gunshots, it took Pinkerton a second to work out what was happening. He saw the muzzle flash from the hall below, and felt his own feet slide on the floor as he tried to turn around to follow the dog back behind the door to his room. He slid heavily onto his back, rolled over and crawled back into his room, his blat gun still in his hand, thinking that this was not the most gentlemanly way to retreat.

Bunce put another bullet into the big man's door, and then saw the next door along start to open. A man with a square jaw and broad shoulders stepped out, with a Twirler in one hand and a sword in the other, so she shot him, and he fell back into the room he'd come from.

Laurel caught Mandell as he was catapulted back from the force of the bullet, and lowered him to the floor.

"What's happening?" she wanted to ask but the silencer was still in place.

Looking down, she saw the bullet wound in his shoulder, and knew exactly what was happening. She tore open his shirt to review the wound, checking Mandell's face to ensure he wasn't going into shock. He shook his head at her with surprise and tried to look down at his wound. She kicked the door closed and reached for some bedding to act as a bandage.

Hilt grunted with effort as he dragged the large bed across the floor, his toes grasping for the cavalry boot he had kicked off in a fit of passion the night before. He got his foot into the rim of the boot and dragged it towards him until he could reach it with his hand, thanking his lucky stars that Elena had secured his bad hand with the handcuffs. He picked it up and turned it upside down, clasping it between his knees to get at the spur. He detached the rowels and brought them up to the handcuff securing him to the bedstead. Putting his fingers against each rowel, he chose the sharpest and thinnest and pushed it between the shackle and the locking mechanism of the handcuff. He paused when he heard the unmistakeable sound of a blat gun, and then the retort of a rifle.

The handcuffs popped open so he replaced the rowels in the spur and started to dress. He heard more rifle fire and a body hitting the floor in a room nearby. He cursed the Professor for bringing trouble to the lodge as he finished dressing, leaving the empty holster on the floor and opening the chest at the end of the bed. He withdrew his old cavalry double holsters and strapped them on, then two stilettos, which he slipped into each of his boots. Without opening the curtains, he peered between them, saw the moon reflect on the armour of an Immolator and opened the window a crack. He took out two pistols from the chest, checked both their sights, placed one in one holster, twirled the other and fired at the Immolator outside. Between the three shots, he spun the Twirler against the windowsill. The first shot struck the warrior's shoulder, the second his armoured chin, and the third pierced the glass covering his eye. The Immolator burst into flames, and Hilt opened the window wide, before climbing out, using the light of the fire to navigate across the roof of the veranda and down to the gravel below.

Teddy watched from his position at the sitting room door as Rickenbacker worked on one of his homemade wonder machines. It resembled a pepper grinder, but with two rounded ends connected to one middle. He twisted the ends carefully, studying the container with his eyes and ears as though he were opening a safe, measuring the amount of wonder and other chemicals in the three compartments. The Professor glanced over at Beasley who nodded and checked his weapon, the small Schrödinger pistol he had pulled on Elena earlier. Rickenbacker held up three fingers and started to count down as Teddy's fist closed on the door handle.

On the other side of the door in the hallway, Spicer and Elena flanked the doorway, Elena still holding Hilt's pistol. Conway crouched next to Spicer, deep in concentration as he wrenched and plucked at his own creation of wonder. Then the door opened a crack.

Spicer raised his pistol, fired twice into the gap, and rammed his full weight against the door. The door flew open and he stumbled into the sitting room. Elena and Conway saw Rickenbacker's device hurtle into the hall as Spicer disappeared into the room, and they immediately dove to the floor for cover as it smashed against the ground. The smell of ginger and sulphur filled the hall as the mixture of Wonder hit the air, and everybody's hearing returned, as though they had all surfaced simultaneously from deep water.

The first thing Spicer heard was an old man in cavalry uniform who smelt of alcohol and tobacco say, "Don't move, sonny Jim."

He looked up from the floor to see the sitting room door slam closed behind him, and the old man pointing a small Schrödinger pistol at his head.

"Drop your weapon," the old man continued, and so Spicer did, as he took in the other people in the room. The old man, in the uniform of the fabled Torchlights, kicked Spicer's Twirler away and it was picked up by the petrified looking boy who had opened and closed the door.

"Professor Rickenbacker. Only you and that fool Mandell would dare attack a regional Trade headquarters. You might as well surrender now."

"And why should I do that, Lieutenant Spicer?"

"Colonel Quine is on his way out here. He's probably marching up the gravel right now with a full brigade. Give me the Gargoyle Key and we can all walk out of here alive."

"Do you know what Quine would do if he had the key?"

Spicer looked up at the Professor from his place on the floor. He had never met the man before and was surprised how old the fellow was. He also looked like a Professor, which Spicer had always thought was an affectation in an attempt to mythologise the man. He was wearing thick tweed and had the long, unkempt hair of a man who had married into books and never taken a mistress. But there was a cold blue steeliness in the man's eyes that betrayed the man's determination. But what was he determined to do? And why?

"Would you mind if I sat down?" Spicer asked.

"You have no need to make yourself comfortable, Lieutenant. I suggest you take your band of troublemakers and leave now," said Rickenbacker, careful to keep some grace to his voice. "I have the capabilities to destroy the key, this lodge and anybody in the vicinity, including Colonel Quine and his cohorts. And please do not mistake alliteration for brevity."

Beasley grinned. He was growing to like this Professor chap. Spicer saw the old man regard the Professor and looked over at Teddy. Spicer's Twirler quivered in the boy's shaking hand.

"Do you have proof of these capabilities of yours, Rickenbacker?"

Rickenbacker pulled his hands from behind his back to reveal the dark orb of the key in one hand and a grenade in the other.

"I'm afraid that…" Rickenbacker started, and then Spicer kicked at Beasley's shin.

The old man twisted on his ankle and fell to the ground. Spicer launched himself at the boy, his head slamming into

Teddy's gut and the force carried them both over the end of one of the sofas. Spicer's hand grabbed the gun and twisted it away from the boy's body. There was a sharp crack as Teddy's finger broke inside the trigger guard and then Spicer disarmed him. They rolled together on the floor, Teddy offering no fight and then Spicer was on his feet, the Twirler already spinning. The large observation window shattered behind him as Beasley fired off a shot from his Schrödinger pistol and Spicer raised his pistol.

"Drop it, old man," he commanded, twirling the chamber.

"Never," replied Beasley, readying his pistol for a second shot.

Spicer dropped the Brigadier with a shot to the head and turned his pistol towards Rickenbacker. The door opened and Elena looked round the doorframe before entering, her gun on Rickenbacker. Conway stood behind her, looking over her shoulder at the Professor.

"That's the famous Professor Rickenbacker?" he said with heavy incredulity. "But he looks so..."

And then they noticed that the old man had pulled the string from the grenade in his hand.

When Pinkerton's hearing returned, the pop of a Schrödinger and the boom of a Twirler reached his ears and he decided this was as good a time as any. He had tied Alexander to his bedstead for his own safety, and he ruffled the dog's fur.

"Wish me luck," he told the wolfhound, before he pulled open the door, threw himself into the gallery above the hallway face first so that he slid on his belly and fired the blat blind.

"Mandell!" he called. "Professor!"

He heard the rifle below and was covered in plaster as the wall above him was hit. He fired the blat over the edge again without aiming.

"Mandell!" he called again.

He heard the woman's voice from the room next to his.

"Pinkerton! In here!" called Laurel, Mandell still cradled in her arms on the floor.

More bullets hit the wall and the barrier separating the gallery from the hall below.

"So open the fucking door!" he cried, his cheek hard against the floor.

He dragged himself nearer the door to Mandell's room and then peered carefully over the edge of the gallery. He caught sight of the rifle just as it swivelled towards him, and then he felt hands around his ankles, and was yanked into Mandell's room as bullets buzzed around him.

As the door closed, Pinkerton looked over his shoulder to see Mandell, ashen faced, holding one foot, and Laurel, flushed, holding the other.

"You've been shot," he informed Mandell.

"We know. What is going on?" Laurel replied.

"I heard a shot, then I went deaf, then I stopped being deaf and heard more shots. That's about it."

"I've been shot," Mandell told them both.

"Who shot you?" Pinkerton asked him.

"Some bugger down there," Mandell replied, pointing towards the door. "Think it's Humps?"

"Humps don't use guns," Laurel answered.

"I saw Immolators," Pinkerton told them.

"Immolators?" Laurel looked worried.

"Shit," said Mandell.

"Where are the others?" Pinkerton continued.

Laurel shrugged while Mandell looked sorry for himself.

"Immolators," Mandell reiterated. "Immolators are horrid. I don't like Immolators."

Hilt stayed close to the house, his Twirlers in their holsters. His boots crunched on glass as he crept past the dining room window but peaking in he could only see darkness. He reached the side door and peered through the slats of the shutters into the kitchen. He saw a big man eating jam straight from the jar with his fingers, empty jars piled around him on the central island. Then he saw the thick puddle of blood and recognised what was left of Alf lying face down on the floor. He carefully tried the handle but found it locked.

So he knocked.

Tork stopped eating when he thought he heard a knock at the side door. This being the tradesmen's entrance, perhaps this was a fresh delivery of something. Perhaps this was a fresh delivery of food, a butcher preferably, strings of sausages around his shoulders and chops in each hand. Maybe it was the caretaker, he smirked to himself, arriving to clear up the mess on the floor.

His hearing had returned and he had heard the gunfire, but he was sure Spicer and the others could looks after themselves. Besides, this jam was tasty. Admittedly anything would be tasty considering what he'd had to put up with recently, but still, blackcurrant, strawberry jams, some other jam, perhaps peach, he wasn't entirely sure, but by golly it was good. Good enough to miss a gunfight for, anyway. He'd already made a kill tonight, so it wasn't like he was being lazy or a coward. And nobody had come to check on him, either. He could be dead right now, with a cleaver in his belly, and none of them would know.

He wiped his sticky fingers on the worktop, then his tunic followed by his trousers. He picked up his blat and then stooped to pick up the cleaver. As he bent over, a shadow passed the window by the sink, but Tork was preoccupied with his new weapon. He liked the weight of it, he thought to himself as he reached the side door. He turned the handle but it was still locked, and he went to check his own pockets, before grinning and looking around the edge of the door for a key. Didn't people leave them hanging on a hook or something? When he came up empty-handed, he shrugged and put his face against the door to listen. Then he heard the kitchen door open and close. He spun around and fired the blat fast, spraying the door.

"Come out come out wherever you are," he suggested, "and join your friend."

He stayed against the side door so that he could see each side of the central island clearly, his blat still trained on anything that moved. The pantry door swung open and Tork let it have it, the blat turning the door to splinters. He thought he saw a swirl of metal in the darkness of the pantry and fired again.

"I can see you," he lied, as the noise of breaking glass abated.

Something caught his eye to the right of the central island and he fired again, his shot splattering a tin of Spam against the wall. Then the jar came at him from the other side of the island, but he was ready for it, and swung at it with the cleaver before it hit his face. The jar smashed in midair, and he was showered with glass and the jar's contents – pepper.

It exploded into his eyes and up his nostrils, sticking in his throat and nose. He choked, spluttered, fired his blat gun and then sneezed. As he doubled over, he felt the blat gun snatched from his hand and he stumbled forward, grabbing the central island to keep himself upright. He swung blind behind him with the cleaver, cutting through thin air.

"How many of you are there?" a voice asked him.

He pushed himself away from the central reservation towards a shadow he could make out through his streaming eyes.

"Fuck off!"

He felt a blade slice through the back of his trousers, cutting into the back of his knee. His leg buckled under him.

"Why are you here?"

Tork reached for his pistol but his holster was empty.

"I've got your pistol," the other man in the kitchen told him, and he heard the Twirler start to spin.

"How many of you are there?"

He swung with the cleaver again from his kneeling position, connecting with nothing.

"You're dead meat, you shit!" he growled.

He wiped his eyes, and his vision started to return. He looked up to see a man standing over him holding his gun. The man leant forward and whispered into Tork's ear.

"This is going to hurt."

He put the pistol against Tork's other knee, pointing the gun down towards his shin and foot, and, before Tork could raise the cleaver, the man fired. Tork felt the bullet shatter his kneecap, shred all the muscles in his shin and destroy the bones in his ankle before it hit the floor, ricocheted up and passed through his foot. He screamed so hard his throat burned and he fell forward, smashing out teeth and crushing his nose on the floor.

"How many of you are here?"

"No," Tork managed to wheeze.

He watched as the man's cavalry boot crashed down into the hand holding the cleaver, breaking most of his fingers. Then the man took the cleaver for himself and rolled Tork onto his back.

"You shouldn't have killed that boy," the man told him.

"Fuh… fuh…" Tork gasped out.

"You're going to go to Hell soon," the man said, and then he chopped down with the cleaver, opening up Tork's belly, leaving his guts open. "First you're going to be in a lot of pain."

Hilt threw the cleaver away and stood up.

"I'm going to kill your friends now," he said to Tork, walking out of the kitchen door without looking back.

Bunce heard Tork's blat and felt uneasy. She couldn't break cover as she knew there were still people above her she needed to keep pinned down. Then she heard a Twirler and Tork's bloodcurdling scream, and she decided to break cover. Forget keeping the others pinned down. As she stood up, her legs felt stiff from keeping her position and then the door above opened. The blat that had been fired wildly previously boomed out, bursting the armchair she had been using for cover.

"Open the door! Open the door!" she bellowed as she moved, the blat above raining down fire.

She fired blind with her rifle as she ran for the sitting room door, which opened before her. She saw Conway's pale face and then she was in.

"Shut the door!" she hissed, and Conway slammed the door behind her.

"What's happening?" Elena asked her, "Was that Tork screaming?"

"I think so."

"I believe our mutual friend Mr Hilt may have joined the fray, Milady Melody," Rickenbacker said, his hand still wrapped around the live grenade, "or whatever your name is."

"Er, so, that's the guy with the sword you were kissing earlier, right?" Conway asked.

Hilt stepped through the kitchen door and saw the shadow from the front door before he saw the Immolator. He drew his Twirler and spun it in one motion, firing at the Immolator's helmet. He felt the heat wash over him as the warrior went up in flames, falling back against the front door before collapsing. He then turned to see the carnage caused in the hall by Pinkerton's blat gun, and saw the man himself coming down the stairs, the blat gun pointing at Hilt's chest.

"Alf's dead," Hilt told the big man.

"The kitchen boy? Where are the others?"

Hilt saw a door above open and Mandell came out, supported by Laurel.

"Not that way," Hilt informed him, flicking his thumb over his shoulder. "Is he okay?"

"I've been shot," Mandell told him, as he staggered down the stairs.

"I saw one of them make a break into the sitting room, but she moved too fast. I think it was one of Spicer's crew. The woman," Pinkerton paused to glance around. "I seemed to have shot a lot of furniture. Sorry, Laurel."

"Yeah, there was an Immolator..." Hilt said, indicating the fire of the Immolator spreading around the front door and across the rugs on the floor.

"I saw one too," Pinkerton said, moving to cover the door to the sitting room.

"I'll go wake up Brennan and the others," Laurel said, leaving Mandell at the bottom of the stairs to go back up to the gallery.

"Where's the Professor?" Mandell asked.

"Probably in there with the Brigadier," Hilt replied, eying the closed door to the sitting room.

"And Elena?" Pinkerton asked.

Hilt shrugged.

"She handcuffed me to the bed and then sneaked down here to let her friends in," Hilt surmised

"But she's one of us," Mandell said, shocked.

"Not anymore."

"Are you sure?" Pinkerton asked.

"Why don't you go in there and ask them what's happening?" Hilt suggested, pointing his blade towards the sitting room.

Spicer spun his Twirler and pointed it at Teddy, his eyes staying on Rickenbacker's grenade.

"Conway?" he asked.

"Are you asking what is in the old man's hand? Like is it an explosive grenade or some other type of wonder that ties our shoelaces or something?" Conway offered.

"I'm beginning to understand why this is the only job you could get, Mr Conway," Rickenbacker chuckled. "Lieutenant, let the boy go."

"I'm a qualified hyperphysicist," Conway insisted.

"Shut up, Conway. So where do we go from here, Professor?" Spicer asked.

"I can smell smoke," Bunce said, sniffing the air.

"I suggest you leave. Go to Quine and tell him you have found me, that I am holed up in this lodge, with the key."

"And in the meantime, you escape into the Chiming Wood?"

"Perhaps. Teddy, come here."

Spicer shrugged and lowered his Twirler. Teddy walked to the Professor's side and cowered behind him.

"What about you give me the key, I take it to Quine and I tell him I left you for dead? I get my money, Quine gets what he wants and you escape with your life."

"The Trade cannot get their hands on this key, Lieutenant."

"Then it would appear we are at an impasse."

"That we are. Farewell, Lieutenant," Rickenbacker said, and then he pulled the fuse and dropped the grenade at his feet.

CHAPTER 6

The Gleave Family Lodge
The Gramarye Region
Grand Quillia

June 1856

Quine watched as Major Franks deployed the platoon to surround the lodge.

"Not long now," he smiled in Axelrod's direction.

"I smell something," Axelrod said, lifting his nose to the air.

Then they saw Spicer and most of his Reclaimers storming out of a large window at the side of the building.

"Hold your fire," Quine commanded and then he felt his ears pop.

A massive explosion rocked the woods as fire engulfed the lodge. The Glasslands rained glass on the Trade platoon as Spicer and his Reclaimers were lifted off their feet and thrown towards Quine in a cloud of smoke, fire and gravel. As they hit the floor, they continued running, Bunce helping Elena to her feet and heading for the cover of the woods.

Spicer paused, glanced back, and scooped up his wig from the floor, holding it to his head as he moved.

"Rickenbacker," Axelrod groaned, as the echo of the explosion abated.

"You think?" Quine snarled back, "Where Spicer's big chap? The one that saluted me? And get up off the floor, Franks."

Franks stood up, his bottom lip trembling and his knees and palms bleeding where he had thrown himself with such force to the ground.

"Bring the lieutenant to me," Quine commanded Franks, who saluted uncertainly, wiping tears from his face.

"Lieutenant!" his shrill voice called. "Over here."

It had been bad enough fighting off the Humps they had encountered, but to be rewarded at their journey's end with a bloody great explosion was just too much. This job would be the death of him, he knew it. If only Mrs Franks would let him retire.

Spicer searched in his jacket for his wig glue while his crew checked each other over and then they approached Franks, wiping detritus from their clothes and picking glass and gravel from abrasions.

"Where's the big one?" Quine asked.

"In there," Spicer replied, pasting glue onto the inside of his wig.

"Bad show. Do you have the key or is that in there too?"

Spicer shrugged and secured his hairpiece to his head.

"Franks, send in the remaining Immolators when the flames have died down. I suppose you might as well go now, Lieutenant. Your ponies served as *hors d'oeuvres* for some Humps, but we lost some men to the brutes so we have some spare rides should you require them," said Quine, waving his hand vaguely behind him.

"If it's all the same to you, I'd like to see if there are any survivors. I lost a good man in there."

"It's up to you, of course."

The Reclaimers and most of the platoon turned to stare at the lodge as it was engulfed by fire. Franks trembled as he approached the four remaining Immolators to give them their orders. Axelrod, in deep thought, rubbed his chin as he watched the flames. He pondered on why he smelt a hint of the brain changing Green Wonder as well as the explosive Red Wonder.

"Send one of the Immolators in immediately," he told Franks. "That fire may not be quite what it appears to be."

Before the explosion, Laurel had just reached Brennan's room when she noticed Kendrick peering through a crack in his door.

"I think you can come out now, Kendrick," she told him.

"Are you sure?"

"No."

"What happened?" the little man asked, opening his door and glancing over the gallery at the hall below.

"We were attacked. The Professor's lady friend betrayed him and opened the door to some scum who tried to take the Gargoyle Key."

"And where are they now?"

"Oh, they're in the sitting room with the Professor, still trying to take the key."

She knocked at Brennan's door and let herself in. The old man was snoring soundly and Laurel felt tears come to her eyes, knowing the news she needed to share with him. She prayed Alf was perhaps just wounded, that Hilt was wrong, but when it came to violence, the man with the sword was never wrong. She reached out a hand and placed it on Brennan's shoulder. Kendrick came to the door, wearing a vest, his trouser braces dangling around his waist.

"Do you know if Alf has washed my shirt?" he asked.

Laurel swallowed a sob.

"I don't know if he did. Perhaps you could go downstairs as I need to discuss something with Brennan. Something important."

And then the explosion happened.

Laurel watched with fascination as fire burst through the open door around Kendrick, swept across her and Brennan, hit the windows and blew them out. She was relieved that her death had come before she'd had to share the terrible news with Brennan, and surprised that death by fireball hadn't hurt more.

Then, as Brennan snorted rudely awake, Laurel noticed Kendrick had wet himself, that the flames had disappeared and that the window was still in place. Fire, however, licked the walls and floor, but she could feel no heat.

"Are we... ghosts?" Kendrick asked.

"Definitely not. I can smell that," replied Laurel, pointing at the stain in the front of Kendrick's pants. "It must be Rickenbacker. He's faked an explosion."

"What?" Brennan said, rubbing his face, "Rickenbacker? Is there trouble?"

"Brennan, it's Alf."

As the explosion illusion moved beyond the hall, leaving just the real flames around the Immolator at the front door, Hilt left Mandell and Pinkerton staring at each other in shock and kicked open the door to the sitting room. He saw the flames licking around the blown out window, bullet holes scarring the books and Rickenbacker and Teddy kneeling by Beasley.

"Who did this?" Hilt asked, pulling his Twirler.

"Spicer, but you can't..."

"Watch me," Hilt spat, heading towards the window.

Rickenbacker stood up and reached towards Hilt.

"If you go out there, they will know the explosion is a fake."

"If I go out there, nobody will live long enough to know anything."

A terrifying heartbroken scream burst from upstairs. Hilt turned and looked at Rickenbacker, his jaw locked, before he spun on his heel and headed back into the hallway, spinning the Twirler.

"Cover that body, Teddy," Rickenbacker told the boy, who was cradling one hand in the other, "and well done."

"What happened?" Teddy asked.

"It's called a perimeter bomb. There is real fire around the outside of the building, but it touches nothing inside. It's possible to jump through it," he saw Teddy looked worried, "but it feels like it gives out a lot of heat externally, so we should be fine. Unless Spicer was right and Quine is out there with his ECO."

Brennan was staggering down the stairs, drunk with grief. Hilt moved up to meet him and the older man grabbed him by his lapels.

"They killed my boy, Hilt. They killed my boy," he wailed, tears and snot rolling down his face.

"I killed his murderer, Brennan. I tortured him and then I killed him"

"Where is he? I need to see my boy."

Hilt grabbed him by the shoulders.

"You can't. The kitchen is on fire. He put up a fight, though. Alf put up a fight. He had a cleaver. He swung it at his killer. He was a hero."

"He's a dead hero. Dead."

Brennan dropped to his knees on the stairs, clinging to Hilt's thighs.

"The Brigadier is dead," Hilt told nobody in particular.

"What the hell happened here?" Laurel asked.

"What are you going to do?" asked Kendrick from the top of the stairs. "I looked out of the window. You're surrounded."

"Thanks for the solidarity," Laurel said.

"I'm just a guest here. I have nothing to do with it. Neither do you. You could walk out now. We could leave here together."

Rickenbacker and Teddy emerged from the sitting room.

"I brought this to your door. I did this," said the Professor.

"You and your fucking key," Hilt said, helping Brennan to his feet.

"If the Trade get their hands on this key, more people will die. More respected old veterans. More young boys."

"Why aren't they attacking?" Kendrick asked.

"I had a grenade called a perimeter bomb. It caused an explosion but only from outside the building. Everybody inside is fine. It should keep the Trade out. They won't realise they can walk straight in."

"Or that we can walk straight out," Kendrick said.

At that point an Immolator stepped through the front door and looked down at the dead warrior. Hilt and Pinkerton brought their weapons to bear, but before they fired, the fire from its colleague caught on the Immolator and immediately it burst into flames itself.

"I could have sworn it was a perimeter bomb," Axelrod said, staring at the burning Immolator at the front door.

"At least it was only an Immolator," Quine shrugged. "So I supposed we wait for the fire to burn itself out and then sift the rubble for the key."

Then they saw an odd little man step across the obliterated window frame where the Reclaimers had come from and walk straight through the flames like a bite-sized messiah. As some of the platoon advanced on him with weapons drawn, he handed them business cards.

"What's this?" Quine asked.

"Kendrick. One of the guests," Elena told them all.

"What are you waiting for, Franks? Bring him to me immediately."

Having taken the measure of the man in the suit and vest, Franks marched up to him, snatched the proffered business card and dragged him physically in front of his Colonel.

"As the lady says, sir, this is Aldo Kendrick, Esquire. Fixer. Entrepreneur. Friend. Oh. That's nice. It says friend."

"And that is indeed what I am. And to prove it, Admiral," said Kendrick, addressing Quine, "I would like to tell you about something called a perimeter bomb..."

"I knew it!" Axelrod interjected.

"Professor Rickenbacker used one, a perimeter bomb, and is in there right now, safe and sound, with your Gargoyle Key, which, I'm sure I must have overheard somewhere, is worth a substantial reward, which I will be happy to claim. Oh hello Lady Melody. Hilt is really quite angry with you."

"Tell the platoon to advance on the lodge," Quine ordered.

"And the front door is actually on fire. Real fire, I mean. One of your Immolators..."

"Tell them to concentrate their fire on the window," Quine ordered Franks. "The window Spicer's men retreated through."

"I have a little something," Axelrod suggested. "Something that will actually burn that place to the ground."

"Let's see if they put up a fight first, old boy," Quine replied, patting Axelrod on the arm.

Spicer and the other Reclaimers glanced uneasily at each other. Elena moved her lips to Spicer's ear.

"We can go in through the veranda," she whispered.

"When can we talk about my reward, Admiral?" Kendrick asked, tugging on Quine's sleeve.

"Someone look after our friend here," Quine ordered as he watched Franks heading off to organise the platoon, and the Reclaimers went their own way.

"He's gone," Hilt reported, coming back in from what was left of the living room. "And they will come at us from that direction. I suggest we get up in the gallery, stay quiet and wait for them to come to us. Rickenbacker, do you have any more dabble?"

"I have bits and bobs but nothing that will keep them out indefinitely."

"What about the cellar?" Mandell suggested through gritted teeth.

"The cellar?" Rickenbacker asked.

"We have a cellar full of equipment left by previous guests. Guests who never came back from the Cathedral," Laurel clarified.

"Let me see," Rickenbacker ordered, and they headed for the door, Laurel lighting a lantern.

They heard the crack of rifle fire as the platoon opened fire. Glass shattered and the whole building seemed to rattle under the onslaught.

"My God, what is this place?" Rickenbacker said to himself as he held the lantern aloft.

"I don't really know. I think they kept captured animals down here when it was still a hunting lodge," Laurel replied, the brevity of her flirting with Mandell long gone.

"The only animals I know those chains would shackle are human," Rickenbacker said as he peered into one of the cells.

Laurel felt herself blushing in the darkness. She had never particularly wanted to examine the history of the Gleave family tree, and the Professor's observations only hardened that feeling, but she felt dumb.

Then she heard a growl from the darkest end of the cellar.

"Do you still keep animals down here?" Rickenbacker asked her, holding the light to her face.

"I've never kept..."

"Then what was that?"

The bullet struck Mandell in the hip, spinning him round.

"Not again!" he roared with anger.

Pinkerton knelt at his side.

"You don't seem to be having much luck today," the large man commented.

"Get him to the cellar," Hilt said, pulling open the door. "You boy, help them."

Teddy was lying flat on the ground, hoping that he would be mistaken for one of the rugs. The smoke was starting to catch in his throat and part of him wished he was Kendrick's manservant instead of Rickenbacker's. He stood up but found it impossible to raise himself to his full height, as if he were standing in a loft, and crept to Mandell's side. Bullets thudded into the remaining furniture that had survived Pinkerton's blat gun.

"I'm going to kill them all," Brennan hissed, a Twirler in his hand, before Hilt grabbed him.

"Don't. Not now. The Professor was right. We need to pick our time. We will take revenge on our terms," Hilt said.

"They killed my boy."

"Trust me. Revenge was my business for ten years. I'll be happy to get back into it."

"That is not a water fountain," Rickenbacker told Laurel.

Laurel found herself clinging to the Professor, her eyes wide with terror, as she stared into the shadows at the dark pitch of the beast at the end of the cellar. Although still black, its eyes seemed to glow with sentience, and there was no doubt it was moving, out of its pitch background, with glistening teeth and claws.

"It's never done that before," Laurel said.

"Stay exactly where you are," Rickenbacker ordered.

The beast moved closer, morphing between serpent, dog and tar, slithering, sniffing and puddling, the sound a combination of a growl and a bubble.

"What is it?" Laurel wondered aloud.

"Gargoyle," Rickenbacker hissed.

It pooled around their feet as Rickenbacker pulled the Gargoyle Key from his bag and held it tightly in white knuckles. As the beast moved from the darkness at the end of the cellar, they could see a corridor beyond the cells, a passage as dark as the creature that surrounded them, with more subterranean eyes and mouths, hellish liquid pouring from mouths to turn into more eyes and teeth and claws, always moving and changing to make more gargoyles.

The goo spiralled up their legs like reverse helter-skelters. "What does it want?"

As it reached Laurel's thighs, it retreated to concentrate on Rickenbacker, spreading across his waist like they'd burst a spider's nest, splitting like fractals and coming back together like puddles. Laurel stepped away from the Professor and leant against a cell door, her hands moving to her mouth to suppress a cry of terror, a yell of sheer horror she prayed would drive back the inhuman alien thing that had lived in her cellar, unknown, waiting for God knows how long.

Rickenbacker felt the beast encase his feet and shins and move up. It felt tight against him, as if he was wrapped in wet towels, and then he felt it enter each pore and spread into his veins, stretching them as though they were filling with dust. The veins seemed to expand to meet the tightening against his skin, and he was aware of chilling coldness and weight. He looked down. As the pitch moved off his feet and shins, it left them as dark shimmering stone.

"Laurel," he cried, realising he was in grave danger, "take the key."

"But I..."

"For both our sakes, take the key!"

He waved it at her and she reached towards the orb, her hand shaking. The pitch moved back off the Professor and he felt the warmth of life returning to his shins. Looking down, he saw flesh and blood where there had been stone.

"Professor?" Laurel whispered, as the pitch spread across her.

"Don't panic, Laurel. You are a Gleave. Gleaves built this place."

"But..." she said, her voice wavering.

As the pitch moved from her skin, it left no mark, made no effect. It caressed her thighs and moved up her back to her shoulders before sliding across her arms towards the Gargoyle Key in her hand.

"What should I do?" she asked, moving nothing but her eyes to stare at Rickenbacker.

"Let it have it," he replied in a soothing tone, "Let it go."

The darkness left Laurel and moved inside the key.

"It's so heavy," she said.

A thick tube of goo burst from the Key, returned to the doorway and became a dark wall again. The gargoyle's face returned, but this time the key was between its teeth. Laurel looked down at her empty hand.

"I did it," she said with relief.

The black gargoyle she had known as a water fountain froze in place before swinging open, like a thick metal door.

"Incredible," Rickenbacker said

Beyond the door where there had been beasts, a stone frieze of twisting gargoyles lined the walls and ceiling. The stone floor seemed to ripple in the light of the lantern, but the Professor kicked a rock forward into the corridor and heard stone on stone.

"Professor, I had no idea I had inherited a secret corridor."

"Laurel Gleave, I think you may have inherited a lot more than a corridor."

Laurel softly embraced Mandell on the cellar stairs and kissed his cheek. His lips moved to hers and they kissed passionately.

"I owed you one," he smiled, "Nurse Gleave."

She couldn't look more different from the nurse he had first met. She had gone through the cellar and looked to Mandell like she was dressed to go mountaineering, with extra guns. She still looked thoroughly desirable, in his eyes, which was one reason why he was willing to give them cover while they escaped. She would know he was a real hero, not some jumped up rich kid who happened to be good with a gun. And a sword. And really good in bed, if occasionally a little selfish. And quick.

"You're my hero," she told him, and made her way down the stairs.

"It has been a pleasure riding with you, Sir Evan," said Rickenbacker. "You have saved my life countless times and enriched every journey. May you go with glory."

Teddy nodded at Sir Evan without looking in his eye, took two steps and then wrapped his arms around the man.

"Look after the Professor, young Teddy."

When Teddy released him, Brennan shook his hand and moved down the stairs without a word. He had Alexander the Western Isle Wolfhound on a lead with him and the dog eagerly licked Mandell's hands as he passed. Hilt handed Mandell a Twirler and patted him on the shoulder.

"This should keep you going when the spinner isn't enough," he said.

"Good luck, Mr Hilt."

"See you later then, old friend," Pinkerton said, firmly shaking Mandell's hand.

"In some bar or tavern…" Mandell suggested

"I suppose the drinks will be on me."

"And the food."

They stood regarding each other, their hands still clasped.

"Look after Laurel," Mandell told him.

"Look after yourself," Pinkerton replied.

Pinkerton turned and started down the stairs.

"Up the Reds," Mandell cried, a reference to an old joke from their years together.

"Down the Blues," Pinkerton said, without looking back.

As the gentleman pugilist made his way into the cellar below, he heard the mosquito buzz of Mandell's spinner. Then the gunfire started.

As the platoon charged the window, Spicer kicked in the remains of the shutters into the dining room, his Twirler buzzing in his hands, Bunce right behind him. They looked at the devastation before them.

"Ever get the feeling Tork has been somewhere?" Conway said as he followed them in.

They could feel the heat coming from the kitchen to their right, and headed to the door into the hall. Conway glanced around and saw a box of cutlery that he eagerly started to empty into his bag.

"Classy, Conway," Elena said, raising her eyebrows as she entered last.

The four of them took positions either side of the door and Spicer opened it a crack to allow Bunce to peer through. Kneeling, she saw Trade soldiers dead on the floor by the entrance to the sitting room and looked up through her rifle sight at the gallery above to check for a shooter. Bullets slammed through the door above her head and she stepped back behind the wall as cover.

"See anything?" Conway asked.

"Not on the gallery."

"There's a cellar," Elena informed them, remembering Mandell mentioning something to her over dinner that she had not wanted to hear.

"Where?"

"To the left of the sitting room."

Spicer and Bunce looked at each other and nodded. The woman lay down by the door and Spicer knelt over her, a Twirler in each hand. With a nod, Conway opened the door and as soon as Spicer saw the entrance into the cellar, he fired both guns without pause. Meanwhile, Bunce sighted down her rifle and saw the sandy hair of Mandell as he slid further down the stairs into cover, and Spicer's bullets thudded around him.

"Wait," she told Spicer, breathing out.

There was a pause. Nobody tried to enter from the sitting room, and for a moment all they could hear was the crackle of the flames at the front door and various Twirlers spinning. Mandell raised his head above ground level, Twirler ready to fire towards the dining room. Bunce squeezed her trigger and the bullet took the top of Mandell's head clean off.

As Laurel pulled the Gargoyle Key from the beast's mouth, she heard the shot that claimed Mandell's life. She clung to the door as it swung closed until Rickenbacker and Brennan heaved her hands away.

"Evan!" she cried, and then the heavy clang of the door shutting signalled the end of them hearing any sound from above.

Spicer raced across the hall towards the cellar door, his weapons drawn. As the door to the sitting room opened he stopped himself from raising his Twirlers. He heard shots and the ground ahead of him pinged with bullets. He skidded to a halt and saw Trade soldiers emerge from the sitting room.

"I'm afraid we have been told not to allow non-Trade personnel beyond ground level," a corporal said, raising his rifle as the other Reclaimers joined Spicer.

"But we cleared the way for you, you useless bastards," Conway said.

"Move the body and send in the remaining Immolators," the corporal said, ignoring the grotty hyperphysicist.

Spicer turned around and, seeing the looks of consternation on his team, he shrugged his shoulders.

"Is there a price on Mandell's head?" Conway asked, glaring at the corporal.

"Yes," Elena replied, watching as Sir Evan's body was dragged across the floor.

"Not enough," Spicer said, thinking of Tork.

He slid his Twirlers back into their holsters as the Immolators entered the room.

Quine watched with satisfaction as the terrorist's body was dumped in the gravel, Trade soldiers spitting at it as they passed. Franks scurried up and saluted.

"The Immolators have entered the cellar, Sir," he informed them, standing to attention.

"And?" Quine asked.

"Well, that's it," Franks replied, sweat on his brow.

"So go back in there and find out if they come back. And if they do, I want you to lead the platoon into the cellar, do you understand?"

"Yes, sir."

Franks saluted and retreated, mopping his forehead with a handkerchief.

"Are you sure it's best for Franks to lead them into the cellar, Sir?" Axelrod asked.

"It is if it kills him."

Franks had not seen much of Spicer and his Reclaimers, but what he had seen had not impressed him. He found it easier to consider other people's faults in testing times such as these, as apparently his self-preservation skills could occasionally paint him in a poor light. Therefore, it was extremely comforting to the Major to witness the Reclaimer's retreat from the lodge. He had to admit that his own predilection for retreat and withdrawal was not ideal for a soldier, but then he preferred to think of himself as a military administrator. One of the back room boys. Mrs Franks liked a uniform, and she didn't care what he did in it, which direction he was moving in. Recently he had often thought he should have become a postman instead.

He stepped through the sitting room window into the lodge and made his way past the troops to the hall just as the last Immolator returned from the cellar. The Reclaimers were seated on the stairs to the gallery, glaring at him.

"Report, Corporal Watson," he demanded.

"All clear in the cellar, Sir."

"What do you mean 'all clear'?"

"Nothing down there, Sir. No-one down there neither."

"But there must be."

"Beggin' your pardon, sir, but there ain't."

"For God's sake, stand aside and let me see for myself."

Franks pushed Watson aside and stepped towards the cellar door. As his foot slid in Mandell's blood and brains, he realised his bravado may have been a little misplaced.

"Can we have a look, Major?"

Franks looked up from the gore on his boots to see Spicer and his dabbler.

"Trade personnel only," warned Watson, raising his hand to scarred man's chest.

Franks was surprised at the presumptuous Corporal. Spicer may be privateer scum and adept as Franks himself at retreating, but he was still an officer.

"Corporal Watson, I think I can speak to Lieutenant Spicer for myself."

"The Colonel said..."

"Corporal Watson, would you like to find yourself on a charge?"

"No, Sir. I just..."

"Then please escort the lieutenant and his hyperphysicist into the cellar."

"Yes, Sir."

"Thank you, Major," said Spicer.

Franks was rather proud of his own initiative and smiled to himself. Colonel Quine hadn't stipulated at which point Franks should lead the platoon into the cellar, so why not make double sure there was nothing down there? He noticed the two Reclaimer women on the stairs roll their eyes in his direction, but decided to ignore it.

Spicer unsheathed his sword as they moved into the gloom.

"You won't need that, Reclaimer," Watson scoffed as he led the way.

Lanterns lit the cellar from the floor, illuminating the junk in the cells.

"Checked each cell?" Spicer asked.

"As much as we need to," Watson said, leaning back against a wall to roll a cigarette. "I don't see how the terrorists could open a secret door and then pull all that crap on top of it again, do you?"

He lit hit cigarette and smirked.

"That looks interesting," Conway said as he saw the blackness of the gargoyle ahead.

"It's a water fountain or something, innit?" Watson suggested, uninterested.

Conway reached into his rucksack and pulled out what appeared to be an egg timer with a small dart at one end. Instead of sand, mixed grains of Wonder could be seen in the chamber. Conway shook it and held the timer to allow the dart to spin.

"What's that?" Watson asked.

"A Wonder diviner," Spicer told the Corporal, as Conway watched the dart start to settle.

"What's it do?"

Spicer ignored the trooper as the dart pointed towards the water fountain. The darkness at its surface seemed to ripple.

"Er, they went thataway," Conway said, taking a step back as the gargoyle's head moved to consider the three men.

Watson drew his Twirler and spun it.

"Leave this to me," said the Corporal, moving towards the gargoyle.

Spicer and Conway continued to move backwards as Watson advanced.

"Is it alive?" Spicer asked.

"It wasn't until I activated the diviner. And I doubt it'll appreciate sonny Jim's Twirler either."

The gargoyle swooped across the floor like a wave of dark clasping hands and engulfed Watson before he could shoot.

"What's happening?" he called as the pitch swallowed him up, so that he resembled some life-size ebony statue, the cigarette still between his lips. As quickly as it had come, the pitch retreated, leaving Watson cast in stone.

"Oh my God," Spicer said from the bottom of the stairs as he watched the stricken soldier.

A breeze blew through the door and came down the stairs, dislodging powdery dust from the brand new memorial. A shoulder slipped out of place and then fell, hitting the floor with a powdery puff. The torso shifted and slid from the hips and the entire top of Watson's effigy collapsed into a cloud of dust.

"Blimey," Conway remarked. "That's got to hurt."

"Know any way past that beast?" Spicer asked as they climbed back up the stairs.

"You mean the gargoyle?" Conway grinned, "Perhaps a Gargoyle Key would do it."

As Hilt led the others down the corridor behind the gargoyle, they didn't notice a new face emerge from the frieze on the wall. The new gargoyle merging and moving with all the others stood out from the crowd. This gargoyle was the only one with a rolled cigarette in its mouth.

PART 2

Subterranean Homesick Blues

PROLOGUE

———— • ————

The Necropolis Dig
(Precise location undisclosed)
The Gramarye Region
Grand Quillia

May 1852

D uring a summer break from the university at Fairport, Professor Hilary Rickenbacker and his manservant Teddy travelled to an archaeological site in a dry basin just a few miles from the Glasslands. The Professor had told the volunteers who had come to join him that this was not about getting inside the graves, but the tombs themselves. Rickenbacker had become obsessed with a language called Angular 4. Nobody had been able to translate it, and the old man knew they needed to find more examples, and where better to find a dead language than a giant graveyard.

Most of the tombs they found were covered in the same dark pitch that had covered the Pyramids of Maisy, and it was hard to differentiate any text from the carved stonework, but the Professor persevered. Then they found the top of the entrance to this necropolis, an archway made of stones as heavy as ten ice yachts, the stones so close fitting it was impossible to get a piece of paper between them. As the team dug down to the bottom of the archway, they discovered bones. Bones of men, women and children that had never been entombed. And although these bones were humanoid, they were not human.

Professor Rickenbacker stopped the dig at the entrance, directing the volunteers to concentrate on their original objective, the tombs themselves, while he examined their new findings.

Teddy had been putting the Professor's freshly ironed shirts into his travel chest when Rickenbacker entered, flanked by two men he had never seen before.

"Of course your discovery is notable, Professor," one of the men was saying, "but I doubt in the way you are thinking."

"And how would you know what I am thinking, Sir?"

"What my colleague is attempting to stress, Professor, is that it is best for some mysteries to remain just that. Mysterious."

"Look, I don't care what governmental department you say you belong to, the fact that you know this mystery, as you call it, could be dangerous, that knowledge of it could prove a threat to the Empire, then that means you already know more about it than you are sharing. So tell me what you know and then I will decide for myself whether I should share my latest findings with the world."

"What makes you think the world would be interested?" asked the first man.

The Professor went to his desk and grabbed his thermos. He poured himself a coffee, thick the way they drink it in the Northern Territories. Teddy kept it topped up from the Professor's private supply, one of the man's few luxuries. He could tell from his employer's disposition that he would not be requiring any more cups to share the unctuous liquid with his guests.

The two men remained at the flap to the large tent. Their clothes were clean, their boots shined, and their hats were pulled down low over their eyes. They looked like they had just stepped off a commuter yacht in the city. Teddy could see no weapons on their persons, but they carried with them a distinct threat of violence. Neither was muscled, but their calm confident demeanour seemed rooted in something dark. And Teddy had never seen the Professor so angry. He felt almost embarrassed for the man, but he was reluctant to leave. For once, Teddy's curiosity was aroused.

"You have found bodies in a graveyard," the first man continued.

"Don't be so facetious, man. I have found a mass grave of families. Families that are not quite human. And the fact that you two have come here to tell me to cease and desist, me, a consultant ECO and well respected academician..."

The second man flipped open a file.

"Professor Hilary Henry Rickenbacker the third. BBA. LSO. LLP. Both parents dead. Sister and family disappeared in Coinerland during the Flint Uprising. Studied Hyperphysics and General Sciences under Professor Grant, who died during an experiment using Blue Wonder. I believe you were there?" the man said, glancing up from his file.

"What is this?" Rickenbacker blustered.

Ignoring the Professor, the man continued.

"A member of the Council of Historical Wonder and occasional setter of The Quillia Dawn's cryptic crossword. Brief relationship with Esther Frankhausen, which ended when her husband returned from his work in the Garrett Islands..."

"You will find nothing there that says I am some dissenter, some anti-government terrorist," Rickenbacker snarled.

"That is what we are here to ensure," the first man said.

"That is for us to judge," added the second.

"Teddy, leave us now."

Teddy nodded, placed the shirt he had been folding and unfolding into the chest and left the three men. As he left, he heard the second man say, "You seem protective of the boy."

The next day, the dig was closed, and they returned to Fairport. Teddy never saw the two men again. As soon as they arrived home, before Teddy had even unpacked for them, he was sent to the Winterbottom Library for various books and treatises. But these aging texts were no longer dry works of academia centring on semantics or semiotics. These works were found in a dark corner of the library that could be labelled esoteric, recondite. Arcane. These were books that some said had no place in a respected scholastic library, covering topics the aesthetes of the capital were currently wittering on about in poetry and painting. Sometimes called fake histories, the bedtime stories told to scare children. The tales referred to in myth.

And the Professor's studies took a new direction when he discovered a place once known as Pearly.

Epic poetry and ancient plays hinted at what the capital of the Gramarye had once been. Hundreds of years after it had been sacked, ancient scholars and explorers described the remains of Pearly, the original capital of the Gramarye. Some said it was named after the Five Great Pearls of the Gramarye, astonishing achievements using both Wonder and human ingenuity.

At the opening to the great harbour stood an enormous stone watchdog with light beaming from its eyes. If it saw sailors in trouble, they were illuminated to aid their rescue. If ships sailed too close to the rocks, the lights would lead them away. And if anyone dared attack Pearly by sea, the watchdog would attack them with its incredible fangs tearing their boats apart, then wash them away with a swipe of its paws.

On the outskirts stood the Necropolis of Pearly, a collection of mausoleums for the high born, the great and good, with friezes playing moments of their lives. Using the same Wonder as the gargoyle in the Gleave cellar, handsome warriors would save beautiful damsels from beasts, charismatic actors would recite their most well-known soliloquies, and expansive choirs carved in miniature would chant a songwriter's worthiest works. Families would visit the necropolis for entertainment, to watch the remembrances and celebration of the lives of the royal, rich and famous.

There were ancient stories that the fabled great Pearly Tower, higher than the clouds, housed at its peak a landing platform for those most skilled in the Wonder, for those who had made their own flying devices, sometimes as small as rugs, sometimes as big as houses.

Pearly also housed the great Library of Senses. From anywhere in the city, the inhabitants could enter a booth, log into the library, and be able to see, hear and feel the records of the great kingdom. All the knowledge was available for everyone, their favourite stories, feelings and sights.

And the whole of the city was run by the Spider Generator, harnessing the Wonder processed by the Pyramids, spinning a web of energy across the area, lighting streets, heating homes, keeping everything going.

Finally a great cataclysm occurred. Nobody remembered why or how. But there was an uprising. After holding back invasions by beasts and barbarians, the people of Pearly destroyed the city from within. Once the Spider Generator was disabled, the rulers were helpless. Men, women, children, fairies, every sentient being in Pearly committed murder or was slaughtered by his neighbours. And then the city was levelled.

The monumental ruins were scavenged. The enormous foundations that remained hinted at the forgotten abilities beyond anything even the Great Quillian Empire would attain hundreds of years later. The remaining Wonder was drained from the canals of the Pyramids. The only thing left standing, besides the pyramids, was the Library of Senses. Without the power of the Wonder from the Spider Generator it was useless, barely holding together with remnants of Wonder, its original use forgotten, and renamed the Cathedral of Tales.

The archaeologists of Great Quillia and other Empires that had come and gone, none of them managed to enter the Cathedral and get out alive. The ground of the Glasslands was unbreakable. Nobody could excavate through the crystal ground to see the city below. And the remains of the Necropolis were now locked down by the Quillian Government.

It was as if someone had willingly and forcefully cut the Gramarye off from its own history, forbade it from its legacy, leaving the Cathedral of Tales, the Library of Senses, a building that once represented the greatest freedom of knowledge, as a warning. And then in one dusty lexicon written in the language Rickenbacker would later translate at the entrance to the Gleave family lodge, Rickenbacker found the first mention of the Gargoyle Key. And in that crumbling book written in a dead language, he also found a clue as to the bodies he had found buried but not entombed in the forbidden Necropolis. The clue was in the form of a nursery rhyme.

A pocket full of Wonder
We can hear the thunder
When elves dance
When elves cry
Then they will fall

CHAPTER 7

Beneath the Cathedral of Tales/ The Library of Senses
The Gramarye Region
Grand Quillia

June 1856

With a lantern in one hand, Brennan steered Teddy past the end of the gargoyle frieze.

"You need to open your eyes now, boy," Brennan told him, and Teddy's eyes cracked open. He was at the top of more steps leading further down into the bowels of the earth.

"Thank you, Mr Brennan, Sir," he said, wiping his eyes.

"You'll be okay, son," Brennan said. His heart caught in his throat, but he knew he had to be brave for this terrified young boy, this defenceless innocent. "Now let's keep up with the others."

Hilt led them, his lantern held high, with Laurel clinging to his sword arm's sleeve. Then came Rickenbacker, pausing now and then to examine the walls of the subterranean

passage with his own light until Pinkerton urged him onwards, one of the big man's hands gripping the dog's collar, the other holding his blat gun. Brennan brought up the
rear, so that nobody would realise he was crying. The fact
that he had to keep an eye on Teddy helped him focus on
the matters at hand, but occasionally he would feel a nauseating wave of pure rage, his breath would grow ragged
and his hand would grip the handle of the hammer he had
plundered from the cellar above. He had thought the blunt
weapon would give his anger something to focus on, but its
weight was already making his belt dig painfully into his
hip. He couldn't remember who had left the hammer at the
lodge, but he hoped it would bring him more luck than its
previous owner.

"Wait up," Hilt called from the front. "Professor, take a
look at this."

The two men stood on the bottom step and took in their
surroundings. It was surprisingly warm down below, and
there was a dry smell, devoid of any human odour, animal
droppings or dampness. It felt incredibly still, and Hilt had
to stop himself thinking of the calm before the storm. Laurel had to flatten herself against the wall to allow Rickenbacker past in the thin stairwell.

"Trap?" Hilt asked.

The steps continued down on the other side of a rect-
angular room, and Hilt would not have paused for thought
except for the fact that the lantern had made out huge metal
spikes jutting out from the walls on either side of them.

"Indubitably," the Professor replied.

Hilt waited for the Professor to continue speaking but the old man was squinting into the darkness where the walls met the ceilings and floors.

"What's going on?" Pinkerton called from behind them.

"They think it's a trap," Laurel told the big man.

"Oh. Can we find a way around it?"

Nobody bothered to reply.

"I can't see any seams that would allow the walls to close in," Rickenbacker said. "Or any sort of trigger mechanism."

"You think they have enormous killer spikes down here for decoration?" Laurel asked.

"Perhaps they are warning."

"Warning for what? More spikes?" Laurel said.

Rickenbacker rubbed his chin in annoyance and glanced over at Hilt, who seemed deaf to Laurel.

"We could send the dog across," Hilt suggested.

"Or I could throw you across," Pinkerton replied in kind.

"I suppose we could hold up here until we think the Trade have left," Laurel suggested.

"You think they won't block the door at the very least?" Hilt said.

"Oh."

"Hold this," said Hilt, passing the lantern to Laurel.

He took a rope from around his shoulder and tied it around his waist. He looked around the steps, the ceiling and walls for something to secure the other end to, his eyes finally falling on Pinkerton, who shrugged and wrapped the rope several times around himself.

"Everybody get behind Pinkerton. Brennan, you and the boy hold onto the big man around his waist. There's no point in securing myself to the big lug if he just gets dragged into… whatever happens."

Hilt stretched the muscles in his legs and arms and prepared himself. Then Teddy pointed over his shoulder, his eyes wide.

"Look!"

They all turned and saw Alexander the wolfhound scampering across the chamber and through the doorway on the other side.

"Alexander!" Brennan called, and the dog trotted back, tail wagging.

"Perhaps we're over-reacting?" Laurel suggested.

"Perhaps we are," Hilt nodded, and he took a step onto the ground of the chamber, testing his weight. He tentatively lifted his other foot from the step and his foot broke through the layer of dust and kept going down, as a thin layer of mud crumbled beneath him.

"Pinkerton!" he called as he tumbled downwards.

"Hold me!" Pinkerton cried as the rope started to tighten.

Teddy and Brennan threw themselves towards Pinkerton's chest to stop the man following Hilt through the floor, and the three of them hit the steps with a thud. Laurel grabbed the rope coming from the pugilist's waist, and immediately realised how they had overcompensated. She pulled quickly at the rope until the severed end was in her hand.

"Oh dear," she said, holding it up in the light of Rickenbacker's lantern.

"Hilt!" Brennan gasped, crawling on his belly to look over the edge of the final step into the dark that had claimed his friend.

Hilt looked up from five foot down, his hand clasping a spike, the rest of his body dangling below him into a deep pit, spikes all around him.

"My sword cut the rope when I fell," he groaned through gritted teeth. "Get me up."

Pinkerton grabbed Brennan's thighs and lowered the man down. As the blood rushed to his head, Brennan reached out for Hilt.

"Give me your hand," he said.

"What hand?"

Brennan looked from the hand gripping the spike to the hand melded to the sword.

"We need another plan," Brennan huffed as Pinkerton pulled him back up.

They looped what was left of the rope under Hilt's armpits and dragged him back up. He lay on the steps wheezing.

"What now?" said Laurel, looking down at the Hilt-sized hole in the floor.

Rickenbacker took the rope, attached it to the loop on the top of his lantern and lowered the light into the hole. He stared into the gloom.

"It's just a pit spanning the width, not the length of the room. We can jump it," he said, pulling the lantern up first.

"Great. You first," muttered Hilt.

And the old man leapt forward, his arms outstretched in front of him, landing on his chest and scrambling forward. Alexander jumped the hole effortlessly and licked the Professor's face excitedly. Everyone looked at each other with surprise, and then at Hilt, who shrugged. Rickenbacker pulled himself to his feet, dusted himself down and turned to face the others.

"So..." and then he shuffled backwards and the floor collapsed behind him. He threw himself forward to cling to the edge of the previous pit as Alexander yelped and leapt through the doorway. Pinkerton, and to everybody's surprise including his own Teddy, leapt the first pit and, taking an arm each, pulled the Professor to safety.

"Thank you, gentlemen. Not all of us are as spry as Alexander, it would appear."

Pinkerton used the butt of his blat gun to check the remaining floor, and found one more pit. He blew a hole into the covering floor and the sound echoed all the way to the spikes at the bottom. And then they were through the doorway at the other side, where Pinkerton paused and looked back.

"Could it really be that nobody has even come this far?" he asked, looking at the booby-trapped room.

"I have never heard of anyone using the Gargoyle Key before, Mr Pinkerton," Rickenbacker said.

They both watched in shock as the surface level that covered the pits reappeared.

"Oh my," Pinkerton whispered.

"Not that that means anything, apparently," Rickenbacker hastily continued, shaking his head.

"I mean, I don't know as well as you do, Professor, but that seems like a rather feeble show of magic from people capable of building something like the Cathedral of Tales," Pinkerton said, shaking his head.

"Perhaps they didn't build it. But whoever did, they certainly knew how to use the minimum wonder for the maximum effect."

Rickenbacker turned and continued down the steps. Pinkerton fired his blat gun at the nearest pit, blowing a revealing hole in the surface.

"Pinkerton! You alright?" Hilt called.

"Yeah. Everything's fine," the pugilist replied, taking one last look around the room before following the others.

"Everything's fine," Teddy repeated as he moved down the steps.

"What's that, son?" Brennan asked from behind him.

"Nothing."

"Tell me."

"Honestly, Mr Brennan, nothing."

Teddy was suddenly aware of how much Brennan had lost in just the last few hours. He felt slight, unimportant, unnecessary, like smoke that could blow away in the slightest breeze.

"Are you scared, Teddy?"

"Yes, Mr Brennan."

"You can call me Alfred, if it'll help."

"I don't understand them, Alfred. The others. They seem to be enjoying all this. Pinkerton just lost his best friend, but everything's fine," he said, quoting the big man again. "Hilt almost died but he comes back from it all like he just stepped in from the rain."

"All these people have seen death before."

"Does that make it less important?"

Brennan stopped and looked at Teddy, who was quaking. He put his hands on the boy's arms.

"Nothing is more important than life itself. Right now everything inside me is broken, torn to pieces. It feels like every sense, every feeling I ever had was sucked out when

Alf was..," he paused, "...when Alf... my son is dead, and I need to stay alive to end the people that caused that death. Until then, all I know is that I am so relieved Alf lived, that my life was so good for sixteen years, that he was happy, that he existed at all..."

Tears started to roll down Brennan's grubby face again, this time leaving rivulets in the dust. He didn't know what he was saying or what he thought, but that seemed to be the point. He'd never known if what he said to Alf made any sense, if it was the right thing to say, but his son had grown and people had told him his son was a good man.

"I'm sorry, Mr Brennan."

"Everybody is. Especially people like Hilt and Pinkerton. They're sorry every minute of every day. They keep talking, they keep walking, but they know all they do is dance with death. They think they spit into the pit of despair but they know, more than most, that every word they utter, every smile they make, every laugh, every show of affection, one day it all will be forgotten, gone, not even missed, like leaves on a windy day. That's why they talk like that. They think life is not even worth forgetting."

He felt his rage balloon in his chest, but he knew that a lack of control, that his anger was the worst thing this poor lost boy needed to see.

"I'm too scared to stay alive," Teddy said.

"And right now, I'm too wounded to keep going, so we need to look after each other. I need you to stay alive, son," Brennan said, taking Teddy's head in his hands. "I need you alive. I need something good. Something right."

Laurel watched the two men embrace and went back down the steps to tell the others that Brennan and Teddy were fine, but they should leave them alone for a minute, wait for them to catch up.

The sun broke above the tree line as Spicer led the Reclaimers out of the lodge, weariness seeping through to his bones. There was no morning song, the only sounds the crackle of the fire at the front of the lodge and the jangle of military kit as the platoon milled about. He kicked at the gravel at his feet.

"Spicer?"

Bunce watched as Elena approached the lieutenant.

"So are we moving on?" Elena asked him.

"I don't fancy trying my hand with that thing downstairs," Conway stated.

"Quine's not going to let us get our hands on anything anyway. We'll never see a penny of that reward. But Tork. We can't just..."

"Let them get away with it?"

Spicer felt a terrible loss deep down in the pit of his stomach, but he wasn't entirely sure that it was connected to Tork's death. He had lost other men in his command, men he valued more, men that weren't out and out murderers like Tork, so he was surprised. He still had a terrible sense of foreboding, of darkness crushing down on him, of doom. Something was wrong with this place. Not just the disfigured woods or the random lodge. When he looked up at the snowdrop spire of the Cathedral above the trees he felt actual heartbreak. For the first time, Spicer realised he had no real control over himself.

Spicer had been scarred as long as he could remember, as long as anyone could remember. He had never felt a real love from anyone but his family, and had put it down to his appearance. He had felt the pain of rejection, the emptiness of a life without love, the bitterness of scorn as children howled with terror at his appearance. And so he had shut down his feelings. They did not matter. He suppressed his inner life. He surrounded himself with bitterness and terror, immersed himself in war. He found respect in command on the battlefield. He met others who had been scarred, who had lost limbs, eyes, ears, loved ones. And then, when he realised even the army, even his commanding officers had problems looking at him, dealing with him, he went freelance, became a Reclaimer. He did the dirty work of the Empire. If he had no chance, why should anybody else?

But ever since he had started on the quest for the Gargoyle Key, he felt like something had been stripped from him, the hardness that he had kindled around his heart had been burnt off, just like the skin of his face. And although his senses told him he was somewhere heart breaking, somewhere that screamed pain, he felt like he had something to do there. Some purpose.

"Let's rest a while, use some military canvas to get some shut-eye and then take advantage of Quine's offer of transport," he said, looking for the platoon quartermaster.

Bunce saw Elena flinch at Spicer's words.

"Are you alright?" she asked the older woman.

"I just…" she shook her head. "That Hilt man, he's dangerous. He's a killer, I mean, that's all he is. And I used him. I made him angry."

She had never seen a chink in Elena's armour. She put a reassuring hand on her arm.

"He might be dead already. Nobody has ever returned from the Cathedral of Tales."

"But we don't even know if that door leads to the Cathedral. He could be right under out feet. He could find his way out of the ground and..."

"I won't let him hurt you," Bunce said.

"I'm not sure you could stop Hilt, Bunce."

Elena shrugged and walked after Spicer, leaving the sniper with Conway.

"I cannot tell you how tired I am," Conway groaned behind her.

"Fuck off, dabbler," Bunce said, following the others.

Axelrod examined Sir Evan's wounds through a magnifying glass, and consulted a thick tome. He opened his large leather case, much like a doctor's bag, and examined some of the phials therein, shaking them carefully, occasionally using the eye glass to double-check the contents. He found three containers of different substances, and laid them carefully next to the corpse. Then he removed a scalpel and a hacksaw and put them on his makeshift operating table. It was time to show everybody that this Rickenbacker buffoon was not the only one who knew how to manipulate the Wonder. It was time to go to work. It was time for some powerful, dark Wonder that would leave a mark. They needed to remind people that the Trade was their superior. And that he, Penfold G. Axelrod, was a hyperphysicist to fear.

Kendrick pulled once more at the handcuffs securing him to the spokes of the wagon and groaned.

"Is there anyone I can speak to about breakfast?" he asked a passing soldier. "Perhaps a cup of tea? I mean, I'm not used to this sort of treatment."

Truth be told, he was very used to this sort of treatment, and he was already feeling nostalgic about a time when he had avoided it, when he could sit down to one of Laurel's breakfasts. But he consigned himself to the fact that he had made his choice for better or worse, and, although he missed scrambled eggs, he was sure this would pay off. He would return to Chinsey a hero of sorts, a man who knew right from wrong, who knew which side to be on.

Then he heard a howl of terror, sadness and anger. A scream that expressed every pain a soul could feel, chilling Kendrick to the bone. The whole platoon paused in what its duties and looked at each other for reassurance. This was a sound from the gates of Hell. It was the first time that day that Kendrick thought that perhaps he hadn't chosen the right side after all.

Only two people who heard the noise understood the real terror. Because when Elena and Kendrick heard it, they both recognised the voice of Sir Evan Mandell. They both knew they were hearing the scream of a dead man.

They walked for about two hours, always heading down. Their calves were burning and their conversation had dried up. And then they reached the bottom of the steps and felt a breeze of sorts.

The one lantern they were using, dimmed to conserve energy, couldn't pick out the walls, ceiling, or any other structures. It was as if the steps had taken them absolutely nowhere. They had climbed down into the night sky. Pinkerton bent down and scooped up something from the floor.

"Gravel?"

"What's that?" Rickenbacker said, lowering himself to the floor to sit down.

He picked up the same bits and pieces from the floor.

"It must have had the same landscape gardener as the lodge," Laurel said.

Her words were swallowed up by the darkness.

"How closely did you examine the... gravel, as you call it?" Rickenbacker asked.

Laurel picked some of the gravel up and let it slip back through her fingers to the floor.

"Well, I didn't. Examining little bits and pieces of rock..."

"These are not rock, Miss Gleave," Rickenbacker explained. "These are chips of bone."

"Bone?"

She shook the last of the gravel from her hands as Pinkerton examined what was in the palm of his hand more closely, and Teddy started to edge back towards the steps.

"Are you sure?" asked Brennan.

"Very old, but definitely. Here's a part of an ankle, a calcaneus. And this is a metacarpal from a hand."

"Hand?" said Laurel. "So they're definitely from a human?"

"Humanoid, at least," Rickenbacker said, holding out his hand so Teddy could help him up.

"What does that mean, humanoid?" Hilt said, kicking at the ground, scattering bone into the gloom.

Rickenbacker chose to ignore Hilt and squinted into the darkness.

"So? Which way now?" Pinkerton asked, rubbing his eyes.

"Hold your lantern by the doorway we entered by please, Mr Brennan. There may be a clue or map or some such."

"Wouldn't that be thoughtful?" Hilt scoffed as the Professor ran his hands around the edge of the doorway.

"Give the man a break," Pinkerton hissed at Hilt.

"You're right, Mr Pinkerton. His incredible leadership skills have so far left two of us dead and his sense of direction has led us into a pit of despair miles from anywhere. We'd have more luck..."

"Laurel, would you be so kind as to pass me the Gargoyle Key please?" asked the Professor quietly, ignoring the two warriors squaring up behind him.

"The what? Oh," she said dumbly, "Of course."

Laurel reached into her bag and passed the dark orb to the Professor.

"Thank you. Now I'm not sure this will do anything..."

And then the darkness lifted. Light flooded the chamber, the sort of light at dusk just before a storm. There was no discernible source, although Teddy thought he had heard the sound of an exhalation, like a long sigh of relief, as the dark disappeared.

"Blimey. Does this sort of thing happen often in these sorts of places?" Laurel said, taking in their surroundings.

"I have no idea," Brennan said, his eyes wide.

"Still think we're miles from anywhere?" Pinkerton asked Hilt.

Crystalline roots from the Glasslands latticed the ceiling above them. Directly in front of them were two trenches, resembling roads or the runs of slideways, full to the brim with bony gravel. The trenches disappeared into two tunnels, both blocked by enormous tumbledown masonry. On the other side of the trenches, another platform the same as the one on which they were standing, with two ascending ramps. Lining the wall on both side of the trenches were mosaics, glistening with what appeared to be precious stones, depicting dancers on a stage, a couple laughing together in a park, a pristine beach by clear seas, all scenes of life from a dead civilisation, subtitled in a language nobody recognised.

"What is this? Some underground art gallery?" Hilt asked, frowning.

As they moved closer to examine the mosaics, they could see shimmering movements, as though they were spying at scenes through a fence or blinds. Laurel stepped forward to touch one of the nearest mosaics, a woman feeding a dog, and heard the bark of the dark echo in her head, before the unknown language gave her unknowable instructions.

"This is incredible," she gasped.

"It's like the theatre, tiny plays and scenes..." Pinkerton whispered, shaking his head in disbelief.

"They are announcements. Living circulars advertising lost treasure from the past," Rickenbacker said, reaching to touch the seaside playing out in front of him.

"I hope we find some better treasure than dog food," Pinkerton said as Alexander leapt up to examine the dog scene.

"And this is all coming from the Gargoyle Key?" Hilt asked.

"The key just provides the power, I think. This is part of something else."

"Something beautiful," said Laurel, moving to the next mosaic depicting a flowing silk dress.

"You forget our friends underfoot," Hilt remarked, kicking gravel towards the trenches.

"What is this place?" Brennan asked, scratching his head.

"I suspect some sort of way station," Rickenbacker answered, regarding the tunnels.

"Like the slideways," said Teddy.

"Exactly, my boy. This was all once a city before the Glasslands. I suspect the citizens did not want the chill of the slideways slicing through their streets and gardens."

"Bringing down the house prices," Brennan added.

"Okay, before we start picking out the furniture, can we all please remember we are just passing through?" said Hilt, one hand on the butt of his Twirler.

"I doubt the ice yachts stop here anymore anyway," remarked Pinkerton, checking the blocked tunnels. "Wherever here is."

"It still feels like a dungeon to me. Or a tomb," growled Hilt.

"I think I know where we are," said Teddy, pointing at a sign.

"It looks like my door knocker," Laurel commented.

"The Cathedral of Tales," said Pinkerton.

"I do know that," Laurel clarified.

Despite the morning sun and refraction of light through the translucent leaves on the trees, everybody in the Trade encampment outside the Gleave lodge noticed the pale blue light emanating from the end of the bent spire of the Cathedral. Although nobody had actually seen the illumination of the snowdrop begin, there was no denying it was there.

The Reclaimers had just finished loading their ponies for their journey out of the woods.

"I get the feeling your friends have hit pay dirt," Conway said to Elena.

"There really is no stopping him, is there?" Spicer said.

"Why are you smiling?" Elena asked the lieutenant.

The Reclaimers turned, and were all surprised to see the leader with his hands on his hips and a slight grin on his face.

"Don't you think it's beautiful?" Spicer asked.

Bunce and Conway exchanged puzzled glances as they regarded Spicer, who for all the world looked like a man taking in the first ray of sun after a stormy winter's night.

"If you say so, boss," Conway shrugged.

"Are you okay?" Elena asked.

"I'm fine. Best I've felt in weeks. And I think I know our next destination," he said, shaking his head as though waking from a pleasant daydream.

"Yeah, you and a whole trade platoon," Conway smirked.

"I thought we were giving up…" Elena said.

Bunce wanted to reassure Elena but now wasn't the time so she decided to speak up.

"I thought you said Quine wouldn't…"

"Fuck Quine. Let's see how these ponies he provided race," Bunce said, mounting up.

"Part of me hopes they are not that fast," Conway mumbled to Bunce, before he climbed into his own saddle.

Rickenbacker had removed the Gargoyle Key and returned it to Laurel. He was relieved to find that the power stayed on. After they crossed the trenches and, despite Hilt's protestations, paused to admire more mosaics, they ascended the ramps, Alexander leading the way, his paws sliding on the shiny surface as the gravel thinned out. The ramps took them through some broken barriers to a level lined with empty serving counters and other, darkened, inactive mosaics.

"Do many tombs have ticket halls in your experience, Mr Hilt?" Pinkerton asked.

"I'd pay to see yours," Hilt mumbled back, as they left the area up some broad shallow steps, entering a huge chamber obviously built for more than just six lost travellers and their wolfhound. Teddy found the emptiness oppressive.

Enormous tendrils of crystal roots hung from the domed ceiling high above like icy stalactites. Clear pillars were reflected in the dark reflective floor, glowing with a pulsing blue light. It was impossible to see where the floor met the walls as they were all the same black pitch. Teddy shivered as he thought of the dark tunnel of Gargoyles. In the opposite side of the expansive chamber, enormous double doors stood ajar, charred and splintered from being forced open.

"This doesn't smell right," Hilt hissed, pulling his Twirler, Rickenbacker put his hand on Hilt's wrist.

"Don't spin it," he warned.

As Alexander started to whine, Pinkerton pulled the blat gun from his back.

"It's all so clean and shiny," Laurel said.

"I wonder who cleans the place," said Brennan, immediately embarrassed by his own flippancy.

And then it spoke to them. Like the shadow seared into a retina by a flashing light or a scene captured through a dirty window from a speeding carriage, the chamber shared something with them.

Crowds of people bustled around them, some hurrying past on their way to somewhere important, some dawdling as they took in the expanse. Children, parents, businesswomen, lovers, workers, tourists, friends and loners went about their day, wearing clothing too foreign to have ever been fashionable, Laurel thought, but with universal glances and cares and insecurities. Some seemed taller than normal, with pointed features and odd shaped ears, others shorter and broader, with long braded beards. A few of the children also wore beards, Teddy noticed, while Pinkerton realised that there was a distinct lack of weaponry. The smell of commuters under cover of soap, the stench of a city thoroughfare wafted over them all, with a strong essence of Wonder. The temperature rose a few degrees with the crush of the crowd.

And in the blink of an eye, the mirage left them. Once again they were alone, contemplating the emptiness. They all turned to one another in shock, Laurel with a smile on her face, intoxicated by city life. Teddy looked flushed.

"Did you just…"

They turned to the Professor.

"I have absolutely no idea what just happened," he informed them, shaking his head.

"We should get out of this place," said Hilt.

"It's like it wants to show us something," said Laurel.

"It just did," Brennan said.

And then the screaming started, the sound of panic, the stench of fear, and a new scene appeared around them.

The Glasslands shook with the thunder of hundreds of feet, the rattle and clink of glass and crystal growing to a cacophony.

"What's happening?" called Elena over the noise, pulling her Twirler.

Conway pointed ahead and reached in terror for his bag of Wonder. Bunce saw what was panicking her fellow Reclaimer, and did what came naturally. She reached up, her gloved hand grabbing a branch, and pulled herself into the nearest tree.

"Get above them!" she called as the ponies started to panic.

Bunce reached out a hand for Elena, who grasped it and clambered into the tree, tearing her clothes on the sharp corners.

"Boss?"

Conway brought his pony alongside Spicer's and caught sight of the lieutenant's face. His eyes were wide, his mouth open in surprise as he experienced something Conway could not see; the living city of Pearly existing in the corner of his eye, and Spicer felt something he had never experienced. Home.

And then the stampede of fleeing Humps was upon them, slamming against their ponies. All the Humps ran headlong through the trees, stricken with horror, howling, stumbling into and over each other. Their eyes were wild, looking back over their shoulders and flickering from side to side as they escaped exactly what Spicer felt embrace him.

Conway reached over and grabbed the reins of Spicer's pony to stop it bolting.

"Lieutenant! Spicer! Lieutenant!" he screamed over the throng.

Spicer only snapped out of his trance as the guns of the Trade platoon opened up at the advancing humps.

"Wait," mumbled Spicer, before raising his voice, "They're not charging! They're running from something!" he called.

"No, don't," Conway said as Spicer snatched away his reins.

"Spicer!" called Elena, and Spicer paused, his pony waiting for the instruction to move. "Don't! Quine will cut you down too," she continued.

Spicer looked at the Humps around him as they continued around them in the direction of the platoon's guns.

"Stand your ground!" he heard Quine scream, before the crack of rifle fire.

"What's going on?" Bunce called down.

"The Cathedral is doing something. It must be," Conway called up. "Right?" he checked with Spicer.

But Spicer's unnerving one hundred yard stare was back, as the Humps' numbers began to thin.

Kendrick cowered inside the wagon where the Trade had secured him, peering beneath the canvas cover. He could hear Twirlers and blat guns firing from the front of the wagon, and the screams of Humps, whom, to his eyes, seemed to be charging but not stopping. With his limited point of view, he could make out the Trade platoon cutting them down with ease as the Humps neglected to defend themselves in their rush to flee.

A warrior stepped directly in front of Kendrick's spy hole, not wearing the Trade uniform, and hacked and cut down the Humps with such ferocity that a pile of corpses started to grow at his feet. He showed no sign of slowing as he spun and stabbed and swiped with sword and dagger, elbow and knee deep in Hump blood. As the warrior moved, Kendrick could also see blood around his collar and hair, and first thought that the man had been wounded. But this blood was darker and drier than the hump blood, from an older cut. As he stared at the blood in the hair, he saw a gash across the entire top of the head, and, as the man moved, Kendrick realised the gash didn't stop. It went all the way round the circumference of the man's skull.

And then the warrior turned and Kendrick looked into the insentient eyes of Sir Evan Mandell.

Spectres filled the chamber, reminiscent of the previous scene, but these people were no longer going about their day-to-day business. They scattered in every direction, with no clear aim but to escape, to leave the enormous space. Husbands gripped to wives, who clung to sons and daughters. Bosses cast their secretaries aside to be trampled underfoot. Best friends kept each other going. Bullies and cowards scrambled for any way out.

From the broken doorway at the opposite end of the chamber came three monstrosities, the size of shire horses rearing up on their hind legs. They were formed of stone and metal; welded, screwed and slotted together into an arched aggressive form that resembled the praying mantis. Each mandible was replaced with three long cogs, tubes with teeth that ground together as they spun. From what would be the mantis' head protruded two huge domes like the eyes of an enormous fly, firing metal projectiles, spinning four-pronged nails. The serrated nails tore into their victims, and, when they fell, the spinning mandibles would swoop down and mash them into a bloody stew.

The murderous contraptions moved on one round ball, stabilised by a tail that was both a twin sided battle-axe and a propellant of liquid fire.

Seconds after they entered the chamber, fifty people lay dead. One of the things held back from the others, not using its weapons. It appeared much older than the other two, moving slower as though its aged joints were aching, its metal a touch rusty, its stone touched by moss.

"Don't look," Rickenbacker warned, attempting to shield Laurel and Teddy from the sight of the massacre. As Pinkerton stared in horror, Alexander slipped from his grasp and shot through the ghost of the crowd, crossing the chamber in no time. Growling, he swerved around the first two things and started barking and growling at the third. Pinkerton started after the hound, trying to keep the dog in view through the doomed inhabitants.

The thing tilted its head down as if to stare at the dog with its bug eyes. Pinkerton saw the first salvo of nails strike the hound across the back.

"What…?" he started and then the scene and hundreds of dead, dying and doomed and the two leading contraptions vanished. Pinkerton watched as Alexander howled in pain, his paws sliding on the shiny floor before the thing struck at the dog with its stone grinders, filling the air with sparks. Alexander's legs kept moving and the dog shot between the grinders. Liquid fire spurted towards him as he slithered through the doors to safety.

For what felt like long minutes, everyone in the now almost-empty chamber froze, staring at the thing that seconds ago had been just another part of the nightmarish mirage.

Hilt was the first to break the trance.

"Run!" he shouted, grabbing Pinkerton by the arm. "Back to the ticket office!"

They all turned, slipping, sliding and skidding on the polished floor, the sound of the grinders behind them, and galloped headlong for the ramps, Hilt pushing Pinkerton in front of him.

"It killed the dog! It killed the fucking dog!" Pinkerton screamed.

"It's killed more than just a dog, now move," Hilt reasoned, shouting over the grinding noise.

Brennan and Teddy took an arm each and practically carried Rickenbacker down the ramp as Laurel reached the bottom and leapt over one of the ticket counters to take cover behind it.

"Keep moving," Hilt growled at Pinkerton, pulling his Twirler.

He turned around, spinning the gun, and was shocked to see how much ground the thing had covered. He let off two shots and heard them both ricochet off the stone mandibles as it continued to approach. He overtook Pinkerton as he ran down the ramp, and he leapt over another ticket counter opposite where Laurel was cowering.

In the dark of the counter, now he was close up, Hilt could make out soot where the liquid fire had been pumped by the thing that had just reached the top of the ramp, grooves and gouges scored the stone counter where the grinders had pummelled whoever had previously hidden there, leaving the bone gravel mingled with four-pronged nails.

Pinkerton rolled over the counter and dropped to the floor beside Hilt. The two men looked at each other, and Hilt pointed at the big man's blat gun then indicated the eyes. Pinkerton nodded and cranked his gun.

On the other side of the ticket hall, behind a similarly battle damaged counter, Rickenbacker emptied his bag of tricks onto the floor between his legs and went through it quickly.

"What is that thing?" Laurel asked, her back against the counter.

"Death itself," Brennan replied, putting his arm around Teddy who was covering his ears. "Got anything, Professor?"

"Not that I... wait a minute. The key. Laurel, give me the key!"

Laurel scrambled in her bag as the machine rolled to the bottom of the ramp.

"Now!" they heard above the rumble of the grinders.

Pinkerton stood up, his eye already sighting down the blat gun's barrel and fired once. He dropped as nails pinged against the wall behind him and ricocheted behind the counter. Hilt and Pinkerton clung to each other as the darts thudded around them, tearing into their faces and clothes.

"Machine!" Rickenbacker called, waving the Gargoyle Key above the counter. "We have the key!"

There was a hiss and fire squirted from the thing's tail, sticking to the wall and the counter. Brennan moved to extinguish it but Rickenbacker held him back.

"Don't touch it!"

The four of them moved to one end of the counter to avoid the scalding heat as the thing moved away from them towards the opposite counter and the two warriors. It continued to fire nails, one eye still functioning perfectly, the other damaged but still able to deliver a payload, while keeping its tail trained on the Rickenbacker and the others.

"Give me a mirror," Brennan said to Laurel.

"What?"

"A mirror. I know you always carry a..."

"Okay! Okay!" she replied, finding a small mirror in the top of her bag.

Brennan snatched it and used it to look over the counter without putting his head above cover. He saw more nails raining down on the other counter, and then the blat gun appeared over the top and fired blind. The shot struck the grinders, forcing the machine back a couple of feet but not breaking through the stone. It continued towards them.

"Bullets have no effect," he said to nobody in particular.

"What do we do?" Laurel said, holding on to Teddy.

Brennan looked at the woman who had believed in him enough to keep him alive and checked the young boy who had nobody but a crazy old troublemaker as a guardian. He thought of his dead son, and knew this could not be the end for any of them.

"Give me your coats," he told them.

Rickenbacker immediately removed his great coat and Brennan poured water from his canteen onto it.

"Take them off," he repeated, "then empty your canteens."

They all did as they were told.

Hilt felt his teeth shudder in his gums as the sound of the grinders grew louder. Pinkerton fired the blat again over the counter. They could hardly hear the gunfire of the enormous blunderbuss. Pinkerton brought the gun back under cover, and Hilt saw that the man's arm was cut to shreds by the nails, but Pinkerton didn't stop. He pumped the gun, and was about to raise it again when sparks started to snow into the area behind the counter, as the grinders thundered across the stone counter top.

Brennan climbed across the top of the opposite counter on his back, wearing the three sodden coats back to front, the collars up so that most of his face was covered. One coat was wrapped round his waist to cover his legs, and he used only one sleeve. The one hand on show was wrapped in a torn shirt, and gripped his hammer with such force his fingers were purple while his knuckles were white.

He dropped to the floor four yards from the thing and stumbled towards it. It vibrated as its grinders skittered across the counter towards Hilt and Pinkerton. He was still a yard away when he heard the hiss of the tail, which he immediately recognised as precursor to the squirt of the liquid fire. He wondered how long it would take the fluid to burn through the coats. Then he saw the flash of Pinkerton's blat gun, firing over the extended grinders, blasting the thing directly in its bug eyes and chest. It was thrown back towards Brennan, and he saw his chance. He slammed down with the hammer, catching the end of the tube and flattening it against the floor. He saw the tube immediately glow bright red, and he threw himself backwards to cower beneath his soggy shield of clothing.

The grinders stopped, and there was silence for a beat. Then the thing burped politely and juddered as though rattled by an invisible hand. Smoke poured from its damaged bug eyes and joints. Through the ringing in his ears he heard Hilt calling something.

"Take cover..."

Brennan shook the three coats from his arms and ran as fast as he could back towards the counter, his legs slapping against the final coat sliding down his thighs. Rickenbacker, Laurel and Teddy grabbed him by the arms and heaved him over the top so they all landed in a heap behind the counter.

They huddled together, waiting for the machine to explode in a torrent of liquid fire.

There was a thud as one of the grinders fell to the ground, and a bubbling as the burning fluid belched from the thing's neck.

They all jumped when Pinkerton fired his blat gun over the counter again, but still the beast refused to attack or collapse. The big man pumped the gun, stood up slowly, with the barrel pointing at the machine, and contemplated the tangled pile of stone, metal and fire before him.

"Yeah. It's definitely dead," he told the others. "I think".

CHAPTER 8

The Glasslands/The City of Pearly
The Gramarye Region
Grand Quillia

June 1856

I t was breathtakingly beautiful, like stars aglow on Earth.

Spicer didn't notice the final Humps pass, the old and infirm, the children and the crippled, stumbling over the ground to follow their countrymen into the barrage of the Trade's guns.

He saw spires reaching into the sky, illuminated from the inside so brightly that it looked as though they had been built around towers of light. The architects and builders of Pearly were not slaves to gravity or other rules of nature. They used hyperphysics to let their skills and imagination run free. Structures arched over and tangled in on themselves forming great stone knots. Roofs appeared to float above their moorings, and walls bowed out like pregnant tummies, or curved inwards like the middle of an hourglass.

186

Emulating the nearby snowdrop of the Cathedral of Tales, some edifices resembled other flowers; geraniums, tulips and orchids. Others seemed to melt into the ground, while others disappeared into the clouds.

In the centre of the city stood a giant glowing stone spider with pulsating strands strung from its head to crisscross the area like silk circuitry. Every street was lit, and many walls illustrated with giant moving mosaics, publicising the beauty, wealth and success of the incredible city. On the other side of the conurbation, Spicer could make out the masts of ships bobbing in an enormous harbour, watched over by an colossal pitch black ebony dog, the eyes of which scoured the waves of an ocean Spicer knew no longer reached this far inland.

Horses, ponies, elephants, camels and other beasts of burden Spicer didn't recognise transported people of all colours and sizes to all corners of the city, and on some roads Spicer caught flashes of speeding carriages that were not being pulled by any animal, man or beast. But the most stunning of all the visions he saw were above him. Even the sky bustled, with flying carpets, windsurfing galleons, winged coaches and other flying creatures, not all with feathers.

Everything was as it should be, the best it could be, all that Spicer had dreamt of. He was suddenly aware he always dreamed of this place, every night countless times, before waking to the nightmare of his ugly battlefield reality.

He felt a tear roll down his cheek, and didn't know if it was from the beauty he could see around him or the sense of loss he knew this illusion would lead to when he woke up.

But this time he didn't open his eyes to find himself in a military crib or curled round a campfire with a boulder for a pillow. It was worse. He saw the world around him change. He saw this city of boundless opportunity die and he was helpless to stop it.

He saw flashes of the last throes of a great civilisation, the dying gasps. He saw riots on its streets, he saw mobs cutting down individuals, sacking shops and burning homes. He saw whole areas ablaze, the flames spreading. He saw the hound at the harbour falling under a rain of cannon fire from an approaching fleet, towers and spires collapsing. He saw the spider's legs explode, the body fall to the ground, and the spider's web of energy flicker into darkness. He saw stone beasts the size of shire horses cutting down men, women and children.

Another jump forward in history now, and he saw the buildings reduced to skeletal foundations, split apart by saplings, trees and weeds, mottled by moss and clasped in the shadows of ivy. Finally even the foundations were buried beneath the great canopy of oak and chestnut and maple trees.

And suddenly the verdant woods were no longer as nature had made them. Spicer didn't know if his vision jumped one hundred years, a decade or just one second, but the green expanse became the colourless angles of the Glasslands, in all their crystal glory.

And all that Spicer could think was, "Where have all my people gone?"

Alexander had returned to them seconds after the demise of the thing, jumping up to lick Brennan's face and barking at Pinkerton, keen to entice him into a game of chase.

They stood in a circle around the remains, feeling the warmth of the liquid fire through the stone and metal, while Laurel bandaged Pinkerton's arm.

"I can't smell any Wonder," Rickenbacker was saying.

Hilt prodded at it with his blade.

"You think it's some kind of…" he searched for the word, "mechanism?"

"I'm not completely certain it's mechanical, I'm just saying…"

"I understand. Whoever destroyed the people of Pearly were wizards of mechnology," Hilt said.

"The ancient texts say Pearly was built by highly advanced hyperphysicists and so the best weapon against them would be something that didn't use the Wonder," Rickenbacker said.

"And this one was left over?" asked Brennan.

"This is the mystery. The Cathedral of Tales and this underworld were sealed off, only to be accessed using the Gargoyle Key, which is a creation of the Wonder. Why allow access to people with a knowledge of hyperphysics only to attack them with something unaffected by the Wonder?"

They regarded the mechanism in silence for a moment.

"This one looks ancient," said Brennan.

"Indeed," Rickenbacker commented, "I do not believe we would have been triumphant against one of these grinders at full speed."

"Imagine an army of the fuckers," said Pinkerton, rubbing his arm.

"We don't need to imagine it," Laurel reminded them, "We saw it."

"How did we see that, Professor?" Pinkerton asked.

"I think the question should be why. Was it a warning?"

"Or was it camouflage so the thing could sneak up and grind us like pepper?" suggested Hilt.

"This place is one big trap," Teddy mumbled.

"I think I prefer it when laughing boy isn't speaking," Hilt commented.

The platoon moved through the Glasslands on foot as they finished off any remaining Humps. Quine looked down at the bodies around him.

"Disgusting things. How did your corpse do?" he asked Axelrod.

"Better than the Immolators," the doctor said with pride.

They looked over at Sir Evan Mandell, who was sorting through a pile of dead Humps, looking for something or someone specific.

"I like what you've done with him," Quine nodded.

The warrior looked sturdier than when he had been living, pumped up a little, except for his face, haggard with sunken eyes and lips drawn back, caked in a mask of his own blood.

"I have to admit, I do enjoy a re-animation, Colonel. They keep some of their basic personality traits, but they are so indebted to their re-animator for keeping them going that firm control is simple."

He glanced over at the former blue-eyed blue blood.

"Come over here, Mandell."

Mandell moved sure-footedly towards them.

"Did you enjoy dispatching the Humps?" Quine asked.

"It made me feel alive," Mandell said, his words monotone, the consonants flat due to his swollen tongue.

"Very good," said Quine, smiling at Axelrod.

"You are dismissed," Axelrod said, watching with pride as his corpse returned to searching through the pile of dead bodies.

"What do you suppose the Humps were running from?" Axelrod asked.

"Who cares?" Quine shrugged, taking a flask from inside his coat.

The two men looked up at the snowdrop of the Cathedral high above them. As they stood there, they grew aware of a grunting just discernible over the noise of scattered gunfire coming from close by. The two men turned, and neither liked what they saw.

"No, Mandell," ordered Axelrod, as though chastising a dog.

Mandell ignored the doctor and continued to sodomise the dead Hump he had chosen.

"It makes me feel alive," he repeated to himself.

Looking back, Elena was surprised how far ahead of the platoon they had come. They were approaching the bottom of the snowdrop spire, where primitive shelters stood vacant next to burnt out fires and charred human bone.

"The Humps really knew how to build a home," Conway commented as they steered their ponies through the empty camp.

"It's enormous," Bunce said, looking around.

"And I think the Trade's guns have now met every resident," Conway joked.

"Shut up, Conway," Spicer shouted at the dabbler.

They all turned in surprise to face their leader, who had been bringing up the rear. His hands covering his face, he glared at Conway through his fingers.

"Nice to have you back, boss," Conway said uncertainly.

"Give it a rest, Conway," Elena moaned, turning her pony to move alongside Spicer.

"Are you okay?" she asked.

"You didn't see it?" he replied, taking his hands from his face.

"What is it?" Spicer asked when he saw his three companion's reaction.

"Your face," Elena whispered, awestruck.

"And your ears," Conway added.

Spicer brought his hands back to his face and traced his fingers over his skin. It felt smoother than before, perhaps more plump. Familiar scars and hard ragged skin tags were missing.

"Your scarring. It's gone," Elena told him, reaching for a mirror from her saddlebags.

Spicer's fingers followed the line of his jaw to his ears. He touched earlobes, which had been burnt off decades before. As he reached the top of his ears, he felt points of gristle standing firmly upwards about half an inch. Not much, but noticeable. Elena held out the mirror and Spicer took it.

For the first time in his memory, Spicer saw his face without his scars. He saw eyebrows and eyelashes, even the beginnings of a beard. His hands moved to his wig, no longer firmly fixed to his scalp, and slid it off to reveal a suede-like fuzz across his head.

And he saw his pointy ears.

"Who…" he started to ask.

"Well, it's you," Conway answered, "apparently."

"How did this happen?"

"It must be something to do with light from the Cathedral spire," Elena suggested. "What do you think, Conway?"

"I suppose," Conway shrugged, ignoring Bunce rolling her eyes.

"What did you see? I mean, before?" Elena asked.

"I saw the city that was here. I saw my people," he replied, emotion welling within him as he looked around the stinking Hump camp.

"That's some mystical shit," Conway nodded, with a serious face.

"How do you know they were your people?" Bunce asked, a little jealous. The only people she counted as her own were her fellow Reclaimers, and one of them was dead and another looked like he was going crazy. And Conway was a dickhead.

"It's like when you remember something that was on the tip of your tongue. Or a smell puts you straight in the middle of your childhood. I just know." Spicer wasn't used to explaining feelings and struggled with his words. "I haven't felt the same since we first got the Gargoyle Key."

"I feel alright," Conway offered, "In case anyone is interested."

"And the light of the snowdrop, when that came on..." Spicer stopped, staring up to the top of the spire.

"What the hell is happening down there?" Elena asked nobody in particular.

"I'm dying for a piss," Pinkerton informed the others, as they reached the large doors in the other side of the chamber.

"Well, have one," Brennan suggested.

"I don't like to in front of the lady," Pinkerton replied, nodding towards Laurel.

"Laurel, are you a lady?" Brennan asked.

"Nope," Laurel replied, as she handed the Gargoyle Key to the Professor.

"But still…" Pinkerton moaned.

"Catch us up," Hilt suggested, as he lit the lantern and lifted it to shoulder height, squinting through the doorway.

The four looked through the large doorway as Pinkerton moved towards a column to relieve himself, his boots echoing on the shiny floor. He caught sight of his reflection in the glassy surface of the column as he unbuttoned his fly. He looked tired, and his whiskers looked somewhat unkempt. Blood was starting to seep through his bandage and his clothes were singed from the sparks of the grinder. He finished up and turned towards the others, twisting his moustaches.

The others had gone, leaving no sign. He knew they had gone ahead but he thought he would be able to hear them at least. All he could see was impenetrable darkness on the other side of the door. He cursed himself for not insisting on carrying a lantern himself.

"Er, Professor?" he called. "Laurel?"

No reply. He put his fingers to his lips and whistled long and loud.

"Alexander! Come here, boy!" he shouted.

His own words echoed back to him. He prayed there would be no more mirages, although he had no idea to whom he was praying. He was simply certain he really did not need to see any more ghosts. And he definitely didn't want to see any ghosts getting killed. He considered himself a man of action tempered by manners. He was not a man of philosophy. He was nothing like the Professor. He was Ten Fingers Pinkerton, the victor of Langtry Common, the Gentleman Pugilist. So far today, he had seen his best friend killed, and had almost met his own end at the grinders of some ancient marionette.

He reached the enormous doorway and looked inside. All he could see was the beam of light and his own shadow created from the open door. He stepped inside and felt his boot crunch down on bone gravel.

"Oh, great," he mumbled to himself.

He unshouldered his blat gun and racked it before taking his first step into the fabled Cathedral of Tales. The darkness seemed to consume him, bringing a chill with it. He paused to let his eyes acclimatise and to listen for footfalls on gravel. Shadows started to reveal themselves in the gloom, giant statues. What you'd expect in a cathedral, Pinkerton thought to himself.

"Professor?" he called again. "Hello?"

Then he heard one single bark from Alexander immediately followed by a yelp. He reached into his pocket for his matches, found the box and pulled them out. He was reluctant to take his finger from the blat gun's trigger and leave himself defenceless, so he moved down onto one knee to take cover behind one of the enormous sculptures.

He struck the match and the flare from the miniscule drop of wonder made him blink. The first thing he saw in his personal circle of light was a tube ending in a battle-axe. The last time he had seem something like that it had been squirting burning fluid at his companions. He cursed, dropping the match, which hit the floor.

His blat gun was right back in his hand and he fired twice, hitting the beast both times. He scrambled backwards, racking the gun again. He lay on his back, waiting for the grinders to start up, for the hiss before the squirt of burning fluid, for the nails to bite into his flesh again. All he could see now in the vague light from the dying match were the silhouettes of the stone and metal praying mantis. He heard a quiet pitter-patter like a dripping tap, getting closer and closer, a rasping breath accompanying it. Alexander planted his paws on Pinkerton's shoulders and licked his face.

The lights came up.

Pinkerton pushed the wolfhound away and got to his feet. The room was a quarter of the size of the previous chamber, more a corridor the width of the gigantic doorway through which they had entered. Flanking the walls stood row after row of grinders, lined up like soldiers awaiting inspection. A few were out of line, including the one Pinkerton had fired at, but none of them moved. At the far end of the room stood his four friends in a small circle, weapons ready, Rickenbacker next to a slot in the wall where he had just inserted the Gargoyle Key.

"What happened?" Pinkerton asked, his arms wide.

All four of the others shushed him, beckoning him over. He tiptoed towards them, aware of every chink and clunk of his equipment. He could feel the bug eyes of each monstrosity on him.

"What happened?" he whispered when he reached them.

"We are trying to sneak past them," Laurel hissed, pointing at the beasts, "but with you shouting, shooting and whistling at everything in sight, I don't think we will be too successful."

Pinkerton looked down at the extinguished lanterns on the floor and then at the dormant things around them.

"I think they've run out of juice or something," Pinkerton suggested.

"You think?" Laurel asked.

"Shall we proceed?" Rickenbacker suggested, as the doors opposite from where they had entered slid open. Rickenbacker detached the Gargoyle Key from the wall and Hilt slipped his Twirler back into his holster.

"Want to whistle some more?" Hilt asked Pinkerton. "Perhaps we could have a singsong. Or there are enough of us to try a barbershop quintet..."

Pinkerton blushed beneath his whiskers.

"So tell us everything," Quine instructed, pouring some liquor from his flask into a tin cup.

"Well, Laurel was a nurse and a dancer, she owned the lodge. I say owned, she got it in a will, she was, what's the word, bequeathed it, by a long lost aunt or grandma or someone she didn't know she had because she was an orphan, had I already said that?" Kendrick paused as he inhaled the cigarillo and reached for the cup of booze. "And Hilt is, I don't really know too much, I mean he tells all these stories but I've never liked history, except he was involved in the massacre at Maisy, in some cavalry or something, his hand is stuck to his sword, you know, and then there's Brennan, who's just a drunk. He pretends not to be for his son's sake, but I suppose he's dead now, the son that is, so..."

"What about the Professor?" Quine interrupted.

"What about the Professor?" Kendrick asked, downing the booze and drawing hard on his cigarillo.

"What do you know about Rickenbacker? Why did he choose to stay at the lodge?"

"Well, everybody on the way to the Cathedral of Tales stops for a final drink at the lodge," Kendrick disclosed as if it was obvious. "And it generally is a final drink, if you catch my meaning."

"So you know nothing about Hilary Rickenbacker," Axelrod reiterated.

"He's quite tall?" offered Kendrick, pushing the empty cup forward for a top up.

"This is pointless, Colonel," Axelrod groaned, "Mandell."

The corpse of Mandell pulled back the flap of the wagon, his sword unsheathed.

"Yes, doctor?"

"Kill this... pipsqueak, will you?" Axelrod told him.

"Wait!" Kendrick pleaded. "Look, the dead man knows Rickenbacker and his gang, I know the people from the lodge..."

Mandell grabbed Kendrick by his hair and pulled back his head to reveal his throat.

"If they have escaped, we can find them."

Mandell raised his sword.

"Stop," Quine ordered.

"I know every Chinsey tavern Brennan drinks in and every music hall Laurel danced in. We were friends. Best of friends," he burbled.

"So it would appear," Axelrod sneered, "considering what you're offering."

"I'm a business man. A pragmatic businessman. If they escape the Cathedral, I will join with the corpse of Rickenbacker's henchman and we will hunt them down."

Kendrick tried to look up at Mandell.

"Together. Right, Mandell?"

"Do I kill him now?"

"Let him live."

"Thank you, Colonel."

"For now. If they die in the Cathedral, and the Doctor will know if they do, then the deal is off. If they escape the Cathedral and one of our patrols captures them the deal is off. If they escape and you do not find them within one week, the deal is off. If the deal is off, Mandell will cut off your head."

"May I bugger his corpse?"

"Yes, Mandell. Any questions, Mister Kendrick?"

"Yes," said Kendrick, raising the tin cup, "May I have a top up?"

CHAPTER 9

The Cathedral of Tales/The Library of the Senses
The Gramarye Region
Grand Quillia

June 1856

"Welcome to the Library of the Senses. We apologise for the current unforeseen outage in the majority of the facility, but please proceed to the main attraction, which remains open to visitors."

They all heard the same message as soon as the doors from the grinders' room closed behind them. Although the message was mainlined straight into their brains, it still carried nuance and a vague accent, a certain burr that none of them recognised. It was a distinct voice, full of flavour like that of a music hall master of ceremonies.

"I would suggest you follow the sound of my voice except I am not currently speaking in the general sense. Therefore I suggest you make your own way. After all, it has worked for you so far," the voice continued, unthreatening, friendly, like a warm-hearted, understanding uncle. "Do take your own time though. I'm sure the six of you have really been through the mill."

"Blimey," said Pinkerton.

"He sounds pleasant," remarked Laurel.

"Who is it?" Hilt asked.

"I have no idea. Whoever it is, they are impressive hyperphysicists."

"Well I don't like the dabble and I don't like whoever it is using it to get in my head."

As soon as Hilt had passed the Gargoyle door in the lodge's cellar, he had been shocked to discover Wonder that actually had some effect on him. Ever since the overdose he had experienced in the Meander Canyon, all but the most powerful or most physical wonder had absolutely no effect on him. Conway's silencer had not worked on him, and, although Rickenbacker was extremely proficient, Hilt had been able to recognise the flames that engulfed the lodge as fake. Blue Wonder was different. He couldn't ignore an Immolator just as the Gargoyle door would have been closed to him until the arrival of the key.

But the false floor in the first room, and especially the mirage, he had fallen for them entirely. And now this omnipresent voice speaking directly into his brain. No matter how friendly the tone may have been, it made Hilt feel vulnerable, out of control. Pliable. There was no way he would share his worries with any of the others, especially Rickenbacker. Despite his apparent decency and their shared hatred of the Trade, the old fool was just another dabbler, underneath it all. A good dabbler with the right intentions perhaps, but his power was still based on other people's susceptibility. Their weaknesses. Like a virus that crept up on the tired and hungry, using them as a springboard to spread to everybody. Hilt saw the Wonder as a disease, and suddenly he was no longer immune.

"If there is anything you need, do let me know," said the voice.

As a hyperphysicist, the Professor was thrilled by their experiences beneath the Cathedral of Tales. As a scholar, his head was reeling with what he had seen, but as a man, Hilary Rickenbacker was starting to feel two things. He was feeling his age, which was frustrating, and he was starting to feel a great weight on his shoulders.

As a hyperphysicist, he should have been examining the methodology behind some of the Wonders they had encountered, parts of a long lost city still working thousands of years later. Despite not being a particularly creative man, he would have loved to learn how to create moving mosaics, to use his skills to bring art to the world. To see the Wonder used in a positive way, not just in defence, made him feel better about humanity and himself.

As a scholar, he would have liked to take notes of everything he had seen. He had been gifted with a glimpse of a long dead culture, something sociologically and historically priceless. But already he was aware of forgetting details, not just the cultural possibilities of the crowds of ghosts, but the anthropological discoveries, the bearded children and tall angular humanoids that matched the corpses from the mass graves.

But his greatest responsibility excluded any possibility he had of sating his hyperphysical or scholastic appetites.

He had seen what the Trade had done when they had discovered the ballrooms and used their secrets to create the Immolators. He had seen the Trade's agents scour the Gramarye to abduct children that could be twisted into the suited mindless killer slaves. The Trade had forbidden his studies in the Necropolis of Pearly at the point he had discovered something proving the horror of which mankind was capable.

He had fought to steal the Gargoyle Key in order to end the rape of the Gramarye, its people, history and reserves of Wonder, but at what cost? People, including friends, were dead, wounded, broken and still the Trade came. The more he saw of the Cathedral of Senses, the more he recognised the potential, the possibilities that the Trade would find here. The moving mosaics, the grinders, the floor illusion, untapped energy that still functioned after a thousand years or more. Blue Wonder, the most dangerous power of all, which allowed transmogrification and mind control, all here to be stolen and used for the Trade's dreams of imperial expansion. Everything here would be broken down to be reverse-designed or shipped off for display in a Grand Quillian museum, where bored school children would answer questions on clipboards and aesthetes would reproduce the artistry and imagery on show for upholstery and wallpaper.

So as the words of the stranger echoed inside his own head, a voice from a distant past that hinted at a new hyperphysical future, the Professor prayed that this whole place would fall, bury all of them and close this world of possibility to the thieves, rapists and opportunists who ruled the land above.

"I am sure you are all quite exhausted from your journey and I notice that your canteens are empty of water so please accept my sincerest apologies when I tell you that the Library of Senses' nourishment facilities are currently offline. Although your visit here may not be culinary related, I wish I could offer you at least a morsel. A little bite to eat."

"Who are you?" Brennan called into the air of the broad stairway they had reached.

"What's the Library of the Senses?" asked Pinkerton.

"Don't talk to it," Hilt growled, swishing his sword irritably.

"Why not?" challenged Laurel. "I think he sounds nice."

"He doesn't sound anything."

"Mister Hilt is right, Laurel. We are not hearing this with our ears," Rickenbacker explained.

"He doesn't exactly come across as evil, however he is choosing to speak to us."

"Why don't we have a sit down and discuss the situation?" suggested the voice.

Hilt's mouth twitched with agitation.

"Thanks," said Laurel.

They were at the bottom of a broad staircase leading into more darkness, with no clue as to what lay ahead. Pinkerton was the first to take a seat, loosening his bootlaces, the blat gun next to him. Brennan and Teddy joined him as Hilt pulled out his canteen and shared it with the others before taking a sip himself. He hoped whoever had been arrogant enough to put voices in his head realised that they had been wrong about something, that he didn't need their nourishment facilities, that he was still capable of some dissent.

Alexander lay down at Pinkerton's feet, his head on the big man's lap, while Hilt took a few more steps up the stairs, his eyes probing the dark. Rickenbacker lent against a wall, aware that if he sat down, his weary bones may not lend him the luxury of standing up again.

Laurel felt too excited to sit down. Ever since she had been entrusted with the Gargoyle Key, she had felt more alive than ever. As a dancer in the music halls, she had felt in control of her young life as she had made her own money and her own choice of friends and lovers, before she had decided to move on. As a nurse she had felt useful, she had been doing the right thing in a world that changed every hour, whereas the day to day of the lodge had become rather tedious, but at least it had given her a taste of her family, her lost heritage. People had made it clear that she was not possessed of the sharpest wit, but she had been brought up to find her own way, but be mindful of others. She had been raised to be good, to deal whatever life threw at her.

Admittedly, she had never expected life to throw secret subterranean cities and voices in her head at her, but one plays the hand one is dealt.

"In answer to your first question, I am the failed saviour of Pearly and the bait in a trap to damn those I was made to save. I am the cursed and forgotten, the last of my kind."

"More bullshit and riddles," Hilt huffed, out of patience.

"And you stand in the Library of the Senses, a testament to Pearly, built to last but long ago stripped of almost all its treasures."

"Treasures?" Pinkerton chipped in.

"Indeed, Mister Pinkerton. All the knowledge of our great city was once kept here, available to all. Cures for all ills, food for thought and recipes for disaster. A whole history written for the future so the same mistakes would never be made again. A once-magical place."

"What happened?" Rickenbacker asked, motioning to Teddy to pass him his notebook.

"Some people are the enemy of knowledge, Professor. The uneducated are a lot more malleable, easier to lead. Subjugate. Control. You, of all people, know that."

Rickenbacker nodded sadly.

"You mentioned being the bait in a trap, Sir," Pinkerton called out, twisting his moustaches.

"I have been the bait for thousands of years, but my captors did not expect me to outlive the trap. You have shown great bravery and strength getting this far, but please believe me, had all the grinders still been fully operational, we would not be having this conversation. And I am sorry to inform you that the trap is not yet fully sprung."

"Great," said Hilt.

"However, if anyone can make it through, it's you."

Pinkerton winked proudly at Laurel, who puffed out her chest.

"Oh good," she said.

"Your bloodstained legacy of evil, of genocide and annihilation, of unrelenting malignancy and atrocity, your birthright of death, Laurel Gleave, means you and your friends have a chance to get out of here alive."

They all felt the voice, the entity that had been in their minds, leave them, as if a barely perceivable background noise had stopped. Brennan turned to Laurel.

"He doesn't like you."

"I definitely preferred the end of that last sentence to the beginning."

The entity had laboured long and hard searching for a name, just in case they survived the final test. It required something dramatic but subtle, intimidating but friendly, familiar yet foreign. It wanted them to both trust and fear it. It had swum in the shallows of their minds and realised that they were all very different people. The Gleave had especially surprised it, not resembling any other members of the damned dynasty it had met through the ages.

It decided it only needed a surname to begin with. It considered Mister Mackinder. The name was romantic and mysterious, implied something magical, but it would intimidate young Teddy and antagonise Widdershins, who had chosen the apt and intimidating name of Hilt for himself. The entity was almost jealous.

Then for a while, it liked Mister Jones. Plain and simple and to the point. But Rickenbacker would see right through the naiveté of it, even if the boxer liked it. It toyed with Mister Guillemot, but it was a little threatening, despite being the name of something as harmless as a gull. For a while the entity settled on Mister White, but it was just so incredibly 'just so'.

Eventually, having gone through and dismissed the names of every hero, villain, statesman and sportsman that Pearly had ever produced, it considered the possibility of presenting itself as female. The choice of being a Missus or Miss led it to Ms, and, although for a second it convinced itself Ms Brumberg was a spectacular moniker, it knew that it had still not found the name it needed.

Then it remembered a childhood tale, and the protagonist seemed apt. Doubtless the visitors would not have heard of two thousand year old fable of the abnormally tiny little boy who convinced everybody around him they were giants, that they were the freaks, not he, but it liked the name.

It toyed with the name as it waited for them in its cell, and the more it rolled it around its mind, the more it worked. It looked forward to meeting them now. It was excited to introduce itself now it had a name. In fact, it found itself growing impatient, and decided it would help them over the final hurdle if needs be.

All of them but the Gleave woman, obviously.

Spicer led the Reclaimers through the centre of the deserted Hump camp to a roughly fortified area built up against the Cathedral.

"Humps have been busy," Conway noted.

"I'm starting to see why none of the treasure hunters ever returned," Elena said.

"What's that?"

"Laurel and the others in the lodge said nobody ever returned from the Cathedral. They'd have to fight their way through the Humps before they even reached the entrance."

"And God knows what's in there," Bunce said, looking up at the enormous doors into the building that stood closed behind the barriers.

"And even if they got in, they'd have to escape back through the Humps."

"Unless you have our Gargoyle Key," mumbled Conway, "and use the back door."

Spicer clambered over the last of the wooden barricades to reach the doors. Since his transformation, they had not spoken of it again. Brothers in arms didn't generally comment on each other's attractiveness, unless they were lascivious wretches like Mandell or creeps like Conway, Elena found herself thinking as she caught sight of the lieutenant's face again. He was undeniably extremely good looking. There even seemed to be a new lustre in his eyes. She realised she was staring and looked away, her face reddening. This was still Spicer, a Reclaimer guilty of a hundred crimes depending on what side you were on, all for money, none for passion or patriotism. A mercenary without a soul, she had always suspected he lived to his own personal code, as she had never seen him attack a child or a defenceless woman. He had never been cruel, but then he had been clever enough to keep someone like Tork around for that. And he wasn't afraid to use threats if the job asked for it. He was a soldier of fortune after all. She had met some who had a definite life plan on how to spend their ill-gotten gains. Others spent it on ladies of easy virtue, which she had experienced at first hand in a previous life. Some frittered it away on expensive gambling and cheap booze. But Lieutenant Spicer never seemed to waste his money. She had never noticed this until now. What was he saving it for?

And why was she suddenly so interested? She'd only been interested in the money and thrills the jobs he offered her presented. Now he looked like that was she really so shallow?

"Elena, can you give us a hand with these doors?" he asked her.

The three of them were using a rusty harpoon to prise open the doors.

"Yes, of course," she said, joining them in their endeavours.

She realised with some embarrassment that she didn't even know his first name. But then she'd never been that interested. She watched his arms as he wrestled with the harpoon.

"Ogle much?" Conway smirked at her.

Major R Franks had had a very busy day. When the Humps had charged the platoon, he had set up his command post in the lodge, safe now the fire at the front of the building had been extinguished. He had posted two of his soldiers at the foot of the stairs and chosen one of the bedrooms, the largest, which smelt of perfume and had a large four-poster bed. He had searched the room for intelligence, and had discovered a wide variety of women's undergarments, some of which he was sure had been worn and not washed. He also discovered a dancer's sequined costume and a nurse's blood-stained uniform. Both had the same odour as the perfume that permeated the room. He checked the dressing table but there were no eau de toilette bottles, just a little powder for the eyes and a little rouge for the lips. He glimpsed himself in the mirror and was sad to see he looked his fifty-two years, his skin tired and perhaps a little drawn. He was definitely lacking in colour and needed a change of clothes. By the time the cracks of the rifles slowed and the stream of Humps past the window thinned, Franks had added a little colour to his mouth and was wearing some fresh underwear, not strictly his own or necessarily created for males, but the Major felt much more comfortable, nonetheless.

"So you have no recollection of any plans Rickenback-er had to aid in his escape from the Cathedral," Kendrick asked his new business partner.

"No," Mandell said.

Kendrick looked up and down at the remains of the once suave warrior, now a blood splattered brute with the black eyes of a shark.

"What's it like being dead?"

"I'm not dead. I'm undead."

"But you were dead."

"But then Doctor Axelrod cured me."

Kendrick held a kerchief to his nose as Mandell talked. The dead man smelt as rotten as a corpse, as one would expect, but his breath carried the stench of Hell itself. The two of them had followed the platoon towards the Cathe-dral and watched as the soldiers were deployed to surround the area. Kendrick had been forced to pause occasional-ly whenever Mandell found a corpse that he took a fancy to, which he would proceed to examine intimately, despite Kendrick's protestations. Indeed, Kendrick was relieved the nauseating foreplay had not progressed further. He was re-assured that his new arrangement had prolonged his life, but did not entirely appreciate his new colleague. He had never had much luck befriending the living, so becoming chummy with the dead was beyond him. Bribery seemed pointless, so, for the first time he could remember, it seemed that Kendrick would have to complete the task he had been employed to execute.

Unfortunately he didn't know the first thing about en-gaging in a manhunt, but luckily he had eavesdropped on many conversations about the Cathedral had by countless doomed treasure hunters.

"Mandell, can you clean yourself up or something?" he asked as he gazed up at the Cathedral, racking his brains for the first step.

"Why?"

And then it struck him. A self-proclaimed daredevil named Ethelred Gibson had bragged about his unique approach in gaining entry to the Cathedral. He had proudly displayed a harpoon powered by the Wonder that he would use to secure a rope in the top of the spire so he could climb into the snowdrop's tip. Obviously, he had never returned, and had doubtlessly failed, but if Kendrick was to find Laurel and the others before anyone else, he had to find a unique approach. And Ethelred Gibson had given him one.

The platoon was now completely encircling the Cathedral, but the snowdrop hung over and beyond their lines.

Kendrick clapped his hands in celebration of his own ingenuity.

"Follow me."

"What's the word of Wonder?" replied Mandell in a singsong voice.

"Oh for God's sake. Please. Please follow me, Mandell," Kendrick snapped. "What are you, a child?"

"Quite the opposite," the undead replied.

The two men headed in the opposite direction to the platoon to wait directly beneath the snowdrop.

As the Reclaimers succeeded in prising open the doors to the Library of Senses, they had no idea they were triggering clockwork as intricate as a snowflake in spider's web. Two thousand year old cogs and weights spun and swung as the trap started to spring.

"What's that sound?" Conway asked as the ticking and turning echoed around the entrance hall.

Opposite the doors they had prised open stood another double door, this one bolted many times. Spicer's eyes drunk in murals depicting Pearly, the spider generator pulsing in the centre, the illustration of the blanket of power lines illuminating the whole hall.

"That's what I could see," Spicer told them, running his hand over his face. "That's the city that used to be here."

"Was it attacked by giant spiders?" Conway asked, stepping through the doorway.

He felt the floor drop an inch or two as he stepped on it, as though it was floating on air, but thought nothing of it as he approached the mural, ignoring the doors at the opposite end.

"You should see this thing," Conway remarked. "There are loads of little fellows pottering about and everything."

Spicer put one foot over the entrance and noticed the floor, uneven and a dark burgundy and sickly brown in colour, like the bottom of a dying bird's cage.

"What's the floor made of?" he asked.

"The ceiling is the same," said Elena, looking up.

"This really is amazing," Conway said, enthralled.

He started poking at the mural, like a child teasing an ants' nest with a stick.

"They even react when you squash them," he laughed, prodding at the miniature buildings. "Bow before your god or I will destroy you all."

Bunce rolled her eyes as she watched the dabbler.

"Bring me your daughters or feel the wrath of my finger!"

Then the floor shot forwards and upwards. Spicer was swept off his feet and fell back through the doorway onto his back as Conway hurtled into the air. Beneath the floor, Elena glanced the giant cogs and wheels of the trap.

The floor stayed horizontal as it was carried through an arc and slammed into the ceiling. When it returned to the floor, Conway had been reduced to a gloopy puddle of brown jelly. It had all happened within three seconds, and the Reclaimers' guns were still in their holsters. Elena's hand went to her mouth until her nausea subsided. Bunce helped Spicer to his feet.

"That was too close," said the Lieutenant.

Apart from the glistening damp patch, there was nothing to differentiate Conway from the rest of the floor.

"I think we can guess what the floor is made out of now," said Elena.

"That puddle owes me money," Bunce informed them.

Pinkerton reached the top of the stairwell and turned to let the others know.

"We've reached a door," he called over his shoulder, turning the handle.

"Wait!" Rickenbacker called, but it was too late.

As Pinkerton pulled back the door, he saw the floor whoosh past him, and glimpsed Conway on his trip into the ceiling. He closed the door again.

"I think we've reached a trap," he told the others.

"Did you see that?" Bunce asked, unshouldering her rifle.

"What? Something besides the Conway thing?" Elena said.

"A door opened."

Bunce knelt down at the doorway and sighted where the wall had opened.

"I can't see a door," Spicer frowned.

"It shut again. It was one of Rickenbacker's group. The big one."

"Pinkerton," Elena told them.

Elena felt a chill. Her mind's eye flashed to his dark eyes and the blade, which he had buried in the wooden floor as they had made love. She found herself feeling a quiver of excitement as she thought of it, and then looked at Spicer. His new face was really quite becoming, and she had never really noticed just how lithe his body was, firm from a lifetime as a warrior. She shook her head, surprised at the teenage-like rush of lust, her heart still beating.

"Well, whatever his name is, he's on the other side of a hidden door over there," said Bunce irritably as she noticed Elena's admiring gaze. "Shall I take him down?"

"Wait," Spicer told her. "Let's see if they know a way through."

Elena pulled her Twirler and exhaled heavily.

Teddy walked slowly up the stairs behind Brennan, who was wheezing loudly. He was thinking about food, toast specifically. Not toast with jam, just lashings of salted butter. And a tea. A huge mug of sugary tea. Teddy really wanted some tea and toast.

"Hello there, Teddy," said the voice.

"Oh, uh, hullo," Teddy replied.

"What's the matter, lad?" Brennan asked.

"Nothing. I just…"

"Don't mention me, Teddy," said the voice.

"Nothing, Mister Brennan. I'm fine."

"That's the way. Now look, I've been thinking about you and I reckon you could do with a little pick me up. What do you say?"

"Toast?" asked Teddy.

"I don't have any, Teddy," Brennan replied.

"You can reply to me without speaking, Teddy. Just think the words."

"Oh. Sorry."

"That's it. Let's give your tongue a rest. I'm afraid I'm not talking toast, but if you do as I say, you'll get out of here quicker and then you can have all the toast you want," the voice chuckled.

Teddy raised his eyebrows, considering the suggestion.

"I'm raising my eyebrows," he thought to the voice.

"Well done, Teddy. Now I really want you and your friends to find the treasure and escape with your lives. And to do that you need get past that trap Pinkerton just mentioned."

"Treasure?"

"Yes, Teddy, treasure. It's not pirates' doubloons or gold bricks, but it's treasure nonetheless. It's something so special it could change..."

"I don't like traps."

"That's why I want to help you, Teddy."

"Are you sure you want to talk to me. The Professor is much better at this sort of thing."

"Don't you want to be a hero, Teddy?"

"No."

"Don't you want to save the day?"

"I don't know. Do I?"

"Yes you do, my boy. You're not just some simple man-servant."

"Yes I am."

"But you could be so much more, Teddy. You could help our companions through this trap and they'll see you differently. You'll go up in their estimations."

"Is that good?"

"Of course it is."

The voice's tone changed. Teddy thought it seemed to be getting agitated. He did not want an angry thing in his head, and resolved to help it.

"Very well, voice. How do I get through the trap?"

"That's it, Teddy. Work with me here. If we work together, it'll be good for both of us. All the women in the world will fall at your feet."

"Do I want them near me feet?"

"You can have manservants of your own. And they will bring you all the toast you want."

"With butter?"

"You're the chosen one, boy. Of course with butter."

"Chosen for what?"

"We're going to change the world, Teddy, usher in a new age of harmony and wonder."

"Are you sure you don't want the Professor, voice?"

"You are about to become the hero of your own story."

"And that's a good thing, I suppose. It's just I'm not great at fighting, and I get nervous around girls. I used to get on well with my cousin Bertha but she had one eye and she used to wee in her hands and rub it in my hair."

"Shall we get you through this trap then?"

"Let's do that, voice."

"Yes. Let's."

"Oh, wait a minute. What's your name, voice?"

"My name? Well thank you so much for asking. My name is Mister Elephantine, Teddy."

"Are you an elephant?"

And it was at that point that the intelligence realised it might have not been too clever in its choice of name.

Nobody was more surprised than the Professor when Teddy pushed himself past the others towards the door to the entrance hall.

"Can I have a look?" Teddy asked.

"Of course," said Pinkerton.

Perhaps this journey through the darkness had made the boy a man, Rickenbacker considered. Maybe he was claustrophobic, and desperation at his situation had led him to bravery. Or was he driven by boredom. The Professor had never know whether Teddy had the facility to be bored, as that intimated that there was something that interested him, and throughout their travels together Teddy had never really shown any interest in anything or anyone, not even the fairer sex– or any sex.

"Hold the dog," Pinkerton told Brennan.

Pinkerton turned the handle and cracked open the door. He did not want to be responsible for the death of the boy the first time he ever showed any side of assertiveness.

His eyes scanned the hall and he saw the mural that had so enthralled Conway. Then he saw the double doors at the entrance and the Reclaimer woman who had almost killed him at the lodge. He closed the door again quickly.

"The Reclaimers are at the door, but they can't get past the trap either."

"Let me see," said Hilt.

"Watch your head," Pinkerton warned him.

Hilt knelt at the doorway and opened it.

"And the good lady Melody is there too," he said, closing the door. "And the leader who killed the Brigadier."

"What are they doing?" Laurel asked.

"Waiting for us to spring the trap," Hilt reasoned. "Saves their bullets."

"What does the trap do?" Rickenbacker asked Pinkerton.

"The floor flew up and squashed their dabbler against the ceiling."

"Straight up or like a pendulum?" Teddy asked.

"The second one."

"I have an idea," said Teddy.

"Really?" asked Hilt.

"If I can just look at the ceiling, I think we'll find a hatch there."

"Oh do you?" said Hilt.

"It makes sense," said Rickenbacker.

"What makes you think there might be a hatch up there?" Hilt asked. "There's something you're not telling us."

"We used something like that on the farm."

Sweat shone on Teddy's top lip.

"Rickenbacker said he met you in the city of Fairport."

"I helped on a farm. My uncle's farm. I helped on my uncle's farm."

Hilt sighed and swept his sword through the air.

"Pinkerton, I have no idea why the boy has decided he is our saviour but I suggest we give him some cover while he finds the hatch like the one on his uncle's farm," said Hilt, glancing over Teddy's shoulder at Rickenbacker, who gave a slight shrug.

Pinkerton racked the blat gun and nodded at Hilt.

"Teddy, Pinkerton is going to kick open the door now and then he and I will fire at the Reclaimers while you lay on the floor on your back. If you see this hatch, point at it. Pinkerton, if the boy points, fire your blat at whatever he's pointing at. Understand?"

Teddy and Pinkerton nodded as Hilt spun his Twirler. He counted down and Pinkerton kicked open the door. Before it was halfway open, the two men started firing.

Bunce had had a clear shot at whoever was next through the door but Spicer's order was to hold fire. If Rickenbacker had got this far, he had reasoned, then the old man may know how to get further through the Cathedral of Tales, in which case he could lead the Reclaimers to his goal, and through any more traps too.

The door halfway down the entrance hall burst open and the light from the mural glinted off Pinkerton and Hilt's weaponry.

"Get down!" called Bunce, flattening herself against the floor as bullets smashed into the door and frame around her. As bits of door and wall rained down around her, she saw a hand pointing up at the ceiling.

"Spicer!" she called over the noise.

She saw the big boxer swing his blat gun upwards, and starting blasting, racking, and blasting away again. She blinked as shot after shot from the blat gun struck a three-metre square, disintegrating it to reveal a hole leading into the darkness above. Then the shooting stopped and their adversaries slammed the door.

"You're right, Lieutenant, they've found a way through," she said, brushing herself down as she stood.

As the door closed, Hilt turned to regard Teddy, who looked flush with fear. He spun his Twirler and pointed it at the boy.

"How did you know?"

Brennan pulled his own pistol and pointed it at the warrior. Hilt flipped the firearm out of the man's hand with his sword.

"Tell me. Have you been here before?"

"No. My uncle's farm..."

"Leave him alone, Hilt. He's just a child," Brennan pleaded, stepping between the boy on the floor and the barrel of Hilt's pistol.

"Brennan, you're not thinking straight. Something is not right here."

"*You're* not right. You're threatening a young boy who just found our way through that trap."

"He's less than useless all his life and then, just after we hear voices, he gives us just what we need?"

"Teddy," said Rickenbacker soberly, his hand on Hilt's arm, "did something or someone tell you about the hatch? Someone in your head?"

Teddy looked up at them all. Hilt's eyes full of suspicion and his steady grip on his gun, the old drunk calling him 'just a child', all in front of this pretty woman who was probably laughing at him. Rickenbacker had treated him well but sometimes treated him like a trained monkey and had almost got him killed hundreds of times. Even his mother had pushed him away. Perhaps it was his time, it was time for him to be a chosen one, as Mister Elephantine said. They were being offered a way out of here and all they did was scoff at Teddy, doubt him. But not Mister Elephantine. According to Mister Elephantine he was special. The chosen one. Did chosen ones almost get eaten by Humps or blown up by crazy Professors? Teddy wasn't sure but he sincerely doubted it.

"Teddy, if you tell them about me," Mister Elephantine said, "I will reseal the hatch and you will be trapped in the bowels of the library forever. For all of your sakes, Teddy…"

"It was the same on my uncle's farm. For the hay. I promise you," Teddy blurted out, tears in his eyes. "You have to believe me, please, all of you…"

Pinkerton popped the door open to see what the Reclaimers were up to. A bullet smashed into the door half an inch from his face, and he stepped back behind the doorframe.

"Does it matter how the boy knows? If we don't act on it soon, the Reclaimers will get to the hatch first," he told the others.

"And if Teddy wouldn't do anything to hurt us, would you, Teddy?" said Laurel, reaching down to help the boy up from the floor.

"Course not, Miss. I just want to get out of here."

"I've got my eye on you, boy," warned Hilt, holstering the Twirler.

"And we still have a problem," mentioned Rickenbacker. "How do we know where to stand on the floor so we will be catapulted into the hatch, not into the ceiling?"

"There must be a mark on the floor or something," Elena said, "but it's covered in blood and guts."

"That's true," Spicer said. "Except if you stood in the right place, you wouldn't be ground into dog food."

"So there must be a spot that is not so smeared with as much…" she searched for the word, "…*remains* as the rest of the floor."

"All the floor looks the same consistency of blood to me," Bunce shrugged.

"Which suggests nobody has found the hatch before."

"I suggest we throw Teddy out there and note where he decides to stand," said Hilt.

"Don't you dare," Brennan growled, his hand tightening on the hammer hanging from his belt.

"The Reclaimers might know something we don't. We need to move now," said Laurel, eager to move the two men on from their discussion.

"Professor?" Pinkerton said, "Anything in your bag of tricks that will delay our friends out there so we can get to the hatch without the sniper girl taking our heads off?"

"There might be," Rickenbacker said, delving into his bag.

"Do you have a bolter?" Hilt asked without looking at the hyperphysicist.

"That's exactly what I was thinking, Mr Hilt."

Rickenbacker nodded at Hilt, pleased to hear for the first time that the Wonder-scarred warrior may concede that he could offer some form of resolution.

"But first you need to get that door shut," he said.

"Pinkerton? Are you in?" Hilt said.

"Sometimes I really wish I had a helmet," the big man replied.

Gunfire echoed around the hall as bullets smacked into both doors. The Reclaimers covered their ears as the doors shook with the impact.

"Why are they still shooting? Can't they see we're not there?" Elena called above the noise.

Spicer's eyes narrowed as he watched the doors edge closer together.

"The doors. They're trying to close the doors," he shouted, grabbing the ancient harpoon from the floor and handing it to Bunce. "Hold the door open with this."

Spicer looked around for something to act as a wedge and spied a skull, no doubt the remains of a Hump's lunchtime snack. Spicer crept forward and rolled the skull into the space between the two doors. They continued to tremble under the onslaught, but did not close any further.

"That's got it," said Spicer, wiping his hands on his trousers.

The shooting paused. Then three shots cracked into the skull, shattering it, and the firing started again. Despite the strength of the doors, proved by the lack of bullet holes, none of the Reclaimers felt comfortable enough to put their shoulders against them, and they shuddered closed.

"What makes them think we won't just open them again?" Bunce asked.

And then their ears popped and the firing stopped.

"Wonder?" Spicer asked.

"Knowing Rickenbacker," Elena nodded.

Spicer picked up the harpoon again and attempted to jam it between the doors, but it was as though the two doors had become one.

"I really hate Professor Rickenbacker," Bunce groaned.

Laurel and Teddy climbed back up the stairs carrying as much bone gravel in a variety of bags they'd pulled together from the whole group.

"Just because we're the youngest doesn't mean we're the fittest," Laurel moaned.

Teddy grinned in agreement, although thinking about it, they probably were the fittest. He definitely felt pretty old himself now though. He hadn't rested since being woken up on a sofa in the middle of the night and now he had descended these stairs once and was climbing them a second time.

"Why are you here, Teddy?"

Teddy frowned.

"We're collecting gravel to find out where..."

"You know what I mean."

"I'm with the Professor, Miss. I go where he goes."

"But why?"

"I'm his manservant, Miss. He pays me."

"When was the last time you saw any pay?"

"I can't remember, Miss, but he gives me food and shelter. He looks after me."

"Is this place shelter?"

"Miss?"

"Is he looking after you now? Sheltering you now? Do you count this underground hellhole as shelter?"

"I suppose not, but I've never done anything else except do what I'm told by my mum and my nana and my sisters. They couldn't afford to keep me, see, so I came to work for the Professor."

"Does it bother you that your mother sent you away?"

"There was an opportunity, Miss. She set me on the road to the good life."

"My parents sent me away and it really hurt. It still hurts every day. When the lawyer found me to give me the lodge, I felt like it was a bad joke, like they only wanted me around when they had gone, when they had left it. When they were dead."

"I wouldn't know anything about that."

"Did you have any friends at home, Teddy? I mean, before the Professor?"

"There was my cousin Bertha."

"Anyone else?"

"I had a tortoise for a while. But she ran away and was crushed by a shire horse."

"What was her name?"

"Michelle."

"How did you know the tortoise was a girl tortoise?"

"She had long nails."

Laurel shook her head. The boy seemed to revel in his lack of depth. He was scared to think for himself, to expect anything better, to consider what he deserved in the past or the future. He was dulled, beaten down, his edges smoothed away like any pebble on any drab beach. All that was special or attractive had been eradicated when he was still in swaddling.

"Will you be pleased to leave this place, Teddy?"

The Professor had said she should accompany the boy alone to collect the bone gravel, see if she could get under his skin. They would use the remains of the long dead to identify where they needed to stand to stay alive and fit through the hatch by scattering it over the entrance hall floor. The hatch that Teddy had found. The boy absolutely lacking in aspiration had ventured forth an opinion.

"Yes, Miss. It horrible down here."

"What was your uncle's farm like?"

"Small."

"But it was big enough to have a barn with a floor like..."

"My uncle really did have a barn with a floor like we saw. I don't understand. I found a way out and everybody is getting angry with me. I thought I was helping. When other people have an idea, people think they are clever and important and heroes and chosen ones, but when I have an idea Mister Hilt puts his foot on my chest and threatens to shoot me."

He stopped and stared imploringly into Laurel's eyes, tears rolling down his face.

"What am I supposed to do, Miss? My mother always told me to do as I was told. And that's what I do. I am told what to do. I was told to be a manservant and I was. I was told to help a crazy Professor who doesn't care if he lives or dies and I did. And when people told me they needed an idea, I gave them one."

"Where did you get the idea though, Teddy?"

"In my head," he said desperately, "it came to me in my head."

Laurel put down the bags of bone gravel and held him by his shoulders.

"It was a brilliant idea, little man. And if you need to be told what to do, then I'm telling you to keep on doing what you're doing, looking after the Professor and coming up with ideas that help us get out of here. Forget Hilt. He's not a real hero. You're the real hero here, Teddy."

"Thank you, Miss. That's very nice of you to say so. I think we should probably keep moving."

Laurel kissed him lightly on the forehead and bent to pick up her bags.

"Keep this up, Teddy," said Mister Elephantine, "and more women will treat you like that. And hopefully they'll have arses as nice as that one."

Teddy was relieved Mister Elephantine was there to tell him what to do, especially if it leads to looking at arses like Laurel's.

As Spicer's eyes traced the smooth neck of the spire to the snowdrop at the end, the first of the Trade soldiers started to climb over the fortifications outside the entrance.

"Is this the entrance?" asked Colonel Franks.

Spicer nodded distractedly and beckoned over the other two.

"Think there could be a way out there?" he said, pointing upwards.

Bunce shrugged as Elena followed the tip of Spicer's finger to the snowdrop.

"The hatch they found led upwards so it makes sense."

"Here comes trouble," Bunce warned as she noticed Quine and Axelrod approaching.

Spicer's hands brushed his face and something told him it would be a bad idea to share his new appearance with the Trade officers. He undid the scarf from around his neck and wrapped it around his face. Then he recovered his wig from his bag and placed it on his head.

"Feeling the cold, are we, Lieutenant?" said Quine.

"Where's your grotty little dabbler?" Axelrod asked.

"He's around," Spicer answered. "Found the Professor yet?"

"I was about to ask you the same question."

"Conway thinks there may be some underground tunnels to other exits so we're going to follow that up," Spicer offered.

"What makes him think that?" Axelrod asked.

"You know dabblers," Spicer smiled beneath his scarf. "They always have a secret or two up their sleeves."

"Indeed they do, Lieutenant, indeed they do," Quine nodded before turning to Franks. "Major, I want those doors open immediately, do you understand me? Immediately."

"If you'll excuse us, Colonel."

"You're excused."

Spicer could feel Axelrod's eyes on him as he headed away from the fortifications, the women flanking him.

"Why didn't you tell them the truth?" Bunce asked.

"I don't like them," Spicer replied as he caught sight of the two remaining Immolators picking their way through the wreckage of the Hump camp.

"There's our travelling companions," Bunce nodded.

"They scare the living breath out of me," said Elena, shivering.

Spicer stopped and felt another wave of regret. A sense of loss filled his soul, as though he had caught a glimpse of a lost love as he looked at the Immolators. He approached them, unwrapping the scarf from his head and leaving the wig on, heedless of whether Quine or Axelrod were watching.

"Spicer?"

The Immolators stopped as he approached and seemed to concentrate on him. He halted when they were toe to toe, and Spicer could see his face reflected in the lenses.

"Who are you?" he whispered. "What are you?"

The closest Immolator raised its gauntlet to Spicer's face. Elena's hand moved towards her holsters but there seemed to be a gentleness in the armoured warrior's movements.

The gauntlet stroked Spicer's cheek tenderly and Spicer raised his own hand to the glove.

"What…" Bunce uttered.

The Immolator moved its hand around the side of Spicer's head and cupped his ear. Then it raised its hand to its own helmet.

"Immolators!" Axelrod called from the fortifications. "Get over here."

The two Immolators didn't move, as though reluctant to leave Spicer.

"Go," Spicer heard himself mumble, and the two armoured warriors moved off in the direction of the entrance to the Cathedral.

"What was that about?" Elena asked.

"I have no idea," Spicer replied, watching the Immolators go.

As they reached the Hump fortifications, one Immolator turned back, and Spicer felt as though he was looking into the creature's eyes.

"Looks like you've made a new friend, Lieutenant," Bunce suggested, before they all turned to head towards the area directly beneath the snowdrop at the end of the spire.

Alexander bounded down the stairs, eager to greet Teddy and Laurel when they finally arrived back.

"What took you?" Hilt asked, seated on the floor.

"Bad news, I'm afraid," Pinkerton reported sadly.

"Oh no. What's happened?" Laurel asked, checking everybody was present as she put the bags of bone gravel on the floor.

"We don't need the bone gravel."

"You must be joking," Laurel growled.

"I am joking. Kind of," Pinkerton blushed.

"We have found where to stand, but we still need to check the size of the hatch," Rickenbacker clarified.

"How did you find where to stand?"

Hilt pushed open the door to reveal a length of rope running halfway across the floor. The majority of the rope was flattened into the floor, threadbare and stained by the aged guts around it, but at the end of the rope, Laurel could make out a full knot, still holding its shape, untouched by the ceiling.

"I see."

"But we still need to make sure we don't overshoot."

"Don't want to lose any fingers or toes now, do we?" grinned Pinkerton.

"Brennan has volunteered to dump the bone gravel you just delivered to the end of the rope," Hilt said, letting the door close.

"Brennan?" Laurel said, her voice breaking.

"Somebody has to," Brennan shrugged, taking her hand. "And I'm the most disposable."

"How can you say that?" Laurel gasped, wrapping her arms around her old friend.

"It's true, Laurel," he sighed, "Without Alf..."

"Brennan will be fine," Pinkerton assured her as Teddy stepped towards the old man, his bottom lip trembling.

"You need to look after each other now," Brennan told Laurel and Teddy, "if I don't make it back"

"Which you will," Pinkerton interjected.

"If I don't make it back you have to promise me you will look after each other."

"We promise to do as we're told," Laurel said, kissing Brennan on the lips. "Don't we, Teddy?"

"Thank you for all your help, Sir," said Teddy.

"Don't you worry, my boy. I'm sure your hunch about the hatch will lead onwards and upwards. Thank God for your uncle's farm or we would be stuck here."

Teddy felt his eyes prickle. He didn't want this responsibility. What if Brennan died? It would be his fault. It would be his fault for listening to Mister Elephantine. Tears came to his eyes.

"Quit blubbing. The old man will be fine," said Mister Elephantine confidently, "as long as his ticker holds out."

"Good luck, son," Brennan said, giving Teddy a hug, and surprised to feel a hearty return.

Brennan stuck out his hand and shook with the three men while Pinkerton loaded him up with the bags of bone gravel.

"And you'll be looking after Alexander, Mister Pinkerton," he said. "Two meals a day and at least ten times around the building before bed."

"You can walk the mutt yourself. Now get going," said Hilt, opening the door.

"Good luck," Rickenbacker said finally, and Brennan stepped through the door, feeling the floor beyond drop a little as he stepped onto it.

He hurried down the length of the rope, the bags of bone gravel hanging from his back and arms. He quickly reached the knot at the end and grunted as he knelt down to empty the bags to scatter the bone gravel around him, the sound masking the ticking of the trap. The others watched from the doorway, transfixed. Teddy could feel his teeth biting into his bottom lip and Laurel's nails digging deeper and deeper into the flesh of his hand.

"This really needs to work, Mister Elephantine," he thought hard through his furrowed brow.

"Don't worry about it," the voice in his head told him.

And then it triggered. The ticking stopped and there was a breath, then a loud slap like an enormous ruler hitting a desk and the floor started to rise. However, this time the speed was not so ferocious. From his kneeling position, Brennan looked up at the others, his eyebrows meeting his hairline as pleasant surprise and relief flooded across his face. The floor clicked slowly and gently towards the ceiling.

"It must have been triggered by the front doors being opened," Rickenbacker suggested as they watched Brennan rise up before them.

Brennan felt an incredible elation as he was elevated towards the roof. As he got closer to the open hatch he could feel the chill of the darkness, and he reached for his matches. It was good to be useful. It was good to be looking after Teddy and Laurel, and every step towards their goal, whatever their goal was besides escaping, was another step closer to hurting the Trade, the Reclaimers and anybody to blame for the death of his son.

One positive aspect of being trapped in this hellhole was the complete lack of booze. Just the thought of alcohol, even some backstreet gin or vodka, made his mouth water. He yearned for the burn of the liquid tearing down his throat and the fire in his chest before oblivion washed across his brain.

Brennan wiped his mouth on his cuff, and lit the match as his head reached the hatch. The darkness and cold seemed to swallow him up, moving down the length of his body. As the bone gravel was ground to dust around him, and his match illuminated his surroundings, Brennan needed a drink more than ever.

Rickenbacker stared at the cogs and wheels beneath the floor in amazement. He knew children's entertainers and con men who used mechanisms when the Wonder would do the job, but he had never seen anything on this scale. From what he had read, Pearly was primarily renowned for its extensive use of the Wonder, and, much like the praying mantis things below, all this mechnology seemed so alien, so different from what he was used to, different even to the advanced Wonder they had seen in the underground way station. The building itself and its graceful spire were at complete odds to this brutalist machinery.

"Watch your head," Pinkerton warned the Professor as the floor clicked back down into place, a clear square of untouched bone gravel discernible where Brennan had stood.

"Where's Mister Brennan?" Teddy asked, looking up the faint candle flicker in the hatch.

"Brennan!" Laurel called up at the ceiling.

Brennan heard Laurel's voice come through the hatch but he couldn't seem to get his mouth to work. The match went out, burning the tips of his fingers. Light from the hatch flickered off the slick pitch of the walls and he could make out the dark silhouettes of heads and hands turning towards him.

"Brennan," he heard.

"Who's there?" he asked.

"Don't worry, Brennan," said the voice, the same as before, in his mind but slightly mocking in tone.

"Are these things what I think they are?"

"Of course they are."

"Will the gargoyles hurt me?"

"No, not while you have the key."

"I don't have the key."

Brennan looked down through the hatch behind him as the pitch slithered towards him.

"Oh dear," said the voice.

"Laurel?" Brennan called out, his voice shaking, "I need the Gargoyle Key. I need the Gargoyle Key *now*..."

Hilt and Rickenbacker were ticking closer to the hatch when they heard Brennan's cry.

"Laurel. Throw me the key! Quickly!" Rickenbacker demanded.

Laurel reached into her bag and peered inside. She couldn't see the key immediately and stuck her hand inside up to her elbow to root around. The floor continued on its journey upwards.

"She's not going to make it and we'll be next for whatever is happening to Brennan," Hilt muttered, swinging his blade.

"Let me help," said Pinkerton, and he grabbed the bag, upended it and emptied the contents on the floor.

"Professor!" he called, grabbing the key. "Here!" He threw the cricket ball-sized key at Rickenbacker's chest.

The old man grasped for it, but it bounced from his palms onto the floor and rolled.

"Hilt," he cried as the key moved from the safe square area defined by the bone gravel.

Hilt leapt forward, his hand grasping towards the key. He missed it, and scrambled on to where it lay fifteen feet away.

As his fingers closed around it, he glanced up to see the ceiling closing in.

"A little help here," he growled, shuffling backwards on his hands and knees towards the safe area. Rickenbacker knelt down, grabbed Hilt by the ankles and heaved. Hilt balled himself up into the foetal position, felt the cold surround him as the floor met the ceiling, and he passed into the darkness.

"Are you alright?" Rickenbacker called, sitting upright in the darkness.

"Apparently," he heard Hilt answer.

It was completely black until the floor ticked back again and a square of light appeared at their feet.

"Brennan?" the Professor called into the cold.

"Help me."

As light broke into the area and they stepped from the hatch opening, Hilt and the Professor saw a pair of stone boots, then a statue's knees.

"Oh no," Rickenbacker groaned, the pain of his own transformation at the door in the cellar fresh in his mind.

"The old chap seems to be in a spot of bother," uttered the voice in their minds.

"Leave us alone, head hijacker," Hilt said.

"What do we do?" Rickenbacker asked, a hand raised in Hilt's direction.

"Do you have the key?"

The light had reached Brennan's waist, no longer flesh but dark and rough like weathered stonework. He had the hammer in his hand, so the still figure looked like a statue that had carved itself out of the rock.

"Yes but Laurel..."

"We don't need the Gleave woman," the voice said. "Find the receptacle in the wall as before. Quickly now, if you value your friend."

Hilt and the Professor looked around and saw the bottom of the black wall of gargoyles, and the stream of pitch that led to Brennan's feet.

"It hurts," Brennan hissed, the pitch as high as his chest, the stone transformation following it up his body.

"Here!" Hilt called as he spied a round hole at the edge of the writhing gargoyles.

The hatch was now letting enough light into the room so that they could see Brennan almost entirely turned to pitch and stone, the ungodly mix now encasing his throat like a neck brace.

"No. Stop," he whispered.

Rickenbacker slammed the Gargoyle Key into the receptacle as Brennan started to attempt a scream as his lungs turned to stone.

"Is it working?" Rickenbacker cried, throwing himself towards Brennan.

Brennan made a noise like a hissing cat before words formed.

"It's going," he gasped, "I can feel it leaving me."

As the floor reached the bottom of the chamber below, they heard calls from the others.

"He's alive," Rickenbacker called, watching in fascination as the stone and pitch retreated from Brennan's body.

Brennan gulped in air and collapsed to his knees as his body regained its flesh and blood. Rickenbacker was by his side.

"Breathe, Mr Brennan. You should be fine."

"The voice," Brennan wheezed.

"Certainly is a little late with advice on occasion, isn't he?" Hilt grumbled, taking in his surroundings.

The floor below started to tick as the last of the group travelled upwards into the ceiling.

Bunce led the way towards the bottom of the snowdrop, her rifle in her hands to give her shoulders a break, and to give her a sense of security. The death of Tork, the exodus of the Humps and Spicer's transformation were playing on her mind, jangling her nerves, and she even missed Conway's facetious remarks. A part of her yearned for the simplicity of the battlefield. She slowed her pace when she heard Elena's voice as she spoke to Spicer.

"Quite a day."

"Indeed," he replied.

"Perhaps we could talk about it?"

"What part of it do you want to talk about, Elena?"

Elena grabbed the lieutenant by the arm.

"All of it. What the hell is happening here? Your scars are cured, you've been crying, for God's sake, the Immolators are flirting with you... It's too much to take, Spicer. If you want us to stay with you, Bunce and me, you have to tell us what on earth is going on."

Bunce stopped and turned. It felt good to have Elena talking for the two of them, as though they were a partnership.

"I don't know what's going on, Elena. All I know is that this place has triggered something in me, physical, emotional, every which way. I don't know if it's Blue Wonder, some sort of weird blood memory, whatever it is, it's trying to tell me something, something about what happened here, something I need to address. There's something I need to do."

He fingered his ears and looked up at the snowdrop.

"That's a lot of somethings."

"I know and I can't ask you to understand because I don't either. If you want to go, get out of this place, leave me here, then that's fine, go. The Trade have corralled their ponies on the way to where we're headed anyway. You can just take off. Both of you."

"I'm not saying that..."

"I don't have a plan. I'm no longer interested in the bounty on Rickenbacker. I don't even care about avenging Tork's death. I need something inside that Cathedral, something Rickenbacker is trying to get his hands on."

"How do you know?"

"I don't," he felt his voice raising. "Except I do. I can't explain it. It's like someone let me flick through a book to the end to see what happens, to give me an idea of what's to come."

"You can see the future?" Bunce asked.

"No, I can feel it. It's like déjà vu. As things happen, it's like I knew they would. Like a story I've heard before."

"And are Bunce and me in this story?"

"Yes. Well, I think so. But not as we are now. I mean, not as Reclaimers."

"What do you mean?"

"Look. I can't order you to follow me and I can't promise you any reward. If you want to come with me, then I..." Spicer exhaled.

"Do you want us along for the ride?" Elena asked.

"I need you. This thing needs you. This journey we are on. It needs us all."

"But you don't know what for, even though you can feel the future?" said Bunce.

"I'm sorry, Bunce."

"Lieutenant…" she started.

"No. I'm not your commanding officer any more. I'm no longer a Lieutenant or a Reclaimer. I'm just Spicer, whoever that is."

"Don't you have a first name?" Elena asked.

"Valentine. My name is Valentine Spicer."

"You can count on me, Valentine," she replied, shaking his hand. "Bunce?"

"Geraldine."

"What?" Elena asked, confused.

"My name. My first name. It's Geraldine."

"Are you in, Geraldine, with Valentine and me?"

Bunce noticed the lieutenant and Elena hadn't let go of each other's hands and felt a pang of jealousy.

"I don't have anywhere else to go," she said, jutting out her chin.

"So I think you've got yourself some help, but then I'm sure you felt that would happen anyway," Elena said.

"That's good. Thank you."

"So let's keep moving then," Bunce suggested, turning away to push on.

"I would never in a million years have guessed your name was Valentine," Elena laughed. "What was Tork's first name? Margaret?"

Spicer smiled vaguely but Elena could see his heart wasn't in it and she let go of his hand. It was a damned warm and firm hand though.

Pinkerton kept a tight hold of both Alexander and his blat gun as they rose into the air. He had visions of the dog bolting beyond the bone gravel square and being crushed into a pancake of dog innards, before he arrived through the hatch himself to find the others turned to stone and him next on the list. As he was lifted through the hatch, he was relieved to find Hilt waiting irritably and holding a lantern, while Rickenbacker was rubbing Brennan's back as though he was trying to relieve trapped wind.

"Is he alright?" Laurel asked, stepping from behind Pinkerton to help the old man.

"Mister Brennan," said Teddy, rushing to embrace him. "I knew everything would be fine."

"He was lucky," Hilt told them.

"What about us? Are we lucky?" Pinkerton asked, looking around as he racked the blat gun.

Lining the room was the same pitch as the Gleave cellar, Pinkerton recognised that much, but these Gargoyles were different. Instead of the demonic writhing of earlier, these figures rose from the wall in veneration towards the room, heads bowed and hands clasped together.

"Friend or foe?" Pinkerton asked Hilt as he regarded the figures.

"My friends are your friends," said the voice.

"Did you hear that?" Hilt asked.

"Of course I heard that," Pinkerton replied.

"No, I mean, did you hear that with your ears?"

"I did," Teddy replied.

"It would appear we have reached our destination," Rickenbacker surmised, stepping up.

"Not quite," said the voice, "but if you'd like to follow me."

All but one of the figures lining the walls stepped back and disappeared, and the one remaining bowed his head and beckoned them to the far wall. The man in the living frieze marched to the wall and as he approached, the pitch swayed and ruffled like curtains. The figure reached the wall and reaching upwards, pulled on a cord within the pitch. The dark pitch split apart to reveal a simple wooden door.

"Welcome to my humble abode," said the pitch figure. "Perhaps you would like to join me."

The four men and one woman all looked at each other in surprise, excitement and relief. Alexander urinated against the wall. Rickenbacker took a breath and reached for the door handle.

"Wait!" Hilt warned, before pulling his Twirler.

The Professor cracked open the door to reveal more darkness.

"They love spooky darkness around here, don't they?" Laurel sighed.

"I'll go first," Hilt offered, stepping towards the doorway to tentatively place his foot on the floor.

"I assure you there are no more surprises. Not unpleasant ones, anyway," said the voice from the figure in the wall next to the door.

"Give me the lantern," Hilt said, "And get the key. I don't trust this fellow, even if he isn't squatting in my head anymore."

Rickenbacker passed Hilt the lantern while Laurel grabbed the key from the wall.

"Just as I thought," Hilt growled as he illuminated the dark, "More gargoyle goo."

And then the darkness dissipated and everything beyond the doors turned translucent. Hilt cursed as he looked down to see his foot resting on glass.

"I wanted to prove to you there are no secrets or traps," the voice chuckled, as the translucence became as transparent as a dusty window.

The pitch seemed to have turned to glass frosted with a slight orange hue, revealing the view from where they stood at the bottom of the snowdrop's stem. A spiral staircase wound its way up the inside of the walls to another door into the snowdrop's flower-like tip, which was still shrouded in white stonework. Hilt squinted down past his foot and saw the Trade platoon directly below assembling a rudimentary battering ram using the remains of the Hump fortifications. Beyond he could see the hump camp, the Trade's corral and the rest of the Glasslands. Through the glistening trees he could make out the Hump corpses. Rising above the woods, a wisp of smoke drifted from the lodge, and, further out, a white scar of the slideways skirting the trees before heading into the distance where Chinsey stained the horizon, belching out multi-coloured smoke from its multitude of industrial chimneys and smoke stacks. Below the snowdrop he made out the diminutive figure of Kendrick seated on a rock, Mandell standing over him.

"It looks like Kendrick is still alive and kicking."

"I'll give him a kicking," Brennan mumbled.

"And your friend Mandell seems healthier than we originally suspected."

"Mandell's alive?" Laurel gasped.

"Good news!" the Professor exclaimed.

"I knew he'd make it," Pinkerton grinned.

"And I can see the Reclaimers, what's left of them," Hilt continued, "They're heading towards Mandell now."

"Can you warn him?" Laurel asked.

"I'm afraid that while you can see out, none of your friends can see inside the library's spire, just as you cannot see inside the snowdrop tip," the voice chimed in.

Hilt looked back at the others and shrugged. He put more weight onto the foot on the glassy step, but felt no give and saw no crack.

"Take my hand," Pinkerton offered, and Hilt acquiesced, holstering the Twirler.

He put his other foot on the step, then moved it onto the next so that all his weight was on the bottom of the spiral staircase.

"It feels like rock," he said, kicking the next step. "Even sounds like it."

"You are perfectly safe. Climb the stairs, join me so that we can all leave this tiring place."

"I am so pleased we used up all the rope," Hilt hissed sarcastically.

"All hold hands," Pinkerton said, and they did without another word.

Hilt led the way, followed by Teddy, Rickenbacker, Laurel, Brennan and finally Pinkerton, while Alexander bounded up and down the stairs excitedly.

"Doesn't he get dizzy?" Pinkerton asked as they ascended the spiral staircase.

"Extraordinary," Rickenbacker said as he drank in the view.

"Can you loosen your grip just a little, boy?" Hilt asked Teddy.

"Mandell seems different," Laurel commented.

"Probably because he hasn't felt the warmth of your embrace, Milady," Pinkerton smiled.

"Think they'll get in?" Brennan asked, looking down at the Trade soldiers.

"The bolter is generally very reliable," Rickenbacker replied, "but who knows?"

"I hope they get through," Brennan spat, "and then the floor will rise up and kill them all."

They reached the top of the spiral where the stairs straightened out and ended at the doorway into the snowdrop itself. Alexander leapt forward, placed his fore paws on the door and barked excitedly, his tail wagging until Pinkerton pulled him back.

The group all quietened as they came upon the door.

"So this is it then," Laurel announced as they let go of each other's hands.

Hilt pulled his Twirler and spun it.

"Stand back," he said, preparing to kick the door open.

"Allow me," Rickenbacker offered, knocking gently on the door.

"Come in," said the voice from beyond

CHAPTER 10

The Cell
The Cathedral of Tales/
The Library of the Senses

The Gramarye Region
Grand Quillia

June 1856

The door opened to reveal a basic but comfortable cell, illuminated by two large round windows, one in the ceiling and another directly below it in the centre of the floor. Books lined the walls of the circular room, although there was no musty odour. A crib sat on one side of the room, sheets folded crisply on top, pillows fully plumped, with a chest of drawers lacking in ornamentation at its base. A pair of curved sofas flanked the floor window, with a worn wooden desk at one end, completing a horseshoe shape. On the desk sat a blotter, reading glasses, a collection of folders, books and notes, and a leather desk tidy holding various writing implements.

Sat behind the desk facing the sofas and the door was a slender figure in odd clothes like those worn by the people in the horrific apparition that had greeted them before the praying mantis attack. He wore his hair long but tied back to keep it off his shoulders, and had a fringe that got in his eyes, high cheekbones, and a long, noble chin. His nose was straight, his shoulders broad and his hands long, his slight frame adding an air of androgyny. His ears peeped from his auburn hair to reveal small peaks. As he stood up he pushed the hair from his face to reveal dark brown, almost black, eyes, framed with long eyelashes and topped with thin eyebrows. Laurel thought he looked how a fairy tale prince should. Teddy discerned a heroic stature to the man. Hilt saw an arrogant bastard.

"Welcome," said the man in a voice they all recognised. "I'm so please you managed to come. How was your journey?"

He raised a hand to be shaken and Rickenbacker stepped forward to take it.

"And to whom do we have the pleasure of speaking?" Rickenbacker asked.

"Of course," said the man, shaking the Professor's hand gently. "How rude of me." He winked at Teddy and moved his attention to Hilt.

The Professor looked at his hand in puzzlement as he withdrew it. It had been like holding a pebble.

"My name is Mister Elephantine."

Hilt looked from Elephantine's eyes to his own hands, one attached to the sword, the other still holding the Twirler.

"Ever the adversary, Captain Widdershins. Good for you," Elephantine grinned. "And Mister Pinkerton, the Gentleman Pugilist, I am truly honoured."

"Well met, Sir."

"Young Teddy, good to meet a hero in the making, and Mister Brennan, I do hope you are bearing up after your loss. My sincere condolences."

Elephantine bowed his head gracefully before ruffling the fur of Alexander's neck.

"How do you do?" Laurel smiled, offering her hand.

"I'm afraid I don't do Gleaves, girl," said Elephantine with a tight and lipless smile, his eyes passing over her hand with distaste.

"Don't do manners either, Elephantine?" Hilt scowled. "Shake the lady's hand."

"There's really no need," Laurel protested.

Hilt raised his Twirler and levelled it at Elephantine's head.

"Do you really think you can kill something that has been dead two thousand years?"

"I can try."

Elephantine nodded quickly in Laurel's direction.

"Charmed," he said, hardly moving his mouth.

"What do you know of the Gleaves, Sir?" Rickenbacker asked.

Elephantine slouched back into his chair behind the desk, gesturing for the group to take a seat on the sofas.

"I have not waited two thousand years to discuss a criminally murderous bloodline."

"What *have* you been waiting for?"

None of them had taken a seat.

"I've been waiting for heroes, for freedom fighters, for the forces of good."

"You're out of luck there then," Hilt said.

"You have always attempted to fight on the side of justice, Mister Widdershins, even if you fight dirty."

"Don't call me Widdershins."

"Why not? It's your name."

"Is Elephantine really yours?"

"I have more than one name, but unlike you, it is not to hide my past." Elephantine leant forward against the desk. "Do please be seated."

"We don't want to get comfortable. We want to get out of here."

"Then we are in complete agreement."

Rickenbacker moved around the window in the floor and lowered himself into one of the sofas. It was cold and rough, as though it had been chilled, nowhere near as comfortable as it looked. Teddy took a place next to him, followed by Pinkerton and Brennan. Hilt and Laurel remained standing as Alexander sat down with a loud sigh at Pinkerton's feet.

"Why do you have more than one name, Mister Elephantine?" Rickenbacker asked, glancing around the room, itching to open any of the books.

"Thank you, Professor. I have more than one name because I am more than one person."

And then Elephantine changed from an attractive young man into a wizened old crone, a crisp middle-aged woman, a bucolic multi-chinned old man, his face and body transforming completely, except for the pointed ears, which remained the same.

"He's a gargoyle!" Teddy gasped.

Elephantine started to change so quickly it became impossible to make out individual people.

"We are the survivors," he said, his voice changing with each syllable, "the prisoners, the bait. We are the city of Pearly, the city that is no more. This is our prison and our castle. We are those who had no future until your arrival."

The switching slowed and the figure at the desk reverted back to the image of Elephantine.

"What makes you think we are here to help you? I just want to get out of here," said Hilt.

"And Brennan wants to avenge his son, Rickenbacker wants to safeguard the people of the Gramarye from the Trade and Teddy was born to be a great hero. I can help with all these things."

"We don't want your help."

"What about me?" Laurel asked. "What about my future?"

"Your future is not known to me, Gleave."

"You can see the future?" Teddy asked, eyes wide.

"Yes, Teddy. I am Elf. That means I can feel the future before it happens."

"Elf?" asked Pinkerton, "Like the things in…"

"Children's stories?"

"Yes."

"What happened to the Elf race?" Rickenbacker asked.

"To explain our end, I must start at the beginning."

"Well, do it quickly," Hilt complained.

"Thousands of years ago, man harnessed the power of magic, or Wonder, as you call it. It changed the world, the first magical revolution happened, and it all started here in the Gramarye, in Pearly, the city of dreams that stretched beyond the horizon in every direction."

"This area is still very rich with the Wonder," Rickenbacker said.

"And rich in history too. The students of magic, those who used it from the raw source, created with it, crafted a world so perfect nobody questioned how it worked, these sculptors of lives..."

"Talk fast, Elephantine."

"The Magi. They suffered for their art. They changed over time. The magic got under their skin, into their minds and bodies. They started to evolve."

"Do you call Humps evolution?" Hilt asked.

"One of these strands of Magi, the ones that used the Blue, they grew into the Elf."

"Fascinating," Rickenbacker whispered.

Laurel suddenly felt a chill that crept up her back. She glanced over her shoulder as the hairs on the back of her neck tingled.

"The Elf could feel the future, yes, but there were other developments."

"You mean side effects. Mutations," said Hilt, his eyes dark.

"I think you may be clouded by your own history, Hilt," Elephantine replied, lingering on the man's name while glancing at the blade.

"We don't have to listen to this," Hilt spat.

"But you do, you see, for you have opened the gates to the future."

"If he is a multitude of people, why did he choose the most annoying personality to share with us?"

"Please, Mister Hilt," said Rickenbacker, raising a hand, "this is important."

"Thank you, Professor. The city of Pearly thrived under the tutelage of the Elf."

"What were these other developments you spoke of?" asked Rickenbacker.

"Heightened senses, an ability to see the shadows of others minds, a certain scent that aids charisma, a clarity of thought that lends itself to leadership. The Blue Magi were raised beyond humanity."

Hilt glanced at Rickenbacker, his face flushed.

"Beyond or above?"

"Perhaps that was a poor choice of words. The Elf were able to feel where the world was going and navigate the best route there. Pearly was the centre of this, the jewel of the earth, the shimmering crown."

"And then?"

"And then darkness. The Elf were betrayed by other Magi, by the people of Pearly, by their own kind. The lights went out, never to be ignited again. Until now."

"Why now?" Pinkerton asked.

"The Gramarye is under threat."

"The Gramarye has been in thrall to the Trade and Grand Quillia for centuries," said Hilt. "It's the bread basket of the Empire, supplying most of the Wonder."

"But there is a new enemy. Greater than the Trade. Bigger than mankind."

"So what are you going to do, Elephantine? Change your faces at them?"

"We need to find the remaining Elf. They still walk the Earth, in shadows or servitude. We need to free them so that we can stand together again, and repel the invader."

"Who is the invader?" Rickenbacker asked.

"The fallout from Pearly magic and its destruction created different forms of humanity. The Elf. The Humps were another. Another strand of the returning Magi are returning and they want the Wonder still buried deep in the Gramarye, safe from grubby hands of the Trade."

"If they are so powerful, can't they find Wonder anywhere else?"

"Who is to say they haven't?"

"The Gramarye has survived the Trade and will continue after them. Who is to say this new threat is any worse?"

"You have only seen a glimmer of what the Elf are capable of. The Threat have waited, biding their time, building an army to destroy the world, tear it open and use the Wonder to transcend beyond reality."

"You've lost me now," Pinkerton admitted.

"We are talking about the end of the world."

Elephantine let his words hang in the air.

"Well, I gathered that much but..."

"What can we do?" Rickenbacker asked.

"We need to find the Elf people and work together to defend ourselves."

"How do we find the Elf?"

"We will need to talk to the fairy folk."

Hilt smirked.

"Really? Fairies? They are hardly any better than the Humps, living in filth and talking in riddles."

"I have answers to their riddles."

"Oh, you would."

"The user of Wonder who followed you here is strong. He will soon be through the doors into the Library of Senses. We need to leave now."

The floor of the snowdrop turned translucent to reveal the Trade platoon below.

"What have I been saying?" Hilt said.

"Once his troops enter, this building will not remain standing for long."

"May I take some of your books on our journey, Mister Elephantine?" asked Rickenbacker.

"Don't you worry, Professor. I will be bringing everything with me."

"All of it?"

"Yes. Teddy will carry it. You don't mind if I utilise your manservant, do you? He is the chosen one, after all."

"The boy?" Hilt chuckled, "Of course he's the chosen one."

"The boy isn't ready, Elephantine," Brennan protested. "Are you, Teddy?"

"I don't think I can carry everything in this room," said Teddy.

"Might I have the Gargoyle Key?"

They all turned to look at Laurel as Elephantine stood up from the desk.

"I don't know," she stuttered.

"Just like a Gleave. Only thinking of herself."

"Professor?" she asked, holding the key in her hand.

Hilt interrupted.

"Don't do it, Laurel. We can find a way out ourselves. We don't need Elephantine."

"But the end of the world..."

"The doors," said Elephantine, pointing through the floor to the Trade below, "will not hold out forever."

They could see Axelrod spinning some form of Wonder as the troops charged with the rudimentary battering ram.

Laurel closed her eyes and held out the key. It flew from the palm of her hand into Elephantine's waiting fist.

"That is the first good decision a Gleave has made in two millennia."

Light and colour faded from the room.

"I advise you to stand up."

The bookshelves and books bled into the key, like a watercolour painting under water. The desk and cot followed. As they stood up, the sofas blurred into non-existence. Except for the windows, the room was unrecognisable from what they had originally entered. The walls were dark and damp, and carvings were scratched into every surface, as though somebody had been counting off the days.

"Our true prison revealed," Elephantine bowed proudly.

"My God," Rickenbacker whispered.

"When we leave here, I should warn you that my power will be severely diminished."

"Some good news at last."

"I will communicate with you when I can, sometimes in this form, sometimes through the chosen one. Step forward, Teddy."

Teddy's eyes grew wide.

"Come, young man, and take your first step to greatness."

Elephantine proffered the key and Teddy, his hands quaking, reached for it. It seemed to leap into his hand and he squealed in shock.

"I shall see you all again when we have found the fairy folk," said Elephantine, and then he closed his eyes. His body seemed to stretch and distort as he was dragged into the Gargoyle Key. Blue light shone from the orb in Teddy's hand.

"It's changing," he hissed in terror.

The Gargoyle Key flashed bright white, momentarily blinding them all. When they opened their eyes, the round key had become a square box, reminiscent of pinewood, with pale coloured patterns on each side.

"It looks like a jack-in-a-box," said Laurel.

"Crush it," said Hilt, reaching for it.

"No," growled Rickenbacker, his face flashing with anger. "If Elephantine's story is true, then we need it intact. We need him."

"How can you trust that thing?"

"Why shouldn't we?"

Hilt and Rickenbacker stood inches apart. The air crackled with tension.

"I suppose we could go to the fairy slums in Chinsey, see how much of it rings true," Hilt shrugged.

"Then are you with us, Mister Hilt?" asked Rickenbacker, his hand outstretched and waiting to be shaken.

"For the minute, dabbler," Hilt replied, shaking the Professor's hand.

"He didn't like me much, did he?" said Laurel, already missing the familiar weight of the key about her person.

"I'm sure you'll grow on him," Brennan offered.

A great echoing crash came from beyond the stem of the snowdrop.

"The Trade..." Hilt hissed.

"So how do we get out of here?" Pinkerton asked.

"Mr Elephantine is arranging that for us now. Apparently we should all stand against that wall," he said, pointing at one side of the cell. Then he paused, frowning as though straining to listen before indicating the opposite wall. "No, I meant that one."

Spicer heard the crash of the Cathedral doors as they were smashed open and turned to Elena.

"That's that then. We'd better be right."

They had reached the shadow of the snowdrop when they first saw two figures in the trees.

"Looks like someone else had the same idea," said Elena.

Then they heard the screams of terror suddenly silenced as a Trade squad was flattened into the ceiling of the entrance hall.

"Sounds like Conway is mingling," said Bunce.

As Kendrick stared up at the snowdrop he thought he saw a shadow pass across the stained window in the underside. He had a good feeling about this. So far he had definitely picked the winning side, just ask the Humps, and although his new business partner wasn't the epitome of charm, at least he was handy with his cutlass and pistol. Admittedly, Mandell had unequivocally lost the fight in the lodge – that was when he had been on the wrong side. Now he was with the good guys, Kendrick was sure everything would be fine. Everything would be dandy. He imagined Hilt throwing down a rope from the snowdrop and climbing down. Kendrick had not worked out how Hilt would manage that with one hand, but the ex-cavalry officer was the determined sort. But whatever, then Mandell would shoot him down as he hung there defencelessly. The others would surrender immediately – naturally, Kendrick would deliver them to the Trade in chains, Laurel would plead for her life and she would be given to Kendrick as a plaything, but she would be so thankful to him for saving her that she would fall desperately in love with him. They would marry in Chinsey, and all Kendrick's friends, or at least those that had always told him he would amount to nothing, they would see him with this beautiful girl, medals hanging from his chest, a hero of the Battle of the Glasslands...

And then the Cathedral of Tales moved. The spire seemed to flex itself, as though testing its muscles.

"Look out, Mandell!" he called, turning to run in the opposite direction as fast as his little legs would carry him.

He waited to hear the thunderous collapse of the structure, for stonework to rain down, a cloud of dust to enshroud him. He glanced back over his shoulder and saw Mandell looking up, one hand shielding his eyes against the sun, the other drawing his Spinner pistol. Kendrick turned to behold an incredible sight. The spire of the building bent over on itself and delivered the snowdrop to the floor. Kendrick would later compare it to a swan on a lake dipping its head to drink.

"Little man, it's time," Mandell said, walking towards the snowdrop now nestled in the crystal grass of the Glasslands.

Bunce shifted her weight so that the branch wasn't cutting into her forearm and sighted down the barrel of her sniper's rifle.

"Wait until they are all out before you open fire," Spicer called up, pulling his own pistol as he leant against the trunk below her.

Teddy wiped vomit from his tunic and quickly checked he hadn't urinated too much in his trousers.

"Everybody alright?" Pinkerton asked, "No broken bones?"

"Extraordinary," the Professor exclaimed, his gaze shifted from one window to the other, both of which were now on the walls, the cell having moved through ninety degrees on its journey to ground level.

"There's Mandell!" Laurel said excitedly, waving through the window at her former lover.

Pinkerton kicked at the window frame, which clicked open, and Alexander clambered out first.

"Down the Blues!" Pinkerton called to his friend as he pulled himself through the opening.

Mandell continued to walk towards his old partner, raising his Spinner to shoulder height, as Laurel climbed out of the window, beaming with glee. The Professor reached the window and as soon as he saw Mandell's countenance, the smile left his face.

"Wait," he warned the others, raising his hand.

"Up the Reds," said Mandell.

"Why are you…" Pinkerton asked, before he was lifted into the air as the bullet struck him.

"Evan?" Laurel called as she saw Pinkerton fall.

Mandell drew his cutlass as he got closer to the woman. She heard the sound of Hilt's Twirler powering up and threw herself to the floor next to Pinkerton. She watched as three bullets struck Mandell in the chest, throwing him backwards onto the floor.

"What's happening?" she heard Pinkerton mumble, laying on his back but trying to look up like a stranded turtle.

"I don't know. Mandell shot you."

"What did he do that for?"

She looked back at the snowdrop and saw Hilt strolling towards them, his Twirler trained on Mandell, and the

Professor carefully making his way out of the window. Then she noticed Kendrick's face pop out from behind the tree he was hiding behind.

"Surrender now and there will be no more violence," he called, before ducking back behind cover.

"Kendrick?" Laurel called, "What are you talking about?"

Bullets from Hilt's Twirler slammed into Kendrick's tree as the warrior approached.

"I never liked you, you traitorous bastard," he called out as he walked.

Laurel crawled to Pinkerton's side and checked him over.

"The bullet passed right through your shoulder," she told him, tearing off a strip of his shirt to stem the bleeding.

"Why?" he asked.

"They did something to Evan. The Trade. They changed him."

"Why? What's going on? Where are the others?"

Laurel glanced around. Teddy was helping Brennan out of the snowdrop window while Rickenbacker checked his bag of tricks. Hilt had holstered his weapon and was continuing towards Kendrick, who was still cowering behind his tree, Mandell's corpse prone between the two men. As she watched, she noticed Mandell twitch and then the hand holding the Spinner rose up to point at Hilt.

"Watch out!" she called as Mandell's thumb spun the chamber.

Hilt threw himself to the ground as a bullet thudded into a tree to his left. Hilt frowned at Mandell laying directly in front of him and looked over at the bullet hole. Remaining flat to the ground, he looked to his right and saw Bunce in her vantage point.

"Sniper!" he called, crawling for cover behind a tree.

"Come on," Laurel said as she dragged Pinkerton into cover, leaving the blat gun where it had fallen.

The Professor, Teddy and Brennan scampered behind the snowdrop as Bunce fired again, causing shards to fly from the tree Hilt was behind.

"It's the Reclaimers," Hilt shouted as he pulled his Twirler.

As the words reached Mandell's ears, he was seized by a wave of elation and anger, emotions stronger than anything he had felt since his death. He sat up and looked in the direction of the firing.

"Her," he said when he found Bunce, flashing a smile that revealed bloodstained teeth. He picked up his cutlass and pulled himself to his feet. His righteousness outweighed anything he was supposed to do for Doctor Axelrod, his saviour.

"Oh my God, it's Mandell," said Elena, "What have they done to him?"

"I thought he was dead," said Spicer.

"He is," said Bunce.

The corpse of Sir Evan Mandell, son of Prince Edmundsen of the Bullen Protectorate, brother of Lord Ethering of the Great Quillia Parliament, raised his cutlass and pointed it at Bunce.

"You. Woman," he called, "You killed me."

Bunce lifted her eye from her rifle and considered the man approaching her, the bleeding scar like a fallen halo around his head, three bullet holes in his chest and Hump blood up to his elbows.

"I'm going to stab you with my cutlass and then I'm going to fuck you while you choke to death on your own blood."

"No you're not," she replied, and put a bullet between his eyes.

His head snapped back as brains burst from his cranium. He straightened up and continued walking.

"The first time you did that to me it was truly life changing," he told her. "Now, not so much."

Then Spicer and Elena stepped from either side of the trunk of the tree and fired their Twirlers at the dead man until the chambers had stopped spinning.

As Laurel reached the snowdrop with Pinkerton's arm draped over her shoulders, Brennan and Teddy stepped out to help them get behind cover.

"Where's Hilt?" Rickenbacker asked.

"I don't know," Laurel replied as they lowered Pinkerton to the floor.

"Where's my gun?" the big man asked.

"I don't know."

"Where's Alexander?" asked Brennan.

"I don't know. I don't know," Laurel replied, wiping tears from her eyes.

"Don't worry, girl," Rickenbacker reassured her, tapping the side of the snowdrop "We're safely behind cover."

And at that precise moment, the spire lifted the snowdrop back into the air and the Cathedral of Tales returned to the shape it had been for two thousand years.

The Trade guard took his rifle from his shoulder as soon as the ponies started to spook. He spun the chamber and looked into the trees around the corral.

"Who's there? Show yourself." he called out.

A large Western Isle wolfhound bounced out of the trees, tail wagging and tongue lolling. The guard lowered his rifle as the dog moved to one of the troughs of water laid out for the ponies and started lapping greedily.

"Thirsty, are you?" the guard asked, and then he was aware of something else emerging from the woods.

"Who goes there?"

"You do," Hilt replied, and then he shot the guard dead with one shot.

Kendrick watched as his business partner's body bounced and juddered under the onslaught of bullets. He considered helping, but this did not really fit in with what he had planned. Not that Kendrick had a plan at this moment beyond self-preservation. He looked towards where the snowdrop had been and saw the Professor and his friends staggering clumsily into the woods. He considered offering his valuable help. Perhaps they would be interested in information about the Colonel and his hyperphysicist, not that he had any. Kendrick could see no problem with swapping sides again, as it were, as he was starting to realise that there was really only one side that was important. And that side was Kendrick himself. Anyway, what hope did they have of escaping a Trade platoon? Two old men, a boy, a woman and a wounded boxer. Then he heard hooves approaching; a Trade advance party, he surmised.

"Farewell, Professor Rickenbacker," he whispered.

Bunce looked up from Mandell's body and scanned the woods for Rickenbacker. Then she felt the tree shudder and recognised the sound of ponies approaching. She looked over her shoulder and saw every single pony the platoon had brought with them galloping towards the group.

"Elena! You two! Climb!" she called, dropping her rifle as she reached down to help them scramble up.

"Again?" Elena said.

Major Franks picked at his crotch as he caught his breath. He watched the remains of the platoon charging away from the cathedral towards the position the snowdrop had dropped into, their own ponies ahead of them, scattering into the woods. He sincerely hoped they recovered at least some of the ponies, as it was a long walk back to Chinsey and these knickers were already chafing.

Hilt squinted into the trees as he guided his pony through the woods, six other ponies tethered in a line behind him.

"Hilt!" he picked out over the noise, and saw Brennan waving his hammer.

As the other ponies continued into the woods, he pulled up and tied his lead pony to a tree.

"Everybody here?" he asked as he released the other ponies from his own and handed their reins to one of his companions in turn. He liked being around ponies again, and the relief in the others' faces served to add to a sense of accomplishment, something he had not felt in a long time. He glanced down at what was left of his filthy cavalry uniform.

"Help me up. I'm shot," said Pinkerton, his arm in a rudimentary sling.

Teddy and Brennan heaved Pinkerton into a saddle.

"Where's Alexander?" asked the big man.

"The last I saw him he was headed back to the lodge. Don't worry about him," Hilt assured him.

"Are you sure?"

"He's doing better than you."

"True."

Hilt checked the others were set and climbed onto his own pony. Pinkerton trotted towards the professor.

"I'm afraid I might not be able to ride as far as Chinsey, Sir, and for that I can only apologise."

"We're not leaving you behind, man."

"Who said we're riding to Chinsey?" Hilt asked, "The Slideway line is only a few miles in this direction."

"But there's no station..."

"Who needs a station?" Hilt asked before he spurred his pony on and led the way towards the edge of the Glasslands.

As the last of the ponies trotted past, Spicer hung from the tree and dropped into a saddle, grabbing the reins as he did so. He blocked two more steeds for Bunce and Elena as they climbed down from the safety of the tree. Bunce picked up what was left of her rifle before dropping the useless object back to the ground.

"We'll get you a new one," Elena said with a smile.

"What with? We're no longer soldiers of fortune. I don't know what we are."

"I know. It's exciting, isn't it?"

And then Bunce embraced her. Elena was surprised but hugged back.

"We'll be fine," she assured the other woman.

"I know we will," Bunce replied, desperate not to let go but knowing she had to. "Sorry."

"Don't apologise," said Elena, letting go as Spicer approached with their ponies. "We'll look after each other."

Bunce watched Elena's long limbs as the woman pulled herself into the saddle.

"Ready?" Spicer asked, leaning over to hand Bunce her reins.

Bunce blushed as she nodded. Something in the lieutenant's face told her he knew exactly what she was thinking.

"Watch out," he said, pulling his Twirler.

She felt Mandell's fingers close on her ankle before Spicer fired twice into the pulped mess of black blood and shattered bone that had been ground into the crystallised floor by the ponies.

"He doesn't give up, does he?" said Spicer as they rode away from the corpse, Mandell's eyes following them from his cracked skull as they left.

Ten minutes later Axelrod and Quine looked from Kendrick to Mandell's corpse.

"Sorry, Doctor Axelrod," mumbled Mandell, struggling to talk with a broken jaw and looking pleadingly up at the man.

"I'll see how I can fix you up, I suppose," said the hyperphysicist, shaking his head.

"Why bother?" asked Quine. "He looks quite finished to me."

"It's no real effort with all the Hump body parts lying around. In fact I think I'll rather enjoy it."

"We are not here for your enjoyment, Doctor."

"Of course not, Colonel."

"Begging your pardon, Colonel Quine," said Kendrick, rubbing his hands together anxiously, "but how am I supposed to find them without my business partner? I need him. For support. For muscle and support."

"Stop whining, man. It's not as if you're any closer to Rickenbacker than we are."

"We were here waiting for them. I didn't know your ponies were going to trample Mandell into the ground."

"Why shouldn't I kill you now?" Quine asked, picking dirt from his nails.

"We have a deal."

"Not worth the hypothetical paper it's written on."

"I can tell you which way Rickenbacker is headed. I was here when he left."

Axelrod and Quine shrugged.

"Very well, Doctor, you have an hour to indulge yourself with that thing. And you, little man…"

"Kendrick. Aldo Kendrick," Kendrick reminded the Colonel, automatically reaching for a business card.

"Our deal still stands. If you reach them first, you live. Now tell me which way the old bastard went."

Kendrick pointed towards the lodge.

"They went thataway."

The Wonder Glossary – for those short of time and/or memory.

AIR – Alien and Insurgent Research – Department of Imperial Operatives investigating foreign and non-human movements within the Empire and beyond. They wear black.

Ashburton Station – The only official and most important Slideways Station in The Gramarye.

Attar Mountains – an impenetrable range of high peaks that separate the Gramarye from The Ditch. It is rumoured to be inhabited by monsters, but so few people have returned, nobody can verify these old wives' tales. Doesn't stop the tales being hailed as truth, though.

Axelrod, Penfold G. Dr. – An advanced hyperphysicist employed by the Trade whose speciality is Green Wonder. His background is not known, but it is suggested he is an orphan.

Beasley, Mycroft – Brigadier– Leader of the Torchlight Cavalry at the Battle of Maisy.

Blat Gun – Named after the noise it makes, a short-range heavy discharge weapon popular with people with bad eyesight.

Blue Wonder – Hyperphysical power – Plentiful in The Gramarye but not so common across the rest of the Empire, Blue Wonder is known to bend people's minds and senses.

Its full capabilities are still being discovered in laboratories across Grand Quillia and in the studies of Fairport. It is suspected that the Gramarye was once powered by a culture with a profound understanding of Blue Wonder, now apparently lost to the ages. It is known colloquially as the "Deep Blue".

Blundstone Hall – Palatial home of Sir Ambrose Willis, Viceroy of Chinsey.

Brennan, Alfred junior – From a family of housekeepers that has run the Gleave Lodge in the Glasslands for generations. Lovely boy, caring, thoughtful, destined for great things.

Brennan, Alfred senior – From a family of housekeepers that has run the Gleave Lodge in the Glasslands for generations. A widower and former inebriant.

Bunce, Geraldine – Ex-Grand Quillian Military sniper, now a member of Spicer's Reclaimer group. Not a fan of lifts.

Chinsey – the Trade Capital in The Gramarye. Once the most important bustling market town in the region, the Trade has demolished the original conurbation and rebuilt it as just another outpost of the Empire. Serviced by the only Slideways in the Gramarye with Ashburton Station.

Conway, Jeremy – Ex-Grand Quillian Military hyperphysicist, now a member of Spicer's Reclaimer group.

Creslow, Teddy – Nephew of a Fairport landlady and currently employed as a manservant. Thoroughly unremarkable. Nothing to see here. Move along.

Ditch, the – The Gramarye's neighbour and previous nemesis until the invasion by Grand Quillia. They are rumoured to be very well versed in Green Wonder, but anybody who has ventured there has either been forced back by the Attar Mountains or has never returned.

ECO – Enchantment and Chicanery Operative – Hyperphysicist employed by the Trade around the Empire to utilise the Wonder as required, sometimes within the realms of espionage and subterfuge.

Elephantine – A charming children's tale about a man who only had nice things to say.

Fairport – Located in the green hills of Grand Quillia, a pretty town that's home to its most important seats of learning.

Franks, Rupert – A Major in the Trade Headquarters at Chinsey, where, much to his own frustration, he has the role of Regional Enchantment Auditor.

Glasslands, the – A forest of glass and crystal, created at the same time as the fall of Pearly.

Gleave – An old and powerful dynasty who once ruled The Gramarye after the fall of Pearly. Not known for their humility or open-mindedness.

Gleave, Laurel – Apparently the last member of the fabled Gleave Dynasty. Known for her humility and open-mindedness, as shown in her work as a nurse, dancer and landlady.

Gramarye, the – A small corner of the Empire ruled by the Trade, who are stripping it of every source of Wonder they can find. It was once the centre of a mysterious culture whose use of the Wonder was far in advance of what the Empire is capable of today.

Grand Quillia – Motherland of an Empire that stretches from sea to shining sea. Made up of people who love pantomime, male voice choirs and subjugating other countries to strip them of resources and quash them with guns followed by bureaucracy. Good gravy; stodgy puddings.

Green Wonder – Hyperphysical power – Rare and very valuable across the Empire but rumoured to be most common in The Ditch, Green Wonder has the power to cure the sick, raise the dead and change the very constitution of the body. It is known colloquially as "Verdant."

Hilt – Survivor of the Meander Canyon Massacre. Some stories suggest he is a hero, some a serial killer, but they all agree he has a sword attached to his hand. It is suggested he got the name Hilt due to this affliction, and not vice versa.

Hyperphysics – The study of the Wonder and how to mix its constituent parts to create the required result. The main factor in an incredible Grand Quillian industrial revolution built around the Wonder.

Immolators – Horrific troops clad from head to toe in thick leather used by the Trade in the Gramarye alone. Humanoid in appearance, they are apparently controlled from afar and burst into flame at death. As you do. They are the dark secret of the Empire.

Kendrick, Aldo – A long-term guest at the Gleave Lodge. Fixer. Entrepreneur. Friend. What a guy.

Library of Senses, the – also known as the Cathedral of Tales, the only remaining building of Pearly in the middle of the Glasslands with a tower that curves like the flower of a snowdrop. Fabled to contain the riches of the Gramarye, many treasure seekers and looters have entered. None has returned.

Maisy – A now destroyed village that stood where Talling is reputed to have been located. The last stand of the rebels of The Gramarye against the might of the Trade.

Mandell, Sir Evan – Son of Prince Edmundsen of the Bullen Protectorate and brother of Lord Ethering of the

Grand Quillia Parliament. Former Grand Quillian cavalry officer. Gentleman adventurer, ardent paramour, swain, wooer and man slut.

Meander Canyon, the – Known for the Last Stand of the Torchlights.

Melody, Lady Elena Drew Hynes Melody (widowed) – A lady of dubious virtue lucky enough to marry into one of the most powerful of Grand Quillian families. Before her marriage, it is rumoured she was involved in the underground network run by the Pick. Since widowhood, she has embarked on a series of "adventures".

Melody, Lord Runciman Drew Hynes (deceased) – Member of Grand Quillian aristocracy, a humanitarian who made his money in offshore gaols, gulags and slave mines. A true philanthropist.

Moon Docks – located in the crescent of a natural harbour, the fishing outpost for Maisy, now deserted.

Pearly – Once the capital of Gramarye, now only one building remains – The Cathedral of Tales, known in its day the as Library of Senses. Its fall from power is a thing of legend. Scholars say its name is from its fame as one of the Five Pearls of The Gramarye.

Pendle, Geoffrey – A Sergeant Major in the Trade, a veteran of many skirmishes, especially in the Western Isles, who has since been working a desk in the Trade Headquarters of Chinsey.

Pick, The – A shadowy underground figure in the Capital said to run most of the criminal gangs, if one believes the lower class penny dreadfuls and less reputable circulars.

Pinkerton, Corporal – aka Ten Fingers Pinkerton the Gentleman Pugilist, the victor at the battle of Langtry

Common against Bill Edlington. Apparently. He has migrated from boxing to general adventuring.

Quine, Edgar – Holds the rank of Colonel and is proud to be the bureaucratic Head of the Gramarye region for the Trade. Well connected in Grand Quillia. Lovely fella. You'd like him.

REA - Regional Enchantment Auditor – Individual employed by the Trade around the Empire to log and if necessary, confiscate relics of the Wonder that may be of interest.

Reclaimers – Mercenaries employed by the Trade to "reclaim" Trade property. Many so named are worse than bandits, pirates and cut-throats.

Red Wonder – Hyperphysical power. Very common throughout the Grand Quillian Empire and the fuel with which they expanded their regions. Harnessed for industry, Red Wonder lights the streets of its cities, transports the ice yachts of the slideways, constructs the buildings, digs the mines and fires the weapons of the Empire. It is known colloquially as the "Blood Red".

Rickenbacker, Hilary – Former ECO and Professor of the History of Wonder. Currently wanted in connection with numerous terrorist activities across the Gramarye.

Simon Insley G Zero – Standard issue rifle for Trade personnel. Boring but functional.

Spicer, Valentine – Ex-Grand Quillian Military. Retired at the rank of Lieutenant. Now the leader of a successful group of Reclaimers. Badly scarred head. Don't eat rich food when he's in view.

Spinner – the first pistol to use Red Wonder, it needs to be spun before each shot to recoup enough energy to discharge.

Talisker, Felix – A hyperphysicist of the Torchlight Cavalry who fought at the Battle of Maisy.

Talling – Once the Wonder powerhouse of the Gramarye, with ancient pyramids unwilling to surrender their secrets to modern archaeologists. An area so strong with Wonder of various flavours, it is dangerous for hyperphysicists to practise their skills.

Tork, Aaron – Ex-Grand Quillian Military, now a member of Spicer's Reclaimer group.

Trade, the – a commercial entity that pursues business across all regions of the Empire on behalf of Grand Quillia. It is empowered to employ and command its own armies to police the furthest regions of the Empire, which is sometimes supplemented by freelancer irregulars, known as Reclaimers. Most shares in the Trade are owned by the aristocracy.

Twirler – The weapon of choice for any violent man. Using Red Wonder to discharge powerful energy from one of its six barrels, it need only be spun once for multiple shots.

Western Isles – A group of islands off the Coast of Grand Quillia that occasionally flare up and rebel against its closest neighbour. The perfect place for the Empire to test its troops and weaponry.

Willis, Sir Ambrose – Former darling of Grand Quillian society and one of the first men of power to see the possibilities of The Gramarye for the Empire and the Trade. Instrumental in bringing down the Gleave family. His reputation may be tarnished, but his power is not diminished.

21701701R00167

Printed in Poland
by Amazon Fulfillment
Poland Sp. z o.o., Wrocław